ACCLAIM FOR MARIO ESCOBAR

"Within the harrowing landscape of both the Spanish Civil War and World War II, Escobar shines a light on hope and humanity through Elisabeth Eidenbenz and her work to create the Elna Maternity Hospital and the Mothers of Elne, saving countless mothers and their newborn children. Descriptions and prose, both startling and lyrical, bring you into the scene and into the lives of both Elisabeth and Isabel as they strive to survive, thrive, and care for others in this gripping tale of destruction, war, and the endless potential within the human heart to endure, sacrifice, and rejoice."

—Katherine Reay, author of *The London House* and
A Shadow in Moscow

"Mario Escobar shares the true story of Janusz Korczak, a respected leader and speaker whose life was dedicated to children . . . Escobar's account draws readers in with compelling, emotional, mind-searing descriptions while delving into human nature, evil, prejudices, and forgiveness."

—Historical Novel Society on *The Teacher of Warsaw*

"In *The Teacher of Warsaw*, Mario Escobar tries to recreate Korczak's complexities, which have largely been erased by his martyrdom during the Holocaust . . . *The Teacher of Warsaw* is a nuanced fictionalization, and it may motivate readers to learn more about the real man behind it—whose tragic circumstances left him unable to save the Jewish children in his care."

—Jewish Book Council

"In *The Teacher of Warsaw*, Escobar's intimate, first-person delivery is flawlessly researched. Its historic timeline unfurls with heightening drama from the vantage point of one selfless man dedicated to the wellbeing of Polish children in harrowing wartime conditions against

all odds and costs. It's a sobering, memorable story taking the reader through tragic events in occupied Warsaw, from September 1939 to May of 1943. An important, sensitive look at the triumph of the human spirit over evil, *The Teacher of Warsaw* is based on a true story and epitomizes the very best of poignant historical fiction."

—*New York Journal of Books*

"Through meticulous research and with wisdom and care, Mario Escobar brings to life a heartbreaking story of love and extraordinary courage. I want everyone I know to read this book."

—Kelly Rimmer, *New York Times* bestselling author of *The Warsaw Orphan*, on *The Teacher of Warsaw*

"A beautifully written, deeply emotional story of hope, love, and courage in the face of unspeakable horrors. That such self-sacrifice, dedication, and goodness existed restores faith in humankind. Escobar's heart-rending yet uplifting tale is made all the more poignant by its authenticity. Bravo!"

—Tea Cooper, *USA TODAY* bestselling and award-winning author of *The Cartographer's Secret*, on *The Teacher of Warsaw*

"This is a powerful portrait of a woman fighting to preserve knowledge in a crumbling world."

—*Publishers Weekly* on *The Librarian of Saint-Malo*

"In *The Librarian of Saint-Malo*, Escobar brings us another poignant tale of sacrifice, love, and loss amidst the pain of war. The seaside town of Saint-Malo comes to life in rich detail and complexity under German occupation, as do the books—full of great ideas and the best of humanity—the young librarian seeks to save. This sweeping story gives us a glimpse into the past with a firm eye towards hope in our future."

—Katherine Reay, bestselling author of *The London House*

"Escobar's latest (after *Auschwitz Lullaby*, 2018) is a meticulously researched story, recreating actual experiences of the 460 Spanish children who were sent to Morelia, Mexico, in 1937. Devastating, enlightening, and passionately told, Escobar's novel shines a light on the experiences of the victims of war, and makes a case against those who would use violence to gain power. Although painful events in the story make it hard to read at times, the book gives a voice to so many whose stories are often overlooked, while inspiring the reader to never give way to fear or let go of one's humanity."

—*BookList*, starred review, on *Remember Me*

"Luminous and beautifully researched, *Remember Me* is a study of displacement, belonging, compassion, and forged family amidst a heart-wrenching escape from the atrocities of the Spanish Civil War. A strong sense of place and the excavation of a little known part of history are reverently handled in a narrative both urgent and romantic. Fans of Arturo Pérez-Reverte, Chanel Cleeton, and Lisa Wingate will be mesmerized."

—Rachel McMillan, author of *The London Restoration*

"An exciting and moving novel."

—*People en Español* on *Recuérdame*

"Escobar highlights the tempestuous, uplifting story of two Jewish brothers who cross Nazi-occupied France in hope of reuniting with their parents in this excellent tale . . . Among the brutality and despair that follows in the wake of the Nazis' rampage through France, Escobar uncovers hope, heart, and faith in humanity."

—*Publishers Weekly* on *Children of the Stars*

"A poignant telling of the tragedies of war and the sacrificing kindness of others seen through the innocent eyes of children."

—J'nell Ciesielski, bestselling author of *Beauty Among Ruins* and *The Socialite*, on *Children of the Stars*

"*Auschwitz Lullaby* grabbed my heart and drew me in. A great choice for readers of historical fiction."

—Irma Joubert, author of *The Girl from the Train*

"Based on historical events, *Auschwitz Lullaby* is a deeply moving and harrowing story of love and commitment."

—*Historical Novels Review*

THE
SWISS
NURSE

ALSO BY MARIO ESCOBAR

Auschwitz Lullaby

Children of the Stars

Remember Me

The Librarian of Saint-Malo

The Teacher of Warsaw

THE
SWISS
NURSE

A NOVEL

MARIO ESCOBAR

HARPER MUSE

The Swiss Nurse

Published by Harper Muse, an imprint of HarperCollins Focus LLC.

Translator: Gretchen Abernathy

Scripture quotation is taken from the King James Version. Public domain.

Library of Congress Cataloging-in-Publication Data

Names: Escobar, Mario, 1971- author. | Abernathy, Gretchen, translator.
Title: The Swiss nurse : a novel / Mario Escobar ; translated by Gretchen Abernathy.
Other titles: Maternidad de Elna. English
Description: [Nashville] : Harper Muse, [2023] | Summary: "The true story of an astonishingly brave woman who saved hundreds of mothers and their children during the Spanish Civil War and WWII"-- Provided by publisher.
Identifiers: LCCN 2022042434 (print) | LCCN 2022042435 (ebook) | ISBN 9781400236053 (paperback) | ISBN 9781400236244 (library binding) | ISBN 9781400236060 (epub) | ISBN 9781400236237
Subjects: LCSH: Eidenbenz, Elisabeth, 1913-2011--Fiction. | Righteous Gentiles in the Holocaust--Fiction. | Spain--History--Civil War, 1936-1939--Fiction. | World War, 1939-1945--Jews--Rescue--France--Fiction. | LCGFT: Biographical fiction. | Historical fiction. | Novels.
Classification: LCC PQ6705.S618 M3813 2023 (print) | LCC PQ6705.S618 (ebook) | DDC 863/.7--dc23/eng/20220930
LC record available at https://lccn.loc.gov/2022042434
LC ebook record available at https://lccn.loc.gov/2022042435

Printed in the United States of America

23 24 25 26 27 LBC 5 4 3 2 1

To the colleagues with whom I traveled to France and discovered the Elne maternity hospital, and for the tears we shed for the lost children of the Second Spanish Republic.

To the dozens of children buried under the sand at the Argelès-sur-Mer beach, whose weeping is forever beyond consolation.

To my parents, war children who faced the hunger, fear, and humiliation of being the losers just for having been born on the wrong side.

The day my son was born in the delivery room at the
maternity hospital, I couldn't hold back my tears.
Everyone thought I was crying from excitement, but only
I knew I was crying for that child I'd seen buried under
the sand at Argelès.

Mercè Domènech, Republican mother

There's a Spaniard who wants
to live and starts living,
between a Spain that's dying
and another that's yawning.
Little Spaniard coming into
the world, may God keep you.
One of the two Spains
will freeze your heart.

Antonio Machado, Spanish poet

CONTENTS

A Note from the Author xv

Prologue 1

PART I: EXILE

Chapter 1 7
Chapter 2 10
Chapter 3 34
Chapter 4 46
Chapter 5 58
Chapter 6 69
Chapter 7 77
Chapter 8 82
Chapter 9 94
Chapter 10 103
Chapter 11 114
Chapter 12 121
Chapter 13 132
Chapter 14 141

PART II: FENCES

Chapter 15 155

Chapter 16 165

Chapter 17 170

Chapter 18 180

Chapter 19 189

Chapter 20 192

Chapter 21 195

Chapter 22 199

PART III: THE ELNE MATERNITY HOSPITAL

Chapter 23 207

Chapter 24 209

Chapter 25 215

Chapter 26 222

Chapter 27 227

Chapter 28 236

Chapter 29 244

Chapter 30 249

Chapter 31 253

Chapter 32 264

Chapter 33 272

Chapter 34 277

Chapter 35 283

Chapter 36 289

Chapter 37 291

Chapter 38 296

Chapter 39 299

Chapter 40 305

Chapter 41 311

Chapter 42 316

Chapter 43 321

Chapter 44 323

Chapter 45 325

Epilogue 327

References 329

Clarifications from History 331

Timeline 333

Discussion Questions 335

About the Author 349

About the Translator 350

A NOTE FROM THE AUTHOR

True freedom consists of escaping the prison of prejudices and conventionalisms and forming our own opinions, even if they go against the grain. This is why, in a world of extremisms and intolerance, writing books about the power of love, respect, and tolerance strikes me as a most revolutionary act. Now that the Spanish Civil War and other twentieth-century conflicts are viewed through various sectarian prisms, it is more pressing than ever to recover the antiquated values of equity, historic rigor, and love for the truth.

The Swiss Nurse is a novel based on the testimonies of dozens of refugees who crossed the French border hoping to escape certain death. The French government published the following statistics in its *Valière Report* from March 9, 1939: of the 440,000 Spanish refugees in southern France at the time, 220,000 were soldiers; 170,000 were women, children, and older adults; and another 50,000 were people with injuries or disabilities.

The Mediterranean beaches of southern France hosted the improvised camps thrown up by French authorities to deal with the avalanche of humanity that became known as the *Retirada*, or the Retreat. The French government had estimated that around 40,000 Spaniards would cross the border at the end of the war, and at a slow rate. Yet the fall of Barcelona at the beginning of 1939 kicked off one of the most severe humanitarian crises of the twentieth century.

The first camps were Argelès-sur-Mer, Saint-Cyprien, and Le Barcarès, in the department of Pyrénées-Orientales. They were barely more than sandy beaches, with a few barracks for camp administration. The earliest refugees had to improvise shelters fashioned with reeds and blankets. With no clean drinking water, poor food rations, and terrible overcrowding, death and disease spread widely.

Among the most vulnerable groups were the children, who always suffer the consequences of the terrible decisions of their elders and the horrors that war produces. Children are the expiatory victims of all human conflicts. The protagonists are their parents, grandparents, and guardians and the adults who decide to flee their countries or are forced to by circumstances. The losers of wars and conflicts go into exile. That may be their decision, but the children themselves have no honor or ideology to preserve. Their exile is in exchange for nothing. Thus they are forever forgotten in history books, novels, and movies.

Elisabeth Eidenbenz, together with the members of the Association to Aid Children in War, knew very well the horror and suffering that were unleashed during the three long years of the Spanish Civil War. She watched as many Republicans fled the Republic, which crumbled by the day. As she saw the suffering of mothers and children in the refugee camps, she decided to take action. Her travels throughout the beaches of southern France showed her the fear and desperation of women who did not even have drinking water to offer their babies. She saw mothers covering their infants in sand to keep them warm and attempting to give them seawater for their thirst. And so she opened the Elne maternity hospital to offer respite and care for pregnant mothers and their babies. Some 597 children graced the halls of the maternity hospital, and their lives were preserved. With the Nazi occupation of France and the arrival of Jewish refugees, the maternity hospital became a hub of shelter and assistance.

I visited the Elne maternity hospital in the spring of 2011. It was at the end of a trip that had taken me across half of France and became the seedbed for my book *Children of the Stars*. On one of the last days, I went with a group of journalists, writers, professors, and Protestant pastors to the maternity hospital. It is now a museum. Our hearts broke as we toured the various rooms and saw the videos and images of our compatriots stranded in a strange and hostile land. When our group met back up in the yard, we were all red-eyed and speechless. The story had been a punch to the gut.

In the summer of 2018, I returned to the area with my family. We visited the Argelès Camp Memorial, and I was once again bowed over with grief and sadness. My maternal grandfather may have been among those desperate souls escaping certain death. After the war he was declared missing.

The Swiss Nurse is the story of the Elne maternity hospital and some of the women who found in that peaceful haven enough hope and strength to keep going.

I hope this book offers a glimpse of what is freest and most authentic about humanity, both in our tremendous humanity and in our destructive inhumanity. This is the story of one dark moment and the bright light that certain people give off in defiance of the darkness of a fanaticized world.

MADRID, SEPTEMBER 1, 2021

PROLOGUE

I had always been aware of the fleeting nature of life. This anxious sensation drove me to rush each minute as if any second could be my last. When we would visit my grandmother Isabel at her house outside of town and by the sea, she would always say that as time marched inexorably on, all the people we had ever loved went slowly and quietly by the wayside. Our parents, friends and teachers disappeared from our lives and never returned. Her words made an impression on me, though I was too young to understand the void of forgetfulness. But I liked listening to her talk. She had a strange accent, and I would listen while staring at the crackling fire in the hearth. That is when I felt safest in life. I have been chasing that sensation ever since.

My parents divorced, and then my grandfather died, and it felt like the ground was splitting open beneath my feet as I navigated dorm life at college. The only thing that made me feel calm and steady was visiting my grandmother. She had been in a retirement home for several years by then, biding her time before going to her eternal resting place. Some Sunday afternoons as we lazily watched the facility's garden, she would talk about the past. Yet she never went anywhere near anything that had to do with the war she had lived through in Spain. Perhaps it had been so painful that silence was the only weapon strong enough to face it.

On one long, chilly winter afternoon, my grandmother closed her eyes briefly and smiled, as if her soul had caught a glimpse of something sweet. I turned toward her and witnessed her last breath, exhaled with deep peace. I squeezed her wrinkled hand—it was still warm—and rested my head on her shoulder. There went my home forever.

The next day, barely a dozen of us gathered for a simple burial. Almost all of my grandparents' friends and acquaintances had died long ago. My mom placed a red carnation on the casket before the frozen clods of dirt started to cover it. My parents left, each going their separate way, but I went back to my grandmother's room to pack up her few remaining personal items.

Along with her condolences, the aide gave me an empty box to take to the room. My chest tightened as I entered. The soul had left the place. I gathered up photos, books, pieces of silver jewelry, a few gold-plated bracelets, my grandfather's old Bible, and an antique fountain pen. Then I sensed that I was being watched. I turned and saw an old woman at the door. Her large dark eyes stood out in the nearly wrinkle-free, dark face surrounded by curly white hair.

"I'm so sorry, honey," she said with a kindness that was reminiscent of my grandmother's.

"Thank you."

"I'm Melody Jackson. My room's right next door."

"Oh, yes. My grandmother talked about you."

"We've never met because my son takes me to church on Sundays and then to eat—I can't miss a week of his famous chicken and dumplings."

"It's so nice to meet you. I'm finished, though, and am headed out."

"You go right along. Young people are always full of things to do and places to go. Around here, time is the only thing we've got too much of," she said with a smile. Though her teeth were worn and a bit yellowed, the woman still retained something of her youthful beauty.

"I'm sure."

"I'm going to miss our dear Isabel. What a hard life she had before coming to our country."

That comment brought me up short. I put the box on top of the dresser. "Did she talk to you about growing up in Spain?"

"It's pretty much all we talked about . . . about how she met your grandfather, how handsome he was, their love story in Barcelona, how terrible the war was, all about France and about Elisabeth, the woman who saved her life."

Mrs. Jackson lowered herself into a sitting position at the edge of the bed, and I sat back in my grandmother's favorite armchair. Hardly daring to breathe, I asked quietly, "Would you tell me that story?"

"Which one, dear?"

"All of them. I want to know everything."

Mrs. Jackson smiled, laced her fingers together, and nodded slightly. "What I've got to tell can't be said in one afternoon or even a week. It's the story of an entire life. I hope I can remember it all and get it in order."

I leaned forward to listen as if to Mnemosyne herself, the Greek goddess of memory and the mother of the nine Muses who inspired all human arts.

"Your grandmother's story could begin so many different

ways, in different times and places, but I suppose the best thing is to start at the very beginning. Isabel was born into a modernist house in Barcelona, at 658 Gran Vía. She had no business being born in such a fancy place, but her mother had worked in that house for over a decade. Your great-grandmother, Ramona, didn't want her daughter growing up as a servant, and I can understand that. I spent my whole life taking care of other people's children. That's why she tried to make a different future possible for her daughter. The world was changing, and Ramona thought it was high time for the Dueñas family to come into their own. What your great-grandmother didn't know was that the twentieth century so many people had dreamed about would end up being one of the worst eras of all times. Men would kill one another for their ideals and their dreams of making a new world. They nearly dragged the entire planet right down into the abyss and managed to turn life into one long night of suffering."

Part 1

EXILE

ONE

Isabel

BARCELONA

January 17, 1939

"If you don't expect the unexpected, you'll never find it." That was one of the first phrases Peter said to me in his wretched Spanish. He loved books and traveling and wanted the life of an adventurer, though he by no means looked the part. His round glasses, his small blue eyes that were always awake and curious, his straight blond hair that was starting to recede from his temples, and his skinny frame did not quite turn him into movie-star glamorous. But he was a fast runner and apparently a marksman par excellence.

We had not seen each other in months. He had asked me to go to Barcelona for safety, doubting that the Republic could hold out for another year of war. I was so hopelessly in love with that gangly Yankee that all I wanted by that point in the war was to spend the rest of my life at his side.

Susana was beside me, sewing military uniforms. She looked up at the roof, then turned to me. Her eyes held a fear and anguish I had not seen in some time. Then we heard the motors of the planes that flew above the City of Counts and the whistle of bombs falling.

We jumped up from our sewing machines and the khaki material and ran. Some twenty-five women were trying to get through the door when a loud bang shook the building and shattered the windows. We covered our faces with our hands and ducked down. Some of my colleagues wet themselves. All our pushing and shoving managed to break the bottleneck at the door. Matilde and Monserrat had fallen, and the others were trampling them in their attempt to flee. I pulled them up and then grabbed for Ana. She was only fifteen, with blond hair and an angelic face, and was so slight I wondered how she was managing to survive. She rubbed her side and groaned, as if a rib had been broken. I supported her on my shoulder, and we ran as best we could to the shelter in the basement of a nearby building.

Fire and smoke billowed up from the building that had been our workshop and home for the past few months. Meanwhile, we took the stairs down to the basement two by two, all the while trying not to trip. My mind raced with what I was going to do now. Peter was at the front somewhere in Tarragona, and here I was in a besieged city that was about to fall into Fascist hands.

The last woman down closed the shelter door, and we all huddled together in the darkness. It was freezing, and we were all so thin. Food had become scarcer and scarcer, and we were constantly hungry and cold.

Susana flicked a lighter, and for a moment we all stared at the tiny blue flame. "We've got to get out of Barcelona. Fermín told me the Fascists are less than fifteen miles from the city. He works in Prime Minister Negrín's office. The Red general has already given up. The only thing that might change things is war in Europe."

I knew Susana was right, but I had promised Peter I would stay in Barcelona. I had no way of getting word to him, and if I left for France, I was afraid I would never see him again.

"Ana is waiting for Mike, like I'm waiting for Peter. But I know we have to get out of here," I answered.

Susana frowned. She was not very fond of Ana and thought her a fussy little bourgeoise with revolutionary airs.

A bomb must have fallen very close because the shelter shook violently, and a rain of dust set us all to coughing. We returned to darkness. Once the bombing stopped, we went back out to the street, and the light of day blinded us. I shaded my eyes with my hand and tried to make out what was left of our building. It was little more than a pile of rubble. Somewhere inside was everything I had managed to save from Madrid, where I had met Peter and where our love story began. Since then, I had been fleeing with no precise destiny—first to Alicante, then to Valencia, and finally to Barcelona, the city where I was born but knew no one anymore.

"I have nothing left," I said, my head dropping low.

"None of us do," Susana pointed out. "But at least we'll travel light."

With the rest of our seamstress colleagues, we watched the fire burn and turn everything back into the dust from which it had come. Then we all realized something at the same time. The sound of shouting reached us from among the flames. We ran as close as we could and tried to see who it was.

"It's Neus!" Monserrat said. Neus was our manager, and both she and Monserrat were from L'Hospitalet. They had known each other since childhood. Monserrat made to go forward into the flames, but the heat was unbearable and the smoke asphyxiating.

"You can't!" I said, grabbing for her hand.

"I can't let her burn alive!" Monserrat hollered and shook off my hand. She braced herself and ran straight into the burning building. We all stood paralyzed, waiting for the remaining structure to cave in at any moment.

"Get water!" I shouted. We scrambled to find things and started throwing buckets of water at the flames, hoping to at least ease their path out if possible.

The smoke blackened our faces, and we were sweating profusely with the heat, but we saw two figures emerge. Monserrat was dragging Neus, and they made it to the street just seconds before the rest of the building crashed. We doused them with water, then wrapped them in wet blankets. It was true—we could not put it off any longer. If we did not get out of Barcelona, the city would become our tomb.

Elisabeth

LA JUNQUERA
January 17, 1939

Elisabeth Eidenbenz sat in the passenger seat of Zwingli, the old bus donated by the Swiss Samaritan Federation. She had not yet been in Spain a full two years and was already escaping while the country fell apart all around her. She wiped her tears with the sleeve of the coat that she wore over her Red Cross uniform. Beside her, Miguel, one of the nine hundred children Elisabeth had helped escape from Madrid at the end of 1937, looked up and asked, "Why are you crying, Miss Elisabeth?"

The young woman did not know what to say. She tried to erase the tear tracks from her face and replace them with a smile. She had been brought up within the strict Calvinist faith, and emotions were to be controlled. Despite how poorly emotional expression was received in Switzerland, her heart was broken by all those children. She knew that most of them would never see their parents again.

"Oh, just for grown-up reasons like the war, you know. We wreak havoc, and you children pay for the plates we break."

The blond-haired, dark-eyed boy wrinkled his nose in confusion at his teacher's words. He had been with Miss Elisabeth for just over a year and had grown very attached to her. Though Miguel missed his parents, the young stranger from another country was the closest thing he had to a mother right then. He could barely recall the faces of his parents or remember what their home in Lavapiés had looked like before the war.

Elisabeth knew that they had been in Fascist territory for a while by that point. Franco's troops occupied most of Castellón and Tarragona, but her group had to cross those regions to get to Barcelona and from there to France. Her boss had given clear orders: all volunteers must leave the country and take with them the children whose parents had not come for them.

She thought back to the bright morning of April 24, 1937, when they arrived in Burjassot, Valencia, with four trucks loaded with three tons of supplies for humanitarian aid. They called the trucks Pestalozzi, Dunant, Wilson, and Nansen. The group of volunteers felt like they were on an exciting trip, having the adventure of their lives.

The Francoists had refused all aid. Elisabeth's boss, Rodolfo Olgiati, had contacted the authorities to assure them of the neutrality of their organization, Service Civil International, since, at the end of the day, orphans and hungry children had no ideology or political party—they were just people who needed urgent care. But Olgiati's offers had been to no avail among the Nationalists.

The SCI workers had turned an abandoned house into their main base. They were all young idealists committed to pacifism, and many were from the Christian faith.

On May 4, 1937, they had headed to Madrid despite the danger. The city was under siege and was being bombed, and the Republican government could not feed the terrified, exhausted population. That had been the first of many trips and had impacted Elisabeth deeply. It was spring and still cool. They had left very early in the morning to get to Madrid, and terrible desperation met them when they arrived. The population did not have the strength to hold out any longer. The SCI workers made their way through a nearly phantasmal city. Grass was already starting to grow on some of the large mounds of rubble from collapsed buildings. They reached the area of the Atocha Station, where they intended to deliver food to the Hospital General y de la Pasión. The four trucks were crossing the plaza when the SCI workers heard the sound of airplanes overhead. They had orders to abandon the trucks in the case of emergency and to seek shelter. Elisabeth jumped out of the truck and ran toward the opening to a subway stop. The bombs started falling on pedestrians, and one hit a bus full of people. It immediately burst into flames, and people were getting out as best they could, some with their clothes burning.

Elisabeth was powerless. It was truly hell. Another plane approached, flying low and firing on the population with machine guns. Bullets were flying everywhere. Elisabeth pressed herself into the ground and watched as debris flew into a woman holding a baby. The woman had been nursing her child on a bench and had not had time to seek shelter. The mother remained sitting upright, her bloodied head cocked backward. Once the plane was gone, Elisabeth ran over to help but saw it was too late. The baby continued to nurse unaware. Elisabeth gently took the baby and held her tight.

"Oh dear God," she had said with a shudder, tears streaming down her milky-white face. The child wailed at being taken from her mother's breast, and Elisabeth rocked and shushed her as pedestrians and nurses from the hospital just a few yards away tended to those wounded in the raid.

Now, a year and a half later as she was trying to escape from Spain, all those memories lacerated Elisabeth's mind. How could she leave behind all those defenseless people to save her own life?

She shook her head and looked out the windshield. All she saw was the back of the truck in front of them and two dark-skinned girls peering out from under the green canopy. The only vehicle that was still working was that truck, which Karl was driving. The one in which Elisabeth sat had broken down, and the third was out of gas. Karl was towing them up the hills that were getting steeper and steeper.

The long line of cars and all sorts of vehicles came to a stop. Karl got out of the first truck, and Elisabeth followed his lead.

"Amparo," she called to the oldest girl in the group, a child of twelve, "look after the younger ones, and don't let anyone get out of the truck." Amparo kept her green eyes trained on Elisabeth and nodded firmly.

Elisabeth went up to Karl as he studied the endless line.

"I'm afraid the truck won't hold out. We're only a couple miles from Le Perthus now. I sure hope the gendarmes help us get to the Saint-Louis Hospital."

"We've got eighty-four children with us, Karl. I don't think they're going to make us spend the night out in the snow."

Karl frowned, unconvinced. "To the French, all these people are just a mass of dangerous Communists. I don't think they understand that the refugees are from every class, ideology, party, and persuasion. It makes things simpler to write them all off together. That way it's easier to keep their conscience clear."

Elisabeth studied Karl. He was not much older than her, but the war had matured and aged him quicker than his appearance let on.

"Well, I need to take some of the girls to the bathroom. Don't leave without us."

Karl smiled. Elisabeth was the only person in the world capable of making him forget the horror all around them. "You'd better hurry. This caravan could start moving again any second."

Elisabeth went and called the girls who had been asking to go. Lourdes and Priscila were beautiful twins, identical down to their blue eyes and blond braids. María was a tiny Roma girl they had found on the side of the road. The SCI workers never learned her name because the child never spoke, so they just called her María. Elisabeth led the girls away from the road into the woods, but there were people everywhere. Some were eating, others were heating up tins of food over a fire, and most were just seated to rest in the snow. As they gazed off into the distance, their gaunt faces reflected the weary sadness of their souls. Their cheeks were sunken with hunger, and their skin was pallid from exhaustion and malnourishment.

To get any privacy, Elisabeth had to lead the girls quite a ways away from the road to a large tree. She stood guard as they took care of their business, and then they made their way back. But the trucks were no longer there.

"Where did they go?" Lourdes asked.

Elisabeth was stunned. How could Karl leave her like this? She was in the middle of nowhere, with no food, water, or money. She and the girls were little more than four shadows cast across a white desert where the snow devoured everything, including the waning strength of their small, defenseless band.

———

Peter

SITGES
January 18, 1939

Peter and fifty of his comrades were all that was left of the Abraham Lincoln Brigade, a group of American patriots who had joined forces with a few Spaniards to rescue democracy in Spain. The brigade was all but disbanded. After the defeat at the Battle of the Ebro and the disappearance of their leader, Robert Hale Merriman, the group had joined other brigade fighters to attempt to halt the Fascist advance over Barcelona. While the last volunteers withdrew along the Paseo Marítimo toward the Iglesia de San Bartolomé y Santa Tecla, Franco's army was pounding them with artillery.

When they reached the church, Peter hopped up on the retaining wall and from there tried to keep his men together.

The young officer had arrived in Spain in 1936 to compete in the People's Olympiad, which had come together as a boycott to the Berlin Olympics organized by Hitler and his henchmen. After a long trek across the Atlantic to London and then another boat ride down to Bilbao, Peter had traveled throughout Spain with his friend Mike. Both were going to compete in sprints and relay races. They were state champions from Ohio, but they had refused to represent their country in Berlin. Mike was a Jew from New York and was incensed that his country did nothing to boycott the Nazi regime.

"Mike, get your head down if you don't want to see it fly across the street!" Peter barked as bullets bounced off the rock facade. The rest of the men were hugging the ground, trying to catch their breath while their captain studied the map and waited for the air to clear so they could get out before the Fascists completely surrounded them.

There was a rumor that Franco's troops did not take prisoners from the International Brigades, whom they accused of being recalcitrant Communists. But Peter knew that the latter claim was just Fascist propaganda. Steve Nelson, one of the political commissars, was openly Communist, but there were plenty of brigade members who merely sympathized with the Republican Party. Edward Carter, one of Peter's companions in arms, was one of them. He was the son of missionaries who had worked in China and India for decades. Peter himself was the son of a Presbyterian minister, though he had to admit that he and his father did not see eye to eye on everything—Peter's fighting in the Spanish Civil War being one. Peter's father, Sam Davis, was an old-fashioned, upright man with whom dialogue was nearly impossible, at least in Peter's experience.

Mike touched his shoulder. "Hey, are you going to get us out of here or what?"

Peter folded up the map. "Yeah, there's a fisherman's wharf not far. I think our best bet is to get away on boat."

"Have you lost your mind, Peter? Do you know how to drive a boat?"

"Well, my dad and I went out on Lake Erie a lot, and he taught me to man the tiller. That should be enough. We're not too far from Barcelona."

Mike motioned to the rest of the men, and they started firing like crazy while, little by little, the troop made its way around the church toward the pier. As the last soldiers turned the corner, a machine gun caught them. Mike fell to the ground.

Peter helped his friend to his feet and propped him up behind the church.

"Go on. Leave me. The battle is over, and maybe those pigs will leave me be," Mike gasped.

"You're joking. They'll blast your head off without thinking twice." Peter dragged his friend as the rest of his men were reaching the boat. Sgt. Robert Martínez picked the biggest boat, though their troop had dwindled to some thirty men. The soldiers loosened the ties and raised the sails, which immediately swelled with the wind. Peter was just a few yards away from the boat. He heard shots close behind him and turned to face a Moroccan soldier from the Indigenous Regular Forces racing toward him with a dagger. Peter put Mike to the side, turned, and tried to block the hit. The red eyes of the Moroccan Regular locked with his, and Peter wondered what in the world an African and an American were doing fighting in this fratricidal war.

The African gained on him, and the dagger was inches from Peter's eye when Peter tucked and rolled and got on top of the Regular. The Moroccan's strength began to give as the knife now approached his own shoulder, and he howled in pain when it dug in. He tried to get it out, but Peter took advantage of the distraction to punch him in the face repeatedly until he passed out. Peter picked Mike back up and jumped with him into the fishing boat.

"It's got a motor!" Robert hollered.

"Then luck is on our side," Peter called, yanking the pull rope. He had to try several times before the motor finally roared to life.

The boat was painfully slow in leaving the dock, and African soldiers began arriving and shooting. Peter's men all hit the deck. The bullets shattered part of the rib but above the waterline. When they were far enough out at sea, they lifted their heads to watch the dock fade away until the town became a small dot on the horizon. Then Peter headed for Barcelona. It would not take long to get there, but his biggest worry was whether or not he would find Isabel. He feared she would have fled to the border with the rest of the refugees and that he would never find her again.

The sun shimmering on the crystalline water made Peter feel something like peace for a few moments. War was constant stress with hardly a moment to breathe. At the same time, Peter admitted he had never felt so alive, despite being so close to death.

TWO

Isabel

I had never walked so far at once. We were exhausted and were barely even on the outskirts of Barcelona. Monserrat and Neus had gone their own way, and Ana had joined Susana and me, painfully giving up the idea of waiting for Mike. It was too dangerous to stay. Our only food had been a bit of moldy cheese and black bread and a flask of water a man with two mules gave us, plus two morsels of chocolate for the three of us to split. The chocolate was the last of what Peter had given me the last time we saw each other. We had gotten to spend one brief night together in a hotel in Barcelona. Part of the building had been caved in by bombs, which meant the rooms were cheaper than usual, and my husband had money from what his mother occasionally sent him. They had always had a good relationship, and he continued writing her behind his father's back. He was the only child they had left. The oldest son had died of tuberculosis and the middle son of polio.

Our magical night together had been all too brief. It had come after months of being separated. His battalion had gone to fight at

Ebro, and only three out of every five soldiers had returned. Peter had lost some of his best friends: idealist students who believed they could keep Fascism from taking over the world. But it was too late. Spain was in Franco's clutches, and Hitler was gobbling up more and more territories in Europe seemingly unopposed. Peter always said that when the British prime minister promised "peace for our time," all he really got was time for the Nazis to get stronger and bolder.

"Should we sit for a while?"

Susana's words brought me out of my reverie.

"Here in the middle of nowhere with all these people around? We need somewhere for shelter. It's freezing, and the temperature's only going to drop," I said.

"Well, we've passed Granollers, and there aren't any more towns until Cardedeu."

Ana starting hopping around, and we both stared at her.

"What's gotten into you?" I asked.

"A truck! There's a truck coming!"

People moved as the truck approached slowly but with enough velocity to run over anyone who did not get to the side. Ana stepped out in front of it, and the driver had to brake suddenly.

"Are you crazy?" the driver hollered from inside the cabin. He had white hair, a bushy beard, and a cap pushed far down over his eyes. He was chewing on a toothpick, and a silver cross peeked out from underneath his open shirt.

"Please, can you give us a ride to the next town? We're exhausted," Ana said.

"It's not my fault you city girls are weak and lazy!"

"No, that's not it," Ana said seriously. Then she opened her jacket and patted her belly. "It's that I'm pregnant."

I stared at her in surprise. She had not said anything about that before.

The driver sighed. "Fine. Get in the back, but hurry or else everybody else will want to get on and I'll have to get my gun out."

I helped Ana up into the truck; then Susana helped me. It was quite dark inside, but soon we sensed human breathing all around. About thirty people were crammed inside, their eyes barely reflecting the dim light that filtered through the canvas roof. The collective body warmth had cut the chill, but the smell was unbearable.

Once the truck was on its way again, I heard the cry of a young child. The woman beside me had a baby with her.

"You don't happen to have anything I could give my son, do you? He hasn't eaten since yesterday, and my milk has dried up."

"No, I'm sorry," Susana said. She was the brashest of us, but I dug around for a mandarin orange and gave a few slices to the mother. The child mashed them greedily between his few teeth.

"Thank you," she said. "I'm Soledad Puertolas, from Calatayud."

"I thought Aragon had fallen a long time ago," I answered.

"Well, I've been in Barcelona for the past year. My husband is a radio announcer, one of those that gives the hourly news report."

"He must have been working around the clock the past couple of years," Susana said with a snort.

Soledad gave the baby another slice of orange and then looked up at us. My eyes had finally adjusted to the dark, but I still could barely make out her face and could not tell for sure what color her hair was.

"He died yesterday. He was at the Ràdio Associació de Catalunya studio during yesterday's bombing. I couldn't even bury him. His body was all over the street."

"Oh God, how terrible!" Ana cried. She had removed the bag that had served as her prop for the feigned pregnancy.

"We'd been together for ten years. Nobody thought we'd make it—an Aragonese woman with a Catalonian man—but the only thing that could drive us apart was the damned war." Soledad broke down crying, and I rested my hand on her shoulder.

"The war's pretty much over now, though."

"I know, but that just makes me angrier. Just a little longer and we would've survived."

"Where are you headed now?" Susana asked.

"To my husband's aunt's house in Figueres. I hope she's still there anyway. She's the only person I've got left in Catalonia."

Susana and Ana both grabbed onto my hands to steady themselves. Every story we encountered along the way reflected the horror of the damned war that so many had greeted with cheers at first, stupidly thinking that war could solve the country's problems. All it got us was starvation and destruction.

"Why don't you stay in Barcelona? Franco's troops probably wouldn't do anything to you now," Ana said.

Soledad shook her head with a renewed sob. "My husband was a well-known journalist. Those brutes wouldn't leave me alone."

"You're right about that." Susana nodded. She belonged to the National Confederation of Labor, the strongest anarchist union in the country. "I've heard that the Moors are raping women and bashing their children against the walls so that Franco can say he's leading a crusade against Communism."

We were quiet after that. We were so exhausted that we dozed propped up against one another, avoiding the interminable terror of war for a few brief moments. We had lost everything but our personal freedom, the last thing we had left. Our only hope was for Europc to go to war and help us kick Franco and his hosts back to Africa where they should have stayed.

———

Elisabeth

THE FRENCH BORDER

January 17, 1939

Elisabeth found a broken-down shack near the border to stay in with the girls for the night. The poor children were freezing. Their light coats and open shoes offered scant protection, and they all huddled close together to share whatever warmth they could. Elisabeth had gotten a small fire going, but it burned out completely within a couple hours. Her threadbare shawl served as a meager blanket, and the tiny María was trembling uncontrollably beside her.

"It's all right," Elisabeth said, holding the child. "We'll be in France soon, and things will get better."

María looked up. Though she never spoke, her huge dark pupils expressed more than words could have. She had been through so much already in her short life. She had lost her parents and was completely alone in the world. Elisabeth could not bear to imagine what the child must be feeling. She herself had been raised in an affectionate family that launched her into adulthood fully prepared with studies and a career as a teacher. Her vocation was children, but a few years before she never would have imagined that she would find herself far from home in a foreign country in the middle of an armed conflict. Her mother's words circled her head. Every night Marie Eidenbenz read Scripture to her children and put them to bed with a prayer. She would end with, "Never forget: We're here on earth to serve the needy."

As soon as the sky started to lighten over the mountains, Elisabeth roused the girls to keep walking. The children were hungry and weak, but there was no one to ask for help even though they were surrounded by countless others. Everyone was in the same misery. Tens of thousands of refugees, perhaps hundreds of thousands, walked like automatons with the shared hope that the French border authorities would allow them to cross.

Elisabeth picked up the smaller twin, Priscila. The child was so worn down she could barely stand. Her bones poked uncomfortably into Elisabeth's hip, and within thirty minutes the young nurse was so fatigued she was only moving by inertia. She tried to clear her head of the exhaustion. She knew they would arrive at the border within hours. Then the column of people they had been walking with halted at the mouth of a tunnel.

"What's going on?" Elisabeth asked an old couple ahead of them. The man was wearing a tailored suit, wide-brimmed hat, and cashmere coat. The woman wore a leather coat and small black wool hat perched at an angle.

"We don't know, honey. Around here nobody lets us know what's going on."

Elisabeth went up to a military vehicle. Seeing that she was dressed as a nurse, the driver stopped, and a lieutenant looked out at her. "Yes?" he said.

"I'm a volunteer with Service Civil International."

"Are the children with you orphans?" the officer asked. He looked too young for his job. His thin blond mustache hardly made up for his boyish features.

Elisabeth nodded. "I got off our truck to take the girls to the bathroom, and we lost sight of the vehicles we were with. We need to get to the border as soon as possible."

A black corporal with thick black eyebrows sighed and said, "Let her move along like the rest of these poor people."

"Oh, come on, Fernando. Don't be an ass. She's a young foreigner who left everything to come help our cause, and we're going to give her a hand. Tell the men to scoot together and put the girls in the back. You"—he looked at Elisabeth—"can sit up here with me." The officer moved to make space between himself and the driver.

Elisabeth gratefully accepted without hesitation. "Thank you so much, Mr. . . ."

"Lt. Ramírez Cuesta, but you can call me Tomás."

"Thank you, Tomás."

"Don't mention it. The sooner we're out of the cemetery that Spain has become, the better for all of us. But we'll be back to give the Fascists what they deserve."

The Renault AGK coughed and spluttered as it started back up. The exhaust pipe popped several times and emitted a large puff of black smoke.

"I hope this piece of junk holds out just a bit longer," Tomás said, patting the dash.

The civilians on foot let the military truck through, and Elisabeth felt herself relaxing just a bit.

"So what brought you into this damned war?" the lieutenant asked while lighting a cigarette.

"Well, I wanted to take care of the children and give them a shot to survive."

A half smile crossed Tomás's face. "Help people you'd never

met before? You're a saint. Really terrible things have happened in this war, but at least every now and then an angel comes down from heaven to remind us all is not lost."

"I imagine all wars are just as bad," Elisabeth mused.

"No—it's for sure that they're all bad, but a war between brothers is especially terrible. At the Battle of the Ebro, I was constantly afraid I was shooting at my own brother and going to kill him. He's on the other side; that's just how it happened. Look, miss, in this war just like other wars there are hundreds of thousands of people in it for their political leanings. But the rest of us, we just sort of got assigned to a side, you see? When the war broke out, the people of our town flushed out all the right-wingers, especially those in the CEDA and the Falange, and they took them on a little walk, shall we say. Against the cemetery wall they shot them all and dumped them in one big grave. They didn't care that the women and children were screaming for mercy. So obviously I joined the Republic's side to avoid that kind of death. The war snuck up on my brother while he was doing his military service in Africa, and he crossed the Strait with the airplanes that Germany loaned Franco. When he got to our town, he had to kill the people who'd executed the right-wingers and plenty of others, too, who were completely innocent but whom his army accused of being Communists. It's a complete shame."

The vehicle approached the border in a long line of other idling cars and trucks.

"Don't you have anything to give those poor children?" Tomás asked some of his men. Two soldiers each took out a chocolate bar, and the girls' eyes lit up.

"Eat slowly so it doesn't give you a stomachache," Elisabeth said, unable to keep the envy out of her own eyes.

Tomás turned to her and handed her another bar. "To get you through the rest of the journey."

Elisabeth said, "Thank you, Lieutenant. I don't know how I'll ever repay you."

"What you've already done for Spain deserves a medal. All we've done is kill people. You help them grow up and become strong and wise so they don't repeat our mistakes."

Elisabeth nibbled a tiny morsel of the chocolate before putting the rest into her bag for the girls for later. The taste on her tongue was a rush of pleasure. It was not like Swiss chocolate, but it tasted like heaven.

The soldiers got out of the truck to walk the last half mile on foot. Three of them carried one girl each and left them in front of the customs post before getting in the military line.

"Thank you for everything," Elisabeth said, shaking Tomás's hand.

"It's been a delight to talk for a few moments with someone civilized. These men"—he waved to his soldiers—"are a bunch of dimwits. They're brave and loyal but ignorant as dirt."

Tomás put his hat on and joined his men. Elisabeth watched them for a few moments. When they reached the border, French police and military officers shouted at them in French to throw their guns on a large pile on the right. Then Tomás's men were searched unceremoniously like criminals.

Fernando balked, and one of the French soldiers smacked him with the butt of his gun. Tomás raised his hands to calm his men down. To a French official, he said, "We're soldiers, not bandits."

"You're Communist Reds, and Franco should've given you what you deserve."

Fernando spat at him, and the soldier hit him again.

Finally Tomás's men were allowed to pass and were led to a row of waiting trucks.

Elisabeth went up to the border with the girls, and a soldier stopped them abruptly.

"You can't pass!" he shouted with his arm stuck out to block the way.

"I'm a Swiss volunteer, and these children have permission to cross. My colleagues must have come by yesterday. We're all headed to Perpignan."

"No," the soldier said, not even deigning to look at the papers Elisabeth held out.

"But the children need somewhere to sleep," Elisabeth said in French.

The soldier frowned. His bushy beard made him look like a shipwreck victim in the middle of a white ocean.

"I'm a Swiss citizen," Elisabeth insisted.

The officer who had given the Spanish soldiers a hard time approached. "What's going on? Ma'am, you can't cross the border without a visa."

"I'm a Swiss citizen, and these girls are under my charge. The rest of my colleagues crossed yesterday and are waiting for us at the hospital in Perpignan." She handed over her documents.

The officer read them carefully, then said shortly, "You can cross, but not the girls."

"That's absurd! These girls have no one but me!" Her voice trembled as her nerves wore thin.

The officer shrugged and handed her papers back. "The border is closed until we get new orders. I doubt you'll be able to get in for at least another week. The Red Cross is putting up some barracks. There's not enough room for all these people," he said, nodding toward the thousands of people all around.

Elisabeth could not leave the girls by themselves, so she decided to wait. Near the border she found a group of Quaker volunteers. Hopefully they could help her until she found a way to get to France.

====

Peter

BARCELONA
January 18, 1939

Peter and his comrades managed to dock the boat in the port of Barcelona. The fuel had run out a few miles from the coast, but the strong winds carried them the rest of the way. Five of the men were wounded, but Mike was the most seriously injured. Peter helped his friend get out of the boat, and they hailed a car that was headed to Las Ramblas street.

"What do you want?" the driver demanded. "The Fascists are right outside the city, and people are fleeing Barcelona. The African legionnaires are mowing down anyone they find with machine guns."

"We've just come from the front. We've got to get some of our wounded men to the hospital," Peter explained.

The militiaman shrugged. "You won't find any open. The doctors and nurses are getting out too. The only ones having a good time are the bourgeoise. I always said we should've taken them out first."

"Well, while you and your people went around murdering at the rear guard, we've been out trying to save the country. These men here have fought for the Republic."

The militiaman made a crude gesture, and Peter's men cocked their guns at him.

"Get out of the car, now!" Peter ordered.

"What, are you a bunch of anarchist idiots?" the militiaman asked, tightening his grip on the steering wheel.

"We're human beings, not like you vermin," one of the brigade fighters said.

Peter's men grabbed and forced the militiamen out of the car and then headed for Hospital Sant Pau. The streets were nearly deserted, and businesses had been sacked and shop windows broken. Peter thought back to October 28, when the International Brigades paraded through these same streets in their last official act. Some brigade soldiers, like him, had stayed to keep fighting. Most who stayed had a Spanish girlfriend or wife or just did not want to go back home and tell everyone they had lost the war, though survival was its own sort of victory.

The sun that autumn afternoon had seemed less vibrant than a few days before when they buried Chaskel Honigstein, the last brigade fighter officially recognized as fallen in battle. Peter knew, however, than many more brigade soldiers had died throughout the long winter that followed. As the brigades marched through the streets of Barcelona, people put flower crowns on the soldiers' heads, and women stopped them to kiss them. José Herrera Petere's poem honoring Honigstein had already become famous, and some were reciting it. Many of the brigade soldiers cried. Others smiled bravely, feeling like the last free men on earth.

The French and Hungarian brigades went first with their clean, elegant uniforms and marched with precise order. The Germans and Poles followed in impeccable formation. Then came the soldiers from the United States, dressed each according to his preference or even in peasant garb, their hands in their pockets and cigarettes balanced on their lower lips.

Milton Wolff led them. Every few steps he stooped to pick up a flower from the street and put it in his pocket or throw it back to the crowd that had gathered to bid farewell to the brigades.

A few days later Peter had read Herbert Matthews's description of the US fighters in the *New York Times*: "They could not seem to keep in step or line, but everyone who saw them knew that these were true soldiers."

People were breaking through the security ropes to hug and kiss the soldiers. Women and children made them nearly lose their balance. For those brief moments, all the sacrifice seemed worth it.

Peter had heard that even Ernest Hemingway cried at the news that the International Brigades were going home. Many of them had enlisted after Hemingway's rousing call to join the brigades during his famous speech at the National Congress of American Writers in June 1937 in New York.

Now, as he and his men were approaching the majestic, modernist hospital, Peter noted how the plaza was pocked with gaping holes from falling bombs and all sorts of belongings people had left behind as they fled. They parked in front of the main entrance and ran inside looking for a doctor. All they found was an abandoned wheelchair, broken jars, and blood-soaked bandages strewn about.

"We need help here!" Peter roared in desperation. He let

his head fall to his chest under the weight of all the pent-up pressure.

"Over here," a short man in a white coat called. They brought the wounded men in, two each per stretcher, and walked quickly down the hallway where they had seen the doctor. Behind an open door they saw the only room that seemed to maintain a semblance of order. A dozen beds were occupied, and many more were empty.

"Put them in the beds so I can look at their wounds," the doctor said and then went around examining each soldier.

Peter stood by, helping. "How is it that you've hung around? Why didn't you leave too?" he asked.

"They're transferring all the wounded to the border, fearing that Franco's soldiers would do away with them. They've only left the ones who can't travel," the doctor said with a shrug.

"You haven't answered my question."

At that, the doctor looked up. His round glasses and longish gray hair gave him the look of a wise, distracted professor. "If the Nationalists kill me for saving lives, that's not a world I'm interested in living in anyhow. You see?"

When the doctor got to Mike, he grimaced. "This one's not looking good. I can give him some penicillin, but it looks like he's already got an infection where the bullet went through him. If he makes it through the night, he might survive."

Peter hung his head again and swallowed back tears.

"Don't worry," the doctor said, placing his hand on Peter's arm. "It'll be as God wills. That he's survived the war this long is already a miracle."

Peter straightened. He had to try to find Isabel before dark.

He grabbed Mike's hand and said, "I'll be back as soon as I can be."

Mike groaned softly but did not open his eyes. Peter let his hand drop. With the sleeves of his fighter jacket, he wiped his eyes, then headed for the plaza. The car had disappeared.

THREE

Isabel

The truck took us as far as Gerona but was headed away from the border after that. It had saved us a lot of walking, and now our group had grown to four women and one baby. Susana was not thrilled that Soledad wanted to join us since she thought the baby would slow us down, but Ana and I managed to persuade her. Soledad was pleasant and helpful. Despite the very recent death of her husband, she was determined to give her son a better life and would face anything in her way. I could not envision myself as a mother. I had been an only child, and my mother had always let me do whatever I wanted. She tried to get me to take school seriously, but I left my studies altogether once the war started, and shortly thereafter my life started revolving around my relationship with Peter.

Gerona seemed to be in just as much chaos as Barcelona. It was an older and smaller city, and the people there looked at us warily. From deep in Catalonia many Requeté militiamen had emerged. Chained to their traditionalist ways and dubious of the Republic since they hoped for a return of the Carlist kings, they had ended up on the Nationalist side.

We found room outside the city in a small boarding house owned by a brusque man with only one leg.

"You'll have to pay with jewelry or food. The Republic's money isn't worth the price of the paper it's printed on," he said in an accent so thick we could hardly understand him. He was eyeing Soledad's gold earrings. She willingly removed them to pay for the night. The owner bit one to make sure it was real gold and then took us to a freezing room in the attic. The ice coating the windows let in very little light, and the place smelled stale and dirty. There were two wrought iron beds side by side. They were not very big, and we would have to double up. In Soledad's case, the bed would have to hold three.

The man shut the door on his way out.

"Well," I said, walking up to a window, "maybe we should air things out a little?"

"Are you mad?" Ana cried, putting her hands over the small window. "It's ten below zero, and we'll freeze to death. Those blankets are as thin as cigarette paper."

Susana and Ana left to look for something to eat while Soledad and I stayed in the room with the baby.

"The poor thing is hungry," I said, stroking his little face.

"He was born at the worst possible time. Damn men and their stupid wars! Why do they want us to bear children? Just to make them kill each other when they get big enough?"

"The war had to happen. The military led a coup and did away with our democracy," I said, a bit peeved.

Soledad scrunched her face up in disgust, then gently laid

her son on the bed and covered him as best she could so he could sleep.

"Our democracy was stillborn. In this country people don't believe in dialogue. Machado was right when he talked about how out of every ten heads, nine fight and attack each other while only one actually thinks."

"But it's that way all over the world. Look at things in Germany, Italy, and all the oldest democracies."

"So then you're agreeing with me, Isabel. People don't want to think. They'd rather follow slogans and obey orders."

Deep down I knew Soledad was right. Until I met Peter, I had never given much thought to any political party. All that mattered to my family was peace, food, and work. During our stays in Madrid, Valencia, and finally Barcelona, things had grown increasingly radical. Infighting within the Republic had led to the rise of the Communist Party and the most extreme wing of the Socialist Party. The war had taught us that there was no place in our country for those who claimed neutrality. If you did not take a stance, you were essentially opposing everyone.

"You may be right, but that doesn't matter anymore. We've got to get to France."

"Stay with me and my husband's aunt in Figueres. You're strong, and you know how to sew. You don't have to flee to another country. Anyhow, what will you do once the war starts in Europe?"

I shrugged. I had no desire to leave Spain. I had no idea what the Fascists were going to turn my country into, but it was the only place I had ever known. Sometimes I thought about my mother and her early death from cancer. Other times I thought about my cousins and the rest of our family. Love is the shortest distance between two hearts, but when I met Peter I had willingly walked away from everything that had ever mattered to me. And now I was alone and desperate.

"All I want is to stay alive. Peter and I will go to the United States and start a new life. There are still exciting things to look forward to, and I might finish school in America."

Soledad stood in front of me and took my hand. "I wish you all the luck in the world, but at the core, every country is the same. The only difference is the scenery. The human comedy unfolds the same way everywhere in the theater of life."

Susana and Ana returned with their findings: stale bread and some rock-hard *fuet* sausage. Susana portioned it out with her knife. She had also managed to find a small bottle of white wine and some grapes.

"There was nothing for the baby?" Soledad asked.

Ana smiled and pulled out two mandarin oranges and a clay jar of cheese curds.

"Oh, thank you!" Soledad cried, much encouraged.

We got into bed after our sparse meal. Given the risk of bombing attacks, we could not turn on the lights. Besides, we were so exhausted that we fell asleep within minutes. The next day we would try to find the buses the Catalonian government, the Generalitat, had outfitted to take people to the border.

We awoke before the sun, straightened our clothes the best we could, and went out to the freezing streets. The snow had frozen solid, and we had to pick our way carefully. The cold seared our lungs. As we approached the bus station, the number of pedestrians increased exponentially. Most were women, children, and older adults. All the men were in the army and were trying to escape however they could. Assault guards had us make lines and let us go through in groups of ten until the vehicles were full. They let Susana and Ana enter with one group but would not let Soledad and me follow.

"But we're traveling together," I told the policeman.

"This isn't a vacation trip. Be thankful you can get on a bus. It's a luxury these days."

I knew the man was right. Our friends waved goodbye and before getting on called out, "We'll see you in Figueres! Don't worry; we'll wait for you at the station. Have a good trip!"

Soledad and I got on the next bus. The baby was even calmer than usual, and she let me pick him up and cradle him against my shoulder. He had the wonderful and unmistakable smell of baby.

The bus made its way out of the city and down the narrow road that wound along the sea. The view of the immense blue Mediterranean burst through the window every so often. The sun shone on the water, and the breeze wafted the smell of the sea toward us. For a few hours we forgot about the war. People began to perk up and even sing popular war songs.

The Ebro army
Ramba ramba ram ram bam!
Crossed the river one night
Oh, Carmela, oh, Carmela!
And gave the invading troops
Ramba ramba ram ram bam!
Gave them a good fight
Oh, Carmela, oh, Carmela!

Long live the Fifth Brigade
Ramba ramba ram ram bam!
That shines in the glory of battle
Oh, Carmela, oh, Carmela!
We fought those Moors
Ramba ramba ram ram bam!
Mercenaries and Fascists
Oh, Carmela, oh, Carmela!

The furor of the traitors
Ramba ramba ram ram bam!
Comes from their aircraft
Oh, Carmela, oh, Carmela!

We had just finished that stanza when we heard the whistling of something headed our way. I looked toward the sea and saw five gray boats with their cannons pointed at our buses.

"Oh God!" I shrieked as everyone started screaming, praying, or cursing Franco's troops.

"They know we're civilians!" a man in a gray suit screamed. But the ship officers cared nothing for the fact that the buses were full of helpless women and children.

The first missile fell short, but the wave that emanated out from the impact shook the bus violently. Another shell fell directly behind us. We covered our ears and ducked down. The windows shook with each explosion, and the smell of dust and dirt filtered through.

I lifted my head just a bit. The enemy fire was growing stronger. I glimpsed a missile flying ahead of us and then one of the first buses flew into the air, split in two, and rolled over to the side of the road.

"Oh God, please take care of us. Take care of this baby," I whispered while clutching the baby in my arms.

"Give him to me," Soledad said. I handed him over and looked up again.

A missile hit so close that flying debris shattered the windshield of our bus. The driver covered his face with his arms, but fragments of glass penetrated his forehead and elbow.

I looked toward the ships. Several columns of smoke were headed our way. A bus behind us went flying into the air. I grabbed Soledad's arm and started weeping. I knew we had come to the end.

"I'm so sorry, my love; I will never see you again," I whispered by way of saying goodbye to Peter, though I did not even know if he was still alive.

I looked in front and saw a missile hit the bus where Susana and Ana were traveling. It rolled over and over across the field next to the road, came to a stop, and exploded into raging flames.

"Dear God! Stop! We have to stop and help those people!" I cried insanely. I wanted to run and get my friends away from the flames, but I knew it was hopeless. Our bus continued traveling as fast as possible until we were out of the line of fire from the ships. Only four buses remained from the original caravan that had left that morning heading north. I covered my face with my hands and wept. Now I really was completely alone. I had no idea where any of my loved ones were. They might all be dead, and I would no longer even be a fleeting memory for them. I had never felt such a powerful wave of loneliness before. It gripped my very soul.

Peter

BARCELONA
January 18, 1939

Peter had to walk to Isabel's uniform workshop and got lost on several occasions trying to find the right street. He had been there before but always by car. When he stood in front of the charred remains of the old workshop, his heart sank. It reeked of fire. He picked his way inside the desolation and saw complete disorder. He gently tapped at some burned fabric but found no cadavers among the rubble. With the haste of fleeing the city, bodies were being left everywhere, but this fire seemed recent, and there was no sign of any human, least of all Isabel. He went back out to the street completely stumped. What should he do? Where could he look for his wife? Was she all right? He crossed the street, and a woman, the doorwoman for the apartment building in front, motioned to him.

"Good sir, *venga aquí*, over here." She had used the formal way of addressing someone, and this puzzled Peter. During the Republic, the formal address had been forbidden, along with any external display of social rank. People generally greeted each other with a simple, "Good day, comrade."

"I saw you go into that building," she said, continuing to address him with the formal verb structure.

"Yes, my wife worked there."

"You are Peter Davis, is that correct?"

Peter nodded, more intrigued than ever.

"Your wife left me a note to give to you. They had to flee after the fire. Today is pretty calm, but we've had a terrible time with the bombings lately."

"Oh, thank you so much; I'm sorry I have nothing to give you in return."

"Oh, don't worry about that. You're a good man. Pretty soon the Moors will be in the city and we'll go back to the same old same old, everything shaken up top to bottom without anything actually changing—isn't that right?"

Peter was unsure how to answer, so he shrugged and thanked the woman again before walking away and starting to read the note. Isabel had let him know she was heading to France but would spend a few days in Figueres, and she was traveling with Ana and Susana.

"Oh, Mike will be relieved to hear that," he said aloud to no one. He kissed the note right where Isabel's signature was decorated with the red outline of her own lips.

Peter made his way back through the streets greatly relieved. He saw a trolley and jumped on. There were very few still operating in the city that seemed more and more spectral. The sound of guns and cannons was growing closer.

As he traveled down the streets, he wondered if there were any militias regrouping anywhere. He had no idea how much was left of the Lincoln Brigade and the few brigade soldiers who had not yet crossed the border. He regretted not having left earlier. Why had he not gotten on a train to the border and headed home with Isabel? But the Republic had tried to hold out a little longer, hoping the Nazis would end up provoking the democratic countries to get involved and help the Republic. If Peter had gotten out in time, he and Isabel would have been in Cleveland before New

Year's Day. He had a sudden ache of nostalgia for Christmas holidays with his parents.

Through the trolley window he saw the building the Communist Party had used in its attempt to organize the city's government. Then he caught sight of a group of brigade soldiers marching in the opposite direction. Without thinking, Peter jumped down from the moving trolley.

"Comrades! Where are you headed?"

"We're going to the meeting," a redheaded English soldier answered.

"What meeting? I thought everything was a lost cause and that the army was retreating."

"The Fascists still haven't made it to Barcelona, and we might be able to hold them off, like in Madrid."

Peter followed the men. He was not one to get cold feet. It was better to go to the meeting before making up his mind. Besides, he figured Mike would be in the hospital several days before they could get back on the road to find Ana and Isabel.

The group arrived at the Plaza de España. At least three thousand brigade soldiers were there, representing every nationality, particularly Germans, British, French, Canadians, Italians, and some from the United States.

Half a dozen brigade officers were standing on a platform around Marty, one of the most fanatical Communists in the International Brigades.

"Comrades, listen to me. I'm not going to lie to you. The Fascists are right outside the city. They have all the weapons and ammunition they need, and we've only got a few bullets and hand grenades. Madrid can't send backup, but we might be able to hold them off, even just a few more months until the war in Europe starts. In

Madrid they managed it with just a few militias that hardly knew how to hold guns. They put their heart into it and won."

One of the Italians called out, "The war is lost! We're better off going home!"

"Franchesco, come on. What's waiting for you at home? Jail. The Fascists have control of your country, just like in Germany, Austria, the Czech Republic, Hungary, Romania, and Bulgaria. Pretty soon they'll attack Poland, and then the world will know that the battle we're fighting here has been for all humanity. It's not about Spain and Communism. It's a battle for liberty."

"Well, you Commies in the Soviet Union don't give much liberty to those who think differently from you," a Frenchman shouted. "And here you've killed all the Trotskyists and anarchists."

"This isn't the time to sow division, comrades," Marty said.

"We've got to get out and take our women with us," a German said.

Marty raised his hands and said angrily, "You want to save yourselves and betray liberty! If you don't fight this final battle, there won't be any place on earth safe to escape to."

Peter was torn between joining and returning to Mike. Beside him, another soldier from the United States asked Peter, "Comrade, what do you think?"

"Marty is right," Peter said, "but I also don't think we can hold out against the Francoists. I've been fighting at the front until yesterday, and they're advancing at top speed. They're in high spirits, and our morale is pretty low."

"So we should leave while we can."

"Well, I didn't say that. You know what happened at the Alamo. Everything was lost, but a small band of patriots held out for the liberty of Texas."

Most of the gathered group stayed, and the Communists started handing out weapons and ammunition. Peter took his gun and asked the sergeant, "Where are we headed?"

"With the Thirty-Fifth Division, to the forests around Barcelona."

Peter slung the gun over his shoulder and followed the brigade soldiers. He would come back for Mike in a few days. This would be his last contribution to the Republic. He did not think they could hold out for long, but hopefully long enough to help more people escape to France. Peter knew the Nationalists were killing prisoners on a large scale. Rumors were already circulating of over thirty-five thousand executions in Catalonia, and Franco's troops occupied barely a third of the territory. Peter's mission was to save lives—even if he had to risk his own again to do it.

FOUR

Isabel

The convoy continued its march. We could not stop to help the wounded. The ships were still firing from shore, and our only hope was to get to the mountains that would protect us from enemy cannons. Everyone in the bus was screaming, children were crying, and some were tending to wounds from shrapnel. I tried to calm down. I did not know if Susana and Ana had been killed instantly, but the likelihood of ever seeing them again alive was next to zero. I regretted leaving Barcelona. This trip was pure lunacy, and I still had no idea where Peter was. I turned toward Soledad and saw she was still slumped over the baby.

"Soledad," I said, shaking her, "are you okay?"

I lifted her by the shoulders and saw that blood completely covered the baby. Her body sagged to the side, and I realized that it was her blood, not the baby's. A piece of glass had cut through her jugular vein, and the blood kept pouring out. I pressed a handkerchief into the wound and started crying again.

"Soledad, hold on, hold on. Is there a doctor here?" I called

46

as loudly as I could. No one responded. Everyone was trying to recover from the attack and shake themselves out of the stupor of fear.

"Take care of the baby," she rasped out. Tears were falling down her cheeks, and I stroked her face until the life disappeared completely from her eyes.

The baby was still calm, too worn out by hunger to be crying. I took him in my arms and cradled him for the rest of the trip.

We came to a town called Sant Pere Pescador. The white stone houses shone in the light of the streetlamps. The passengers started to get out, taking no note of Soledad and her baby. Then an old woman came up and said in a sad tone, "Great heavens, we're losing our humanity. Look at this poor mother and baby. My name is Inmaculada. Let me help you, child."

She took the baby and changed his diaper, then searched Soledad's bag until she found clean clothes. She changed the child with such tenderness and care that I wept again. The innocent baby smiled at me when I picked him up and nestled him under my coat. We got off the bus while the driver took care of Soledad's body.

"Come with us, sweetie. My husband and I are headed to my sister's house here in town. We couldn't stay in Gerona."

Inmaculada's husband was wearing a black beret and a green corduroy jacket. He was already carrying two heavy suitcases, and his shoulders drooped even further when he saw me. His face expressed his displeasure.

"Don't worry about him. He barks but doesn't bite. He's got a good heart deep in there."

"Inma, that's two more mouths to feed," the man said gruffly.

"God will provide."

"Don't bring God into this," he retorted. "He damn well could've stopped this war and kept our sons from fighting in it."

"These are men's affairs, not God's," she spat back.

We walked to the outskirts of the town until the couple stopped at a two-story stone house, opened the gate, and went up to the porch. They knocked, and in time a woman who looked very much like Inmaculada appeared.

"Come in quickly!" she said sternly and hurried us inside with none of the sisterly affection I had expected to see.

"Thank you for taking us in, Dolores," Inmaculada said.

"We're blood, Inma. If we don't take in our own kin, who will we accept?"

A man with a robe over his clothes walked into the foyer and eyed us up and down. "Who's this?" he demanded. "Not one of your sons' Esquerra lovers, I hope? We won't have any of that anti-Franco independence nonsense here."

His wife cut in. "Matías, let's watch our tone!"

Inmaculada's husband dropped the suitcases abruptly.

"Oh, dear me," Dolores said, turning to me. "I'm so sorry, child. You must be freezing. Come over to the hearth."

The tension in the room eased up slightly. I sat in a comfortable velvet armchair and watched the bright flames while the two sisters headed for the kitchen.

Matías sat on the other side of the fireplace and kept his eyes trained on me, as if he expected me to steal something any minute.

"Very cold out?" he asked. I was not sure if he was speaking to me or to Inmaculada's husband, so I nodded noncommittally.

Then he let out a deep sigh and said, "Poor thing, I'm sorry about the way I've been acting. We're all on edge. Now that the liberating troops are on their way here, people are escaping like rats—everyone who has been cheering for their Communist, atheistic Republic, that is."

Inmaculada's husband crossed his arms tightly over his chest and was about to say something but bit his tongue instead.

Matías continued, "Don't think it doesn't tug at my heart to see people like yourself and all the poor children. The war is hard on everyone. We've lost a son ourselves. He was killed just a stone's throw from here by two men just like that one's sons."

He jutted his chin at Inmaculada's husband, who retorted with, "You know I'm against the violence, and your sons have killed plenty of innocent people as well."

Just then the two women returned to the dining room, carrying a tray with cut meats, steaming soup, and sliced bread. We sat at the table, and Matías prayed to bless the food.

No one spoke as we sipped the soup. Eventually, Dolores said to me, "Let me hold the baby so you can eat. You have a very handsome son."

Inmaculada explained, "It's not her son. He belongs to her friend, who was killed on the bus. The journey here was unspeakable."

"Oh, I'm so sorry," Dolores said. She went to the kitchen and returned a few minutes later with a bottle of milk. "I still have everything from when mine were little. To me, they'll always be my babies." She choked up as she spoke, and we all felt the impact of the son she had lost. "Our daughter lives in Barcelona. We hope and pray she's been spared from the bombs."

At that point I understood something more clearly than ever before: We were all cursed. We had defiantly thrown our proclamations in life's face, and now she had abandoned us to our destiny. All the hundreds of thousands of deaths had been for nothing. No ideology, however just and true it may be, was worth such a price. The fratricidal war was almost over, but the wounds would be deep and lasting. The hatred would open up anew every time we remembered any of the horrible things we had lived through.

————

Elisabeth

Elisabeth approached the Quaker aid tent hoping to find Alfred and Norma Jacob, missionaries who had opened a soup kitchen for children in Barcelona right after the war started. Instead, she found a group of women trying to help children who had gotten lost on the journey to France and orphans who had lost their parents along the way.

"Hello. I'm Elisabeth Eidenbenz, a Service Civil International worker. I got separated from the vehicles taking us to France, and now the French officials won't let me cross with the girls under my care."

Two women studied Elisabeth for a few seconds and then turned to the girls. The young Swiss woman before them looked completely exhausted and beaten down. Elisabeth's eyes were ringed with dark circles, and her pale face held none of its youthful vigor.

"Of course. Please let some of us tend to the children. I'm Kanty Cooper, and this is Lucy Palser."

It took Elisabeth a few seconds to let go of the girls' hands, but she did and then followed one of the Quaker women to a tent. Once she was seated in the folding chair, she realized just how tired she was.

"We've got some hot chicken soup that will do you good. Your hands are blocks of ice," Lucy said, rubbing them gently to get the blood flowing again.

Kanty brought in a steaming bowl and set it on the folding camping table. Elisabeth just looked at the women and then burst out crying. Lucy wrapped her arms around Elisabeth and tried to cheer her.

"Don't worry; we all feel that way. The war has been cruel and long, and now this exodus is absolutely hellish."

Elisabeth just stared blankly at them, and Kanty put the first spoonful of soup into her mouth. "You've got to eat to get your strength back."

After slowly sipping the warm broth, Elisabeth started to feel calmer.

Lucy said, "We'll take care of the girls and take them wherever you tell us to. I think you need to go back home."

"I can't. The girls need me, and so do thousands of refugees stuck in this no-man's-land. How could I just walk away and leave them?"

Kanty stroked Elisabeth's face. "Sometimes we have to leave part of the work up to God, don't you think? We live in really challenging times, and the worst is yet to come. Rumors about impending war in Europe are everywhere. There will be *plenty* of times in the future to help out, but the important thing right now is for you to recover. In the state you're in, you can't help anybody. One of the things I've learned in this war is that we can't love others if we don't love ourselves. And even helping our neighbors can turn into an act of idolatry. We'll find space for you in one of our transports. We're part of the British mission, but there are Swiss sisters sending a truck to Geneva soon to bring more supplies."

Elisabeth shook her head to protest but no longer had the strength to remain upright. They laid her gently on the cot and covered her with blankets. As her fever began to rise, Kanty and Lucy gave her medicine. They could not send her home in her state.

Elisabeth rested in fevered sleep a full forty-eight hours. On the third day, she woke up and looked around.

"Lourdes, Priscila, and María—where are they?" she croaked with her dry throat.

Lucy had stayed by Elisabeth's side, changing out the damp cloths on her forehead and watching over her. She smiled now.

"Thank God. We've been praying for you to pull through."

"But where are the girls?"

"Already in France with your colleagues. We sent them a letter to tell them you were all right and you're with us, and they wrote back."

At that, Elisabeth started crying in relief.

"It's all right, friend; everything is okay. The orphans are all at the hospital for the time being." Lucy pulled the letter out of her apron pocket and settled a pair of small, round glasses on her nose.

Dear Elisabeth,

Thank God you're all right. We were sick with sorrow when you didn't come back with the girls, but we had no option but to move on with the caravan. Knowing you, I had complete confidence that you'd find a way to cross the border and meet back up with us. I'm so sorry we haven't been able to go back and look for you. We've spent days trying to find somewhere for the children to stay.

The Quaker sisters got word to us about your illness. The exhaustion and the cold have taken a toll on your health. Please, I'm begging you, go back home for a while. Once you've regained your strength, you can come back. I'm afraid we're only at the beginning of an unprecedented avalanche of refugees.

We all hope you get better soon, and we're so grateful for how lovingly you serve others. You're an example to us all.

With the affection of all your colleagues,
Karl Ketterer

Elisabeth was quietly weeping by the time Lucy finished reading. Lucy hugged her and said in a gentle, calming tone, "The French have opened the border, and the columns of refugees have started to move. Soon they'll all be safe in France. I'm going to bring you some soup now. We've decided that I'll go with you to Geneva. We don't want you traveling alone."

"You don't have to do that. I'm already feeling better," Elisabeth insisted. But her attempt to stand ended in a weak slump.

"Impatience is never a good counselor," Lucy cooed.

Elisabeth stretched back out on the cot and closed her eyes. She could not keep the images of the war from flashing continuously before her. She had believed herself to be above the suffering, but the accumulated horror had eroded her physical and psychological reserves. The exhaustion was kept at bay as long as she was moving and working, but she could not go on. She thought about her home in Stäfa, near Zurich. A gut punch of homesickness washed over her. She missed her parents, who had spent their lives pastoring churches in Switzerland. And she missed her five brothers and sisters. It had been months since she had heard news of them.

The next day, Elisabeth and Lucy set off for Switzerland. As the car passed the endless columns of refugees, Elisabeth could not stop crying. Lucy held her hand tightly and whispered, "Have faith, dear one. There's no greater certainty than believing in what we can't see."

Peter

Word reached Peter the next day that Mike had died. The ensuing rage energized Peter to fight with more hatred than ever before. He wanted to kill, wanted to obliterate the Fascists down to the last man. They had robbed the world of one of the best men he had ever known. Many of the best men died while the political commissars and opportunists hid in the rear guard, killing off dissidents or enjoying the privileges and advantages of their positions.

Manresa was even more of a ghost town than Barcelona. The fighting was intense in every street and every plaza. The volunteer Republic army was trying to hold Franco's troops off, but they had scarce equipment compared to their well-armed enemy. While Prime Minister Negrín's government retreated to Figueres, the volunteers were sacrificing their lives to buy time.

Anthony, a young man with horn-rimmed glasses and a per-petual nervous laugh, came up puffing to Peter. "We've got to retreat. There are tanks headed this way, and we don't even have hand grenades."

"If we fall back, the Fascists will get to the city center and own the place. Who will protect the civilians?"

Anthony shrugged. He had come to Spain two years before more for the adventure than for any ideology. Now that the war was lost, he just wanted to go home. Yet he needed to save up a bit more money to buy a ticket for his girlfriend, Gloria.

The tanks started firing at the buildings and hit a nearby church. Under cover of the resulting cloud of dust, a group of bri-gade soldiers ran to the other side of the plaza. The Moroccan soldiers opened fire, and two brigade fighters fell dead.

Peter and Anthony ran up a street while bullets whistled over-head. They knew they would never make it to the end of the street before the ammunition found its target. Then a door opened, and a voice called for them to come in. Not hesitating for a moment, they took refuge in the house.

The young woman who had opened the door for them lifted a rug in the hallway and motioned for them to help her open a trapdoor.

"Get in, quick!"

Peter and Anthony hurried down a ladder and crouched behind some casks. The sound of gunshots retreated, and they let out their pent-up breath in relief.

"That was close," Anthony said with his wide, childlike smile.

"Don't think we're out of the woods. At best, we're now be-hind enemy lines, and you've surely seen that the Moors take no prisoners."

"But we're US citizens. The Geneva Conventions . . ."

Peter flicked his lighter and pierced Anthony with a look. "In this war, the only rule is that there are no rules."

They heard noises from above and crouched back down in silence. Someone was beating on the door. After a few hesitating steps, the young woman went and opened the door.

"Where are the Reds?" demanded a Regular.

The young woman did not respond.

"Catalan cow, don't you speak Spanish?" the officer growled.

"There's no one here but me and my sister."

From the cellar, Peter and Anthony heard the boots of several soldiers tromp all over the house. A while later, one called out to the first officer that there was no sign of the men. There was a sound of scuffling and a second woman protesting.

"Where did you hide them?" the officer demanded.

"Leave us be! We've done nothing!" she cried, trying to get to her feet.

"My men are going to have themselves a good time with you until you tell me where those Reds are."

The women started screaming. At that, Peter took his gun and whispered, "We've got to go up."

"They'll kill us," Anthony protested.

"Those girls saved our lives. You push the door up and I'll do the shooting."

Anthony screwed his eyes shut as he pushed against the trap-door. He could not bear to see what was about to happen. Peter nudged the tip of his gun out and looked toward the dining room. Three soldiers and an officer had their backs to him. The screams of the women were growing louder. Peter took aim and fired at the officer, who crumpled upon impact. The three soldiers turned immediately, and Peter fired again. A second man fell. Anthony had decided to join, and the third Fascist sank to the floor after his shot. Peter jumped up from the cellar and, before the last soldier could reach him, Anthony's bullet had blasted the man's chest open.

Peter skirted the corpses and helped the young woman on the table to her feet. "Are you all right, ma'am?" he asked.

The girl nodded, but then her face froze in terror. Peter turned to find a gigantic Moroccan soldier lunging toward him. He had no time to react. The soldier tried to slice through Peter's neck with his bayonet, but Anthony grabbed him from behind. The huge man managed to shake Anthony off and made to jump at Peter again when a shot rang out. The younger woman had grabbed the officer's pistol from the floor and aimed at the Regular, but she hit Anthony instead. He collapsed on the floor with a sickening thud.

The Fascist's bayonet came close to Peter's neck as they struggled. A wave of outrage over Anthony's pointless death pulsed through Peter, and he managed to turn the soldier's hand back toward his own body. The sharp stiletto plunged into his chest, and soon the floor was covered with the Moroccan soldier's blood.

FIVE

Isabel

FIGUERES

January 19, 1939

I had slept better than ever before. On the journey to happiness, there are too many stations of pain and suffering. That was my last thought as I lay my head on the pillow the night before. The fluffy bed and clean sheets fully enveloped me. That mattress was not stuffed with straw but with soft feathers. I had fallen asleep instantly, trying to forget everything I had endured in the last few days. The next morning I woke at a cock's crowing. For a brief, wonderful second, I thought I was a child in my grandparents' small town, back in the only country we ever truly abandon—childhood. But then the dark room with strange figures on the brown wallpaper brought me back to reality. I stood up and went to the window. Nothing was stirring on that quiet street outside of town, but a ways off I could see a long line of refugees making their way toward Figueres. The smell of coffee and freshly baked bread lured me downstairs.

"Awake already?" Inmaculada asked. "I didn't want to disturb you. The rings around your eyes are too dark, and your face was nearly blank last night. Have you rested well?"

She was rocking an old cradle. Her sister was beside her.

I nodded and asked, "How's the baby?"

"Oh, young ones are always grateful. All they need is to be clean, well rested, and well fed. In a few days he'll gain all the weight he needs and will be bright and happy again. At least he'll never remember what happened to his poor mother."

That comment disturbed me. I could not stay in Spain any longer. I did not know where my husband was, but I had to cross the border as soon as possible.

"I have to look for a way to get to France today."

"But you're exhausted. Rest up for a few days. The baby needs . . ."

I looked inside the cradle and choked up at the sight of the child's face. His expression was so innocent and peaceful. He was completely alone in the world, like all of us at the core.

"I'll have to leave him at a convent or an orphanage. I can't take charge of him." I finally said aloud the thought that had tormented me since I realized the blood in the bus was Soledad's. I broke down crying again.

Inmaculada came up and hugged me. I needed to feel the warmth of a human embrace. I was carrying so much suffering with me that the tears were choking the breath out of me. After a few minutes Inmaculada motioned for me to sit down at the table, and she brought me some coffee with a touch of milk. She set a plate down in front of me with freshly toasted bread covered with a tomato and olive oil. It tasted absolutely divine, and I made short work of it.

"Dolores and I will take care of the baby for now until all of this calms down. Then we'll see about what institution to take him to," Inmaculada said.

"Thank you," I said, wiping my mouth with the cloth napkin.

"My brother-in-law can drive you into town. There are several buses and trucks going on to France. I took the liberty of packing you a change of clothes or two, a bit of bread and Catalan sausage, and cans of tuna and condensed milk. It's not much, but hopefully it'll see you through to France."

I stared at her in speechless gratitude.

In the bathroom, I changed clothes, brushed my hair, and took a good look at myself in the mirror. All traces of youth and beauty had disappeared. My eyes were sunken, my lips parched, my face as pale as the moon, my formerly chubby cheeks gaunt, and my neck a spindly, bony thing I hardly recognized. The dress Inmaculada had picked out for me was simple but elegant. The shoes were comfortable, and the coat was thick, much better than my own. I went out to the hallway, and Inmaculada held up Soledad's baby for me one last time. I knew I would never forget his huge, expressive eyes. I swallowed back tears as I kissed him, and we made our way to the door.

"Such a pity to have met under these circumstances. The war has made us all so cold and unfeeling, but that, too, will pass," she said.

"Thank you, Doña Inmaculada. And please thank your family for taking care of this tiny, helpless baby."

We hugged one last time, and I folded myself into the old black Renault. Matías did not open his mouth to speak for the entire trip. When we arrived at the station, the voice of the president of the Generalitat, Lluís Companys, was blaring over the speakers. Only then did Matías mutter, "Damned brute," in Catalan.

I got out of the car, and before I could turn to thank him, Matías sped off. The plaza was packed with people listening intently to the president's speech.

"People of Catalonia! We must resist! We cannot allow the Fascist troops to enter Barcelona. At the French border tons and tons of weapons are waiting approval to be transported to Catalonia, and with them we will stop Franco's soldiers. We cannot give up. We will never give up!"

As the crowd applauded, I tried to swim my way through the multitude. I felt small and insignificant and terribly alone.

I headed for the union building, hoping to find some sort of help there.

"Comrade, I've come from Barcelona. My husband is a soldier with the International Brigades, and I'm trying to get to France, but I don't know what to do," I explained to a thin man with gray hair and a gray mustache. He eyed me up and down as if my words were hard to understand. I took out my papers and handed them to him.

"All right. The women and children are staying here, and the men in the military barracks. Come on in, and they'll serve you something to eat. Tomorrow you've got to go to the consulate and try to get a visa. In a few days, more buses will be heading to the border. It seems the frogs have finally opened their customs checks. Apparently they were afraid of a Spanish invasion."

I went inside the building. It was a lovely old place but scantily furnished, with just one office desk and a few chairs. Women and children lined the walls. There must have been two hundred people on the first floor alone, most of them reeking of sweat and stinky feet, but I soon got used to the smell. I found a spot next to a girl reading a book. She looked to be around eighteen or nineteen years old.

"Mind if I sit here?" I asked.

"Go right ahead—this wall isn't reserved," she said with a lovely smile. Her eyes were blue and her skin milky white. Her black hair was pulled back in a bun, and she had a leather traveling case beside her.

"I'm Isabel," I said.

"And I'm América. Are you hungry?"

"No, I actually had a decent breakfast today." It was the first time in a long time that I was not hungry.

"That sounds nice! All I had was some disgusting coffee early this morning and a bit of soup a few minutes ago."

I felt a bit sorry for this girl. She reminded me of a cousin I had not seen in years.

"Are you traveling by yourself?" I asked.

Her face fell, and I regretted my question.

"I left Barcelona three days ago. My parents . . ." Her voice trailed off as her head dropped and the tears started flowing. She tried to catch her breath.

"I'm so sorry, I didn't mean to . . . ," I stammered.

"We lived on Paseo de Gracia. A bomb hit our building, and most people were killed, including my siblings and my parents. I wasn't home at the time. I was at a friend's house."

"So why are you fleeing to France? You're young. I don't think you'd be in danger in Barcelona. They aren't killing off the women, and you could start a new life."

"I've lost everything. I don't have any family left, and my father was a deputy in the Generalitat."

I put my hand on her shoulder. "You really should go back."

"I was in college, but women won't have any opportunity

in Franco's Spain. Now my dream is to study at the Sorbonne and see Paris." Her face momentarily lit up as she spoke of this future.

"I understand. I hope you get what you're after."

"But enough about me," América said. "What about you?"

I told her my story, and she stared at me, soaking up every word. When I got to the part about the bus trip from Gerona, her face contorted with pain.

"Oh, I'm so, so sorry, Isabel. I don't know what will happen after the war, but there are too many lives being destroyed. We've all taken to the streets hoping to escape the world that's out to get us, and we just want a fresh start. How many of us will actually get it? I've never seen so many needy people."

We looked around us: dirty, flea-infested children; desperate mothers with no milk to give their babies; older adults quietly muttering on the damp cold set about ruining their bones. We were a mass of castaways in a raging sea.

———

Elisabeth

STÄFA, SWITZERLAND
January 23, 1939

Elisabeth could not help but feel defeated. All her work seemed to have been in vain. Throughout the two-and-a-half-day journey, Lucy kept encouraging her and trying to help her get her strength back, but Elisabeth could not stop weeping and thinking about the children she was leaving behind. Her mood shifted slightly once they got to Switzerland. The memories of her own childhood rekindled a bit of happiness within her.

"Oh, I had forgotten how beautiful this place is!" she exclaimed, watching the countryside go by out the passenger window.

"We should be in your city by tonight."

"Stäfa is a small town on Lake Zurich, and the only thing it's ever been famous for is its wine. My father has been a pastor there for years. Everyone knows him, and that can sometimes be a burden for the family."

"I'm also a pastor's kid. It's not always easy to be in the spotlight."

"I had always dreamed about living in Zurich, so I left Stäfa the first chance I got. I studied in the big city, then went to Winterthur to teach in a school for working-class children. Some say it's the ugliest city in Switzerland."

Lucy raised her eyebrows at Elisabeth and said, "So you've always had a heart for the less fortunate."

For the first time in a long time, Elisabeth smiled. "Well, what's life good for except for giving it for others? A lot of people are happy just warming a church pew, but I prefer going to where the needy are, like in the Bible."

Lucy nodded. She saw a great deal of herself reflected in the slight young woman beside her who looked common enough on the outside but who was brimming over with passion for humanity on the inside. "So how did you end up in Spain?" she asked. "I bet all of us volunteers have a similar enough story."

"I was in Denmark, taking a summer school class at Danebod, and Willy Begert from Service Civil International reached out to me with an invitation. I didn't have to think about it for long. I joined up with a humanitarian aid group traveling to Valencia. I'm sure you can guess the rest."

"I'm with the British Quakers. There are some with us from the United States and other places too. Our community is all over the world. In 1937, we received a request to help open a children's hospital in Valencia, which is where a lot of refugees had gone. First we opened it in Alicante and then moved it to Polop de la Marina."

"It's odd, isn't it? We've been so close to each other but didn't cross paths until we got to the French border," Elisabeth mused.

Lucy shrugged. "Not to mention the miracle that we've both survived. Many of our brothers and sisters have paid with their lives for the desire to help the Spanish children."

They arrived at Elisabeth's town in the evening. The young woman happily pointed out the street where her parents lived beside the church and ran up to knock on the door while Lucy got their bags from the car and followed slowly.

Marie Eidenbenz opened the door. To Elisabeth, she seemed older, but her dark eyes shone brightly when she saw her daughter.

"Oh, Elisabeth!" she exclaimed, drawing the young woman to her. Elisabeth's three younger siblings still lived at home and were soon covering their sister with hugs and kisses.

"Where's Dad?" Elisabeth asked.

"At the church," her mother said, nodding with her head to the building next door.

After introducing Lucy, Elisabeth took her leave and headed for the church. Her father was kneeling in the front row, praying. Elisabeth slid silently into the pew beside him, not disturbing his prayer. After a few moments, Johann Eidenbenz looked up.

"Elisabeth?"

"Father."

"So you're back, my dear?"

"Yes, I've just arrived."

"And is the war in Spain over?" he said, turning to look her full in the face.

"No, but we had to evacuate the orphanage and flee to France."

"And what brings you back here?"

Wondering the same thing, Elisabeth was not sure how to answer. "To get my strength back," she said at last. "It's been quite difficult."

Johann rested a hand on his daughter's shoulder and then said in a gentle tone, "We can't escape our destiny. God doesn't want you here, my child. I've dedicated my whole life to others. In this little town people are suffering, too, but I've always felt that I've wasted my life in a way. I'm not a very good parish priest. I always wanted to go out on the mission field."

"But, Father, your work here in this small town has been wonderful."

The old man tried to hide his sadness. Elisabeth sensed his exhaustion, as if the relentless routine had worn him thin.

"Let's go home," he said, pushing up to his feet. "Your mother was preparing a delicious cake when I left, and there's so much for you to tell us."

They returned to the parsonage arm in arm. There was not a man on earth whom Elisabeth respected more than her father. Though well aware of his defects, she always hoped she could one day find a husband as upright and selfless as Johann Eidenbenz.

Peter

BARCELONA
January 20, 1939

"The Fascists are right outside the city," Sergeant Braum confirmed to his men.

"We've got to get out," Klaus, one of the few friends Peter had left alive, said.

"For that, we've got to find a vehicle."

Peter had decided to go back to the front and try to postpone the inevitable defeat of the Spanish Republic. He and his two comrades had been separated from the rest of the division. The Republican army was disintegrating by the moment. They managed to make it on foot to the Sagrada Familia basilica, where they came upon an abandoned truck. One of the tires was flat, but between the three of them they got it changed, and Braum sat behind the wheel. They drove for several hours. The truck's motor was none too strong, but it got them to Mataró. There they bedded down for the night, taking turns to stand guard lest anyone try to steal the vehicle. The next morning they headed to Blanes. As they neared the town, ships from off the coast were launching missiles at civilian transports and foot traffic. Peter and his companions decided to follow the roads inland to avoid the coastal attack. Yet on the outskirts of Gerona, a German fighter plane dropped down suddenly from the skies and opened fire on them. They jumped out of the truck just before it burst into flames and ran to hide in a nearby forest.

Gerona was full of refugees. The men found something to eat and lodged in an old army barracks with only a thin blanket for cover. They next day they intended to get to Figueres. Peter could think of nothing but finding Isabel. He figured she had taken more or less the same route he was now traveling. Surely he would come upon her at some point. After all, it had been pure circumstantial luck that brought them together the first time in Barcelona a few years before. He was a tall, pale North American and she a small, dark Spaniard. What were the chances of finding a soulmate thousands of miles from his hometown?

As Peter tried to sleep, he envisioned his beloved receiving him with open arms on the other side of the border. Somehow or another, he had to survive and take her back home so they could start a new life together, far away from all this suffering.

SIX

Isabel

FIGUERES
January 20, 1939

My body was throbbing with pain when I woke. The humidity
had sunk into my bones, and my stomach was growling. I glanced
over at América, who seemed to be sleeping peacefully enough.
I recalled the fluffy bed from the night before and wished I had
acquiesced to stay longer and get my strength back. I could not
shake the images of my friends and their terrible deaths. It all
seemed so unreal, as if everything were a nightmare and surely I
would wake soon. I tried to stand, but my sides were so stiff and
sore it was hard to move. My attempts at movement woke América.

"Where are you going?" she asked. "It's still dark."

"I need to eat and want to try to get my visa."

"I'll go with you."

Outside, it was raining and very cold. We stood under a porch
awning, and I pulled out some of the bread and cheese Inmaculada
had packed me. I sliced off two pieces with my knife and shared
with my new friend. It was soon finished, and we walked toward
the consulate. The line already wrapped around the building. Part

of me wanted to give up and come back another day, but we took our place at the end of the line and started talking.

"Why do you want to go to France?" América asked.

"Well, my husband is from North America, and from France we can travel to his country."

"Is he Mexican?"

"No, he's from the United States."

"Oh, a Yankee," she teased.

"Why did your parents name you América?" I asked.

She smiled, and it lit up her face. "Well, my grandparents were Cuban. After the war, they left the island and settled in Barcelona. My grandmother begged my father to name me América."

"It's pretty," I said.

The night gave way to a day as cold and cloudy as the one before it. The rain did not let up, and we were soaking wet. América was shivering, and I feared she would get sick.

"Why don't you go stand under that porch? There's no need for us to both wait here in line."

"No, you're older; you should go."

I gave her a wry look. "Do I look that old?"

"No." She smiled. "I'm guessing you're around twenty-five."

The past three years had flown by. I could hardly remember my life before Peter: my mother's unmet hopes for me to go to college and my work as a seamstress.

"I've been married for three years, but I've only actually been with my husband for about six months of that time." The words came out with the bitterness I felt. The war had stolen that too: the sweetest years of our life.

América begged me to tell her the whole story of how we had met.

"My mother was the doorwoman for a really nice building in a well-to-do neighborhood, and she'd sent me to a good school. One of the women in the building, Doña Agatha Morales Pujol— she was the widow of a steel tycoon—paid for my education. But I always felt like a fish out of water, a poor wretch in a room full of rich girls. Everyone wore uniforms, but they all knew perfectly well that I didn't have a father and that my mother was a doorwoman. Doña Morales wanted to pay for me to go to college, too, and I really wanted to be a nurse. But she died just when I was about to start taking classes. Then my mother got sick. She wasn't very old, but everything started with bad pain in her stomach. After a few weeks, we went to the doctor. He said she was retaining fluid and that she might have ovarian cancer. It turned out the cancer had already spread throughout her womb, and operating would do no good. Besides, it was too expensive. She died just a few months later, and the rest of the people in the building asked me to leave."

"Oh, I'm so sorry," América said, resting her hand on my shoulder.

"Yeah, that's life for you. It's never easy." I drifted into silence. Remembering all of that pushed me deeper into sadness than I already was.

"But then everything changed when Peter came along?" América chimed in. "Or am I just being a romantic?"

"Peter made life light up again completely."

"Oh, tell me about it!"

I smiled, thinking back to the day. "Sometimes I feel like life is made up of thousands of coincidences. If things had gone just a tiny bit differently, we would've become different people or maybe not even have come into this world. So that morning I was

71

rushing out of the room I was renting with my friend Marta. Life was pretty dull and bleak."

"Oh, it must be so exciting to find true love. I hope I do someday!" América interjected.

"Yes, it really is. Marta and I had met at the seamstress shop, and she had offered to let me share her place and split the rent. It was a small room in a big house owned by a woman whose husband had died in the Rif War. Like I was saying, that morning I overslept, so I was running to catch the trolley, and I missed it. I decided to take the Metro, and as I was running down the stairs, I slipped and tumbled all the way to the bottom. Nobody helped me, can you believe it? But a tall, skinny young man with very blond hair and beautiful blue eyes gave me his hand and helped me up. The war had just started two months before, but it was down in Barcelona. After the uprising, everything went back to normal for a while, you remember? That guy asked me if I was okay. My ankle was hurting, so he helped me get inside the station, and he sat beside me on a bench on the platform. He introduced himself and told me he'd come to Barcelona for the People's Olympiad, the games they'd arranged to boycott the Berlin Olympics, but when the war broke out, he decided to enlist as a volunteer and fight for the Republic. He seemed so romantic, handsome, and put together that I let him escort me to my shop. He asked me what time I'd be done with work. I never talk with strangers, but I went ahead and told him I'd be finished at six; and that evening, there he was, waiting for me."

Just then, a woman started yelling to a group of girls in front of us in line, "There are buses leaving for the border, and there aren't many seats left!"

"We don't have visas," the girls answered nervously.

"The French have opened the border, and now everyone can get through!" she answered.

We ran with the rest of the crowd to the plaza. Everything was mayhem. The first buses were already leaving, and there were only a few trucks left. The sides were tall, and it was hard to get on. I helped América scramble up into one, but as I tried to join her, I slipped and fell flat.

"Stop!" América called to the driver. "My friend fell off!" No one paid any heed, and she jumped down while the truck was in motion.

"Are you crazy? You should get out while you have the chance," I said.

"Look, there's one more over there." She pointed.

We ran over and were among the last few people to get on just before it pulled away. We made room for ourselves to sit at the back where we could look out and catch a bit of wind. We knew the air inside the truck would quickly become nearly unbreathable.

From Figueres we headed to La Junquera, but the driver followed the rest of the transports down a secondary road toward La Vajol. The main route to France was impassable because of the number of people trying to cross the border.

The clattering of the truck jostled us all into one another. Children were crying. The older adults all wore a similar look of resignation, as if asking themselves why they had not just waited to die in their own beds instead of heading off into the unknown.

The route took us into a forest. Some inside the truck started singing to cheer up the journey, but then we heard a dreaded sound. Two planes were headed our way from the mountains. We all ducked and stayed silent, as if that would change anything.

We could hear the bombs falling and the machine guns roaring. The first pass overhead took out one of the buses, but the gunfire barely grazed our truck. We hoped they would move on, pleased enough to have murdered a few civilians.

"They're Italians!" one man called out. "Damned Fascists!"

Seemingly in response to his comment, the planes came back. On the second round, they hit the truck in front of us full on, and then our motor started burning.

"Everybody out!" our driver yelled.

We jumped out and headed for the woods right before the truck went up in flames. Children were screaming and crying, and their mothers held them as tight as possible in defiance of death's grasp. Our driver, the only one of us who was armed, joined the group América and I were with.

"Let's find an abandoned house to take refuge in. We're about four hours from the border, but night will fall before we make it," he said.

We followed him dumbly, unable to hide our fear and worry. The border seemed to be getting farther and farther away the closer we got.

Elisabeth

It only took Elisabeth two nights to get her spirits and strength back once she was home. Elisabeth's physical and mental exhaustion had given way to renewed enthusiasm and momentum. The more that grown children cease to belong to their parents, the more they put into practice what they learned from their progenitors, for better or for worse. Elisabeth's parents knew that their daughter's place was with the orphans. So she set off with Lucy for France, where French Quaker churches had collected food and clothing for the Spanish refugees crowding the border.

She and Lucy went from church to church, collecting the aid, and left the next day for the southern border. All the French newspapers had stories about the flood of refugees as well as the tension between Germany and the rest of Europe. Some of the headlines portrayed the Spanish refugees as a dangerous Communist invasion, while others clamored for the government to help the countless women, children, and older adults exposed to the cold and rain at the border.

Lucy and Elisabeth arrived in Perpignan the following day. The city was in complete chaos. The army and the gendarmes were patrolling the streets, and many of the townsfolk had locked themselves inside for fear of venturing out. Without too much trouble, they located the hospital where Elisabeth's friend Karl Ketterer was staying with the children in what was clearly an unsustainable situation.

Inside the small, worn-down building, Lucy gave the hospital director some of the supplies for pregnant women and newborns. Then she and Elisabeth opened a set of double doors to find two hundred children crammed into a space with around thirty beds.

"Elisabeth!" Karl exclaimed, running up to her. She hugged her friend and then went around to hug and kiss each of the children, who all greeted her with "Hola, Señorita Elisabeth."

Elisabeth, Lucy, and Karl went out into the hallway to talk.

"Thank God you've come," Karl began. "We can't stay here any longer. The hospital needs this room for those sick and wounded in the war. We've got one week left."

"Don't worry. People in Switzerland and France gave us money, and we've brought food and other supplies. We'll find a place."

"And God will help us!" Lucy said with a smile.

"Forgive me, Karl; I haven't introduced Lucy. She and her Quaker sisters helped me when I was alone at the border. Then I fell ill, and Lucy escorted me back home."

"I'm so pleased to meet you," Karl said, shaking Lucy's hand.

"And I you." There was a flush in Lucy's cheeks that made it clear she truly was pleased to meet this attractive, good-hearted man.

"Well, catch me up on everything over hot chocolate," Karl said, leading them down the stairs.

Elisabeth felt the same as on her first day in Spain, like her life had suddenly lit up and everything made sense. Right then she understood the Bible's words about how all who are weary and burdened should come to the Lord. Sometimes people had to be at the end of their strength to understand the source of life's true strength.

SEVEN

Isabel

We never know what we have till we lose it. In the security of our own homes with the people we love, we presume those moments will last forever and that we are immune to death, ruin, and misfortune. Yet this is a simple denial of reality, like the frightened child hiding underneath the bedsheets to keep the nighttime terrors at bay.

The night in the abandoned country home was more challenging than any of the previous nights. Part of the roof was caved in, and snowflakes drifted through once the snow began. No one actually slept, and in the morning we discovered that one of the babies in our group had died. The mother was overwrought and could not be comforted. We all wondered when the horror would end.

We bought some eggs from a peasant woman who lived in a nearby house. We had no choice but to eat them raw. Then we set off on the trek to the border. The driver from our ruined transport led the way alongside a man in a worker's uniform. The way was steep, and the snow was mounding up. Two hours in, it was hard to keep walking. Shivering and nearly frozen, América and I paused to rest in the shelter of an old shack that had half a roof left. The path ahead crossed a rushing creek, and we needed to gather our strength for that.

"I can't keep going," América said as the rest of our group continued on. Her face was bright red from the cold, and her nose was soaked.

"Just a bit more and we'll be in France," I said to cheer her up, but her skinny legs could barely hold her up any longer.

"I don't know if it's worth it anymore."

"That's the exhaustion talking." I gave her some water and bread. We had not had anything since the raw egg. Just then an old woman passed us with two children. I had not noticed her before, as she had been in one of the other transports hit by the planes.

"Come on, girls. You've got to cross!" she called out, trying to keep her balance on the slippery rocks. The creek was not very deep, but the nearly freezing temperature of the water was danger enough.

"I'm scared, Gran," the younger girl said. She could not have been over five years old. Her freckled face was frozen stiff, as was her red hair beneath her soaked wool hat.

"We'll be there soon, and the French will give us all a mug of hot chocolate!" the grandmother answered. She held one hand of each granddaughter, but the youngest one slipped on the wet rocks and fell into the frigid water. I ran to them, and América followed. She steadied the grandmother, and I lunged for the girl. The water came up to my knees, and everything it touched was instantly numb. I pulled the child out of the water and helped her across. The grandmother covered her with a blanket and started rubbing her body to get the circulation going again.

"There's a fire over there," the other girl said, pointing through the trees.

We could just make out smoke rising, and we headed in that direction with the hope of finding warmth. Three Republican soldiers were sitting around the fire while two others were working on a truck. They were surprised to see us but motioned for us to come to the fire. The old woman put the youngest girl right up to the flames and kept rubbing her until she was able to relax and move again.

I slapped at my legs and stamped my feet, changed my socks, and put my shoes close to the fire to dry as much as possible. I could not stop rubbing my hands together.

"Do you have any food?" the youngest soldier asked. He looked no older than eighteen.

I pulled out more of Inmaculada's bread and a can of tuna. The soldiers whooped with delight and made short work of the meager lunch or dinner. Night was about to fall.

"The truck broke down," a gray-haired soldier with a receding hairline explained.

"Do you think you can fix it?" I asked.

"That's what Hermida and the corporal are trying to find out. There's not a long way left to go, but our feet are blistered, and it's hard to keep walking. We've been marching for ten days now, from Castellón. We got out by some miracle," the younger soldier said.

An hour later, the truck was fixed, but it was too late to start out. We all lay down in the truck bed and waited for morning. Now at last it seemed like nothing would keep us from getting to France. We foolishly thought our nightmare was coming to a close.

Peter

Peter had been traveling for two days. He had had luck and had gotten a ride on a truck to Figueres. His search for Isabel had been fruitless, which he interpreted to mean she was already in France. The next day he left for the border. The convoy of trucks he was in took the route to La Vajol and passed by several vehicles destroyed in a recent attack. He glimpsed an abandoned country home and then was met with a very long line of cars. The truck he was in had to wait several hours to get close to the border.

The border guard and French military men ordered the refugees to make two long lines. One was for civilians and the other for soldiers. The few brigade soldiers left lined up in an orderly fashion. By that time everyone just wanted to get out of Spain as quickly as possible.

"What are you going to do when you get across?" Philip asked Peter. Philip was an African American man who had spent two years fighting with the brigades, though he and Peter had rarely overlapped in their placements.

Peter smiled as if already imagining it. "I'm going to find my wife and take a good, long shower. What about you?"

"I'm going to take the first boat I can find for Louisiana and order gumbo and red beans and rice as soon as I get there," Philip said.

"All you ever think about is food," Peter chided him and handed back the cigarette they were sharing.

A group of women were causing a bit of a ruckus in the civilian line as they jostled to be first. Peter and Philip turned to see what the commotion was about, and Peter recognized one of Isabel's workmates from the seamstress shop.

"Ramona?" he asked.

She turned and studied the American soldier blankly. Of course she could not recognize him with his thick, unkempt beard.

"I'm Peter, Isabel's husband."

"Oh, good heavens! Your wife has been looking all over for you. You know the shop was bombed and we had to flee. We all got separated as we left Barcelona, but I saw her in Figueres. One of the other girls told me she was planning to wait for you there."

"In Figueres? Are you sure? I was there yesterday and couldn't find her anywhere."

"Yes, I think she was with a woman who had family there."

The French guards prodded the line of soldiers to keep moving, and they had to place their weapons in a big pile.

Peter looked around at his comrades. "I've got to go back."

"Are you crazy?" Philip asked, not bothering to temper his opinion. "If the Nationalists catch you, they'll shoot you on sight or stick you in a concentration camp. You know the horrible things that happen there." He shivered.

"Isabel's waiting for me. I have to get her out of Spain before it's too late."

Peter broke out of the line and started running in the opposite direction as the truck Isabel was in rolled toward the border.

EIGHT

Isabel

When our truck revved up and started moving, we all cheered. We could not believe it. Just an hour later, despite the throngs of people and the snow, we arrived at the border. About a mile away we had to leave the truck and continue on foot. América and I helped the old woman with her two granddaughters. Two of the soldiers picked them up and carried them piggyback. We all started cheering again as we drew close to French soil.

Soon, though, we realized that our euphoria was overly optimistic. Senegalese soldiers, French gendarmes, and customs agents were treating the refugees roughly and refusing to let them pass.

One of the soldiers with us went up to the fence, studied the situation, and came back to report. "I don't like the look of things. They're having all the soldiers throw down their weapons before being loaded into trucks. The civilians are going on foot, being pushed around and hurried, with no care for the children or the older adults. They're being taken to a neutral zone, but it's still Spanish territory. You still won't be safe there."

I stared at the young soldier with a blank face. We could not go back. Franco had arrived in Barcelona, and the rest of the cities would not hold out much longer. His troops would be at our heels within weeks.

"We're going to cross," I said, taking América's arm. The youngest soldier joined us, and the grandmother and grand-daughters did as well. The others opted to wait on the Spanish side of the border.

We walked the last few yards with anguished determination. We were walking toward the complete unknown. We had lost our rights, our country, and almost our dignity. The only thing we could hope for was compassion from the French.

The line moved forward slowly, just a few yards every quarter hour. We could see the first Senegalese soldiers. They were tall and thin, and their dark blue uniforms were hardly distinguisha-ble from their dark skin. The Senegalese soldiers were escorting Republican soldiers to the trucks after stripping them of their weapons. Meanwhile, the gendarmes beside them were dealing with the civilians, shouting at the refugees and pushing them to one side or another.

As we approached the border police, my legs were shaking. I had never been so scared, not even during Fascist bombing raids.

"Do you have papers?" the agent asked in poor Spanish.

I handed them over, trying to keep my hand steady.

"Visa?"

I shook my head.

"Over there." He flicked his head.

I was pushed into a group of women as he turned to question América. A few seconds later we were together again. The grand-mother and the two girls were taken to the other line. The young soldier insisted on escorting them, but the Senegalese beat him back and forced him into one of the trucks.

As a group, we walked forward about a hundred yards. There were a few Red Cross tents, and people were handing out bread and soup. We gobbled ours down. We were still shivering with the cold. A few minutes later I told one of the soldiers I needed to go to the bathroom. He pointed to some bushes a ways off.

I sought as much privacy as possible behind some tall shrubs but heard footsteps. A French soldier was heading my way, eyeing me. I got up quickly, and he disappeared into the brush.

Elisabeth

The surrounding neighborhoods in Perpignan were by no means overly nice or well equipped, but they would surely offer something better than the hospital room. Elisabeth asked Lucy to help her look for a suitable house for the children. They took Rocinante, one of the old vans the SCI had used in Spain, and the two women scouted out the area. The van spouted smoke and made a terrible racket, and the townspeople eyed it warily. Many Spaniards had slipped through to Spain by mountains and woods, and the region was full of strangers. Local farmers reported that food was being stolen, and every manner of legend had grown up around the "fearsome Spaniards."

After driving around for an hour, the two women arrived at

a small town called Brouilla. It was only about ten miles outside of Perpignan, which was close enough to get a sick child to the hospital or go shopping for whatever they could not find nearby. They drove along the streets south of the town. Country homes were scattered throughout the area, hidden between gardens and fields of grapevines.

The rain started falling harder, and they drove by a two-story house that looked to be abandoned. From the outside, it looked strong, and the roof seemed to be intact.

"It's got stables in the back," Lucy said, cleaning one of the windows enough to allow her to peer inside.

"It's outside of town, and there's a garden. We could grow vegetables and even keep a few cows."

"You don't strike me as a farmer," Lucy joked.

They covered up with their coats and ran back to the car. They had not gone far when they came upon an old Ford driven by a white-bearded man.

"Bonjour, monsieur. Do you know if the house with the red shutters is for rent?"

The old man stopped his car and lowered his window. They repeated their question, and he stared at them.

"Why do two foreigners want an old house?"

"We're volunteers, and we're taking care of a group of Spanish children. We need somewhere for them to stay," Elisabeth explained.

"Oh, the Spaniards, what a shame. That war is inhumane. I'm glad it's coming to a close, but I've no idea where all those people are going to go. The radio says there's thousands of them at the border. I fought in the Great War and saw plenty of French escaping south, but I think some of my compatriots have forgotten all about that. Humans tend to have a very short memory, don't you think?"

The two young women nodded.

"That house and farm belong to Xavier Durand. People say it's cursed, but I don't believe in superstition myself. The only things that are cursed are human beings. I served on a ship off the African coast. You wouldn't believe what supposedly decent people were doing to the population. Up here we talk all about liberty, equality, and fraternity, but those French values are conspicuously absent in our colonies."

"We're too easy on ourselves and too harsh on others," Lucy offered. The man nodded.

"Xavier died years ago, but his son Pierre lives in the village. He's a veterinarian and didn't want to keep his dad's farm. Taking care of farm animals is hard work. You have to feed the beasts every day, keep them clean, watch over the births . . . it's not a job everyone's fit for. I've just come from feeding my cows."

"Where exactly does Pierre Durand live?" Elisabeth asked.

"Follow me," he said.

Elisabeth and Lucy followed the man's Ford in Rocinante. Five minutes later they were parked in front of a beautiful home, clearly the most elegant of the town. The old man knocked at the front door. A maid with a bonnet came out to meet them. They asked to see the veterinarian, and the maid showed them in to a small sitting room off the foyer.

"This is where people wait with their animals," the old man said, settling into a velvet chair.

"It's rather fancy for a veterinarian," Elisabeth commented.

"Pierre was in the colonies for a while and came home quite well-off. The veterinary clinic is just something he does to keep from getting bored. Money has little use once you've got it," the man said, smiling. He was wearing old, dirty work clothes that looked to be his daily uniform, and his boots were caked with mud.

"Marcus, I've been told . . . ," Pierre said, walking in, but he stopped abruptly when he saw the two strangers.

"These women are volunteers with the Spaniards, Pierre. They want you to rent them your dad's old place."

Pierre ducked his head in greeting but kept studying them with his eyes.

"Are you Spaniards?"

"No, sir. I'm from Switzerland, and my friend is British."

He raised his eyebrows at that, trying to understand why two young foreigners were interested in helping the Spaniards.

"What do you want the farm for? Not to house a bunch of refugees?"

Elisabeth frowned, and Lucy spoke up. "It's for orphaned children. We got them out of the country and are looking for somewhere for them to stay as we care for them."

"But why would you do that? The Spanish authorities would've taken charge of them. You're uprooting them from their homeland."

"We've been in Spain for the past two years. What's going on there is much worse than a war—it's pure massacre. The Francoist troops are nearly at the border. Most people are just trying to escape for their lives." Lucy's hackles were getting raised. It was easy for people to have an opinion about a situation they did not actually understand.

"I've read about the Republicans murdering plenty of innocent people as well, in their so-called *checas*, the improvised 'police' force of the militia. You know how it goes: an eye for an eye, tooth for a tooth."

"We're more in the camp of those who turn the other cheek. We're not interested in debating the war in Spain. My father taught me that being guided by other people's opinions is the quickest way for humans to get lost. God gave each of us a conscience. What does yours tell you?"

Pierre seemed unruffled by his conscience. He simply stated a price, which the women countered by half.

"Pierre," the aged Marcus said from his chair, "I've known you since you were playing with my own kids in the pigpens. You've got enough money to last you several lifetimes. God will remember you for this deed."

The vet touched his chin and looked off as if contemplating his eternal future, then held out his hand to the women. "I hope I don't come to regret this."

"You won't!" Elisabeth said, relieved.

They thanked Marcus as they returned to their cars.

"It's nothing. I like to hassle people like Pierre who forget where they came from. There are a lot like him, and my own son is one of them. It's a shame, but that's human nature for you," he said, shrugging.

As they drove back through the neighborhoods, Elisabeth thought back to one of her first classes in Denmark just before heading for Spain. In that phase of life, she was questioning everything her parents had taught her. Their small realm of faith and certainty seemed so insignificant compared to the university and the vast world outside their town. One of her professors in Copenhagen had said that, for many philosophers and intellectuals like Goethe, the nineteenth century had been all about the freedom of human beings. Goethe had his hero rob fire from the gods in the poem "Prometheus" to showcase humans determining their own fate. What the poets and intellectuals did not realize was that, by distancing humankind from the divine, they were severing themselves from the sanctity of what it means to be human. They were animalizing the human race and turning the act of killing into a simple matter of survival. At least that was her interpretation of the way things had gone.

As they drove through the countryside in the rain, the war and the refugees seemed so far off, like a nightmare they were waking up from. They were aware that this was how many people viewed the tragedies of others, as mere stories told around the fireplace or overheard from the radio, soon to be forgotten.

Peter

GERONA

January 23, 1939

Peter fell in with a group of military men who had refused to give up their weapons at the border and become French prisoners. The five men found an abandoned truck and returned to Figueres. After another full day of looking for Isabel, Peter was deflated. He slept fitfully in the nearly empty army barracks and intended to continue searching the next day. He woke at dawn and had some coffee and dry bread. Just as he was leaving the barracks, a Republican army captain entered and ordered Peter and the other men from the barracks to get into some trucks outside. The

Republican government had moved to Gerona and was trying to hold out while waiting for a shipment of weapons that were stalled at the French border.

"Captain, I request permission to speak," Peter said while waiting in formation before entering the trucks.

"Speak, soldier."

"I'm a volunteer with the International Brigades. Our units have dissolved. I rejoined the fight a few days ago and went back to Barcelona, but it's pointless. The Fascists are much better equipped than we are. All we're doing is dragging out the inevitable."

"Is that so, soldier?"

"Yes, Captain."

"You came here to defend the Republic, isn't that right?"

"Yes, Captain."

"Well, the Republic is still alive. In a few weeks war might break out in Europe, and then the French will join us. You know what that would mean?"

"But, Captain, we've been hearing that for the past two years. The French aren't going to join any war, and . . ."

The captain pulled out his gun and aimed at Peter.

"We're finished with soldier committees. We're not anarchists. We're Communists, and we know how to respect hierarchy and the chain of command. If that had been the case from the beginning, things would look a lot different now, wouldn't they?"

"I'm not a Communist, Captain."

"I don't care. You're a vet, and we need you so Gerona doesn't fall."

"But I need to find my wife."

"Forget your wife! Do you want to leave her a widow? Right now I could order a war council and a firing squad for you."

Peter stood at stiff attention and followed the rest of the men to the trucks. As he sat beside his fellow men-at-arms, some of whom were boys of fifteen or sixteen years, he cursed his fate.

A few hours later they were in Gerona. They were ordered to help build barricades before the Francoist troops arrived. Peter's squad was assigned the duty of placing sandbags along the streets. He found himself working next to a young soldier named José, from Andalusia.

"So how did you end up here, José?" Peter asked, lugging a bag over.

"The Fascists recruited me in Priego de Córdoba and sent me to fight in the Battle of the Ebro, but as soon as I got the chance I came over to the Republican side. My family has always been poor farmers, and we've got nothing to thank Franco and the military for."

"Well, you chose the losing side," Peter said.

"I've always been with the losers. I'm used to it. For hundreds of years we've been told not to try to move up from where we belong. It's easy enough for them; they've always been on top. But a lot of people like me are tired of obeying the fancy little masters and of being little more than slaves."

Peter admired the young man's bravery, but he knew that anytime one master is done away with, another rises to fill the space. Peter no longer believed in the nobility of war. He had seen too much.

At the end of the day, they were exhausted. He sat and shared a cigarette with José. Then the captain came up to them.

"Englishman, come with me."

"I'm not an Englishman, Captain. I'm from the United States."

"Same thing. You speak English, don't you?"

Peter nodded. He was taken to the quarters where the government was currently housed and led through several improvised offices where employees were scurrying about trying to get things in order. The captain stopped at a door at the very back and knocked. When it opened, Peter saw Prime Minister Juan Negrín. His wide face and open forehead held an intelligent but sad look as he glanced up from the papers on his desk. He gestured for the men to sit.

"With the government's move, we lost our English translator. You speak English?" Negrín asked.

"Yes, Mr. Prime Minister," Peter answered in a cowed voice, intimidated by the man he had heard so much about.

"Well, do me the service of reading this letter from the British ambassador. I could read it myself, but my mind these days—it's too much to keep up with all the documents."

As Peter read, the prime minister huffed and tsked. At the end, he leaned back and massaged his scalp. "You know the Spanish refrain about how everyone's a flea to the skinny dog?"

"I haven't heard that one, sir."

"The democracies have never supported us, and we had to throw ourselves into the embrace of Stalin, which is like letting a wild bear pet you. I'm a doctor. I've spent my life saving people, and now I send them to the front to die like cannon fodder. I've proposed a ceasefire and a negotiated peace time after time to Franco, but do you know what he answers? Only unconditional surrender. He won't even promise to respect the lives of my soldiers after surrender. Everyone blames me—quite Spanish of them. They accuse me of being a Communist, which I'm not, and others say I'm a conservative. In our country no one tolerates those who aren't sectarian, those who simply love their country and are heartbroken to see it divided and destroyed by the people who should be protecting and caring for it."

The prime minister regained his composure and looked at Peter before continuing. "You're a foreigner; you'll have seen what I'm talking about. We're a wild, medieval, cruel people. Well, that's not the whole story. We can also be wonderfully joyful, loving, and disciplined. Forgive me for going on and on. I haven't slept for forty-eight hours."

"Can I help you with anything else, Mr. Prime Minister?" Peter asked, getting to his feet.

"Stay close by. There's more correspondence to get through. There might still be hope to stop the war or to hold out until war breaks out in Europe. It's terrible to think that for us to win, other countries have to suffer."

Peter left the office, and the captain asked a corporal to take him to the room where government employees were being housed. They offered him a bed with clean sheets and served him dinner.

"Are there bathrooms?" Peter asked.

The corporal gave him soap and a towel and showed him the way.

As the water washed over his body, Peter thought again of his beloved Isabel. He felt like some inexplicable force was keeping him away from her. For the first time in years he said a short prayer. He whispered that if a higher being would reunite him with his wife, Peter would be a better man. He thought about his father and what Sam Davis would say if he could see his son weeping in the shower in a foreign country.

NINE

Isabel

LA VAJOL
January 27, 1939

The cold of those interminable nights gripped us to the bone. Most of us were sleeping outdoors on the crunchy snow. A few privileged refugees had managed to fashion a shelter with sticks and blankets, but they, too, were soaked as soon as the snow started falling again. América and I slept curled up together. We were each other's only support right then. I was desperate, confused, friendless, and had no idea what to do. I needed to find Peter, but he was probably still fighting somewhere in Catalonia, trying to hold the front a few weeks more with the vain illusion that war would start in Europe.

As I watched the multitude of desperate women, children, and older adults, I understood that poverty has no history and that soon enough the world would forget the hundreds who had fallen dead along the road; the world would forget those who had returned home with fear forever etched in their bodies and knowing it would be their last trek; and it would forget the soldiers of the people's army whom their enemies considered murderers and who had nothing but ignominious defeat and death by firing squad to look forward to.

"What are you thinking about?" América asked. Her innocent expression moved me. Something compelled me to protect her. This adolescent would not survive in the chaotic place the world had become. She was a student full of dreams who could have become a wife and mother in a nice part of Barcelona—now she was just a skeletal, terrified girl.

"Well, the truth is I'd rather not be thinking at all. Every time I look back on life I get the feeling that something like what happened to Lot's wife will happen to me."

América scrunched up her face, not following me.

"Ah, it's obvious you were raised during the Republic. I had to learn catechesis and take First Communion. I'm guessing you didn't. What I mean is that it's dangerous to look back because you might get paralyzed forever."

"Oh, my parents said something similar. They didn't want me to go backward, which is why I always try to be optimistic, though I don't really see much point in that anymore."

We got up. We needed to find some privacy to go to the bathroom, but there was little to be had in that improvised camp.

"You watch first," I asked América.

She moved back a bit, to the beginning of the path. Without stockings, her legs were chapped and red beneath her skirt. I turned and squatted under a tree. I had barely started when I heard a shout. I got up immediately and looked toward the path, but América was no longer there. I ran to where I heard muffled shouting that had dwindled to a murmur. A gendarme was crushing América with his weight beside one of the shrubs. She was trying to wriggle free, but he held her down with one hand while the other covered her mouth.

"Let her go!" I screamed, jumping on him. He threw me off, and I fell back hard to the ground. I got up as quickly as I could and looked around for help. There was a rock half buried in the snow. I wrenched it out of the ground and smacked him hard on the head with it. He whirled around to me in a fury. The blood was pouring down his face and soaking his combat jacket. He took two steps forward. I thought he would pull out his pistol and shoot me, but he collapsed. The snow around him was turning red.

"Is he dead?" América asked, straightening her clothes. We could still smell the man's sweat and the alcohol from his breath.

"I don't know," I said, grabbing her hand and running.

"We're headed away from camp," América said.

"We can't go back. We've got to try to get across."

We were fenced in, but we found a small hole by a nearby stream. The freezing water immediately cut off our circulation, but the terror coursing through our blood pushed us to keep going. We passed under the fence and were in France.

"Now what?" América asked.

I shrugged. I would have liked to have an answer, but I knew that whatever we found next could not be worse than what we were running away from.

"We need to try to get to Perpignan. We'll be less noticeable in a city. We can look for work and try to survive the winter. When Peter gets here, I'll ask him to take you with us."

América stopped and turned to me with her big, bright eyes. "Seriously? You would do that for me?"

I nodded, and she hugged me. Her stiff, frozen clothing made me shiver anew, but her embrace made me feel close to another human being for the first time in a long time.

"I thought I'd never matter to anyone again," she said.

"My child, my sweet child," I said as we both wept. In the face of adversity, there is no greater comfort than feeling connected to a kindred soul. For me, América was the younger sister I never had.

===

Elisabeth

ELNE
January 31, 1939

Turning the old, abandoned homestead in Brouilla into adequate living quarters was no small job. The entire SCI team worked around the clock, but almost nothing about the house worked the way it should. The pipes had burst, the electricity was shot, the chimney for the coal-burning stove was blocked, and the roof had so many broken tiles that twenty buckets were not enough to catch all the water that dripped through.

Elisabeth and Lucy worked themselves to the bone. Besides taking care of the children alongside the rest of the workers, they had to source food for everyone in the middle of winter while the large-scale arrival of refugees had already exhausted the region's supplies. Given the high prices and how much the authorities confiscated, they had to go through several towns just to get the bare minimum that would allow the workers and children to survive the winter.

Elisabeth had learned to handle all of Rocinante's tricks,

though the van still sometimes froze up on longer journeys. Lucy kept her company singing in the passenger seat, trying to enjoy their little ventures and the moments of peace amid the wearisome work of surviving. At any point in time, Elisabeth and Lucy could have gone back to their homes and started their lives over again. Yet they were committed to that obscure quagmire that the French border had become.

"It looks like the sun might be trying to come out," Elisabeth said. She was back in full spirits now, thanks in large part to Lucy. Elisabeth had not found such a dear friend anywhere else in her journeys. She and Karl were close, but their temperaments could not have been more different. Karl seemed to be above all the circumstances and immune to the suffering around them, and Elisabeth carried the weight of the world on her shoulders.

"The sun gets hotter here than in Switzerland or England," Elisabeth went on, "but there's no sun like in Spain. I miss those long, warm afternoons along the Mediterranean and how alive it made me feel."

Lucy agreed wholeheartedly. Spaniards had a host of defects, but they knew how to live life. They had a joyful, unworried disposition despite great adversity. They were not afraid of death, and they laughed at the future. Many blamed the country's misfortune on the people's indolent attitude, but Elisabeth and Lucy did not agree. The Spanish people worked hard, but they did not live to work. They enjoyed celebrations and sharing time with their family. Their hospitality was legendary. Yet they were in the grip of the same spirit of the twentieth century that had poisoned half of Europe: damned ideologies that promised prosperity and a better future but that dragged humanity into a bottomless abyss.

"I just wonder what will become of Spain in a few years," Lucy mused.

Elisabeth looked over at her friend and shook her head in answer. The war had caused so much suffering that it would take a very long time for the hatred to dissipate. A deep wound had opened among the Spaniards, and it would not heal easily.

"Only a miracle can heal all of this," Elisabeth said, gesturing to the column of refugees escorted by soldiers.

"Wait! This means they've let them through the border!" Lucy exclaimed.

The refugees had been waiting for days in a no-man's-land. The group that Lucy and Elisabeth saw now could only mean one thing: the French had finally opened the border. The constant drip of people who'd been entering the country secretly would soon turn into a flood of tens of thousands.

"Dear Lord, what are we going to do? Our little hole-in-the-wall is barely big enough for us and the children. What are we going to do with the hundreds of children who need help?" That reaction was typical of Elisabeth. Always thinking one step ahead, she often ended up tortured by situations and realities that never actually came to be.

"We can't do anything about it." Lucy shrugged.

"Should we follow this line of people?" Elisabeth suggested.

They drove Rocinante several miles ahead, following the human column that was heading to the sea. There the army had thrown up a few makeshift shacks, a fence, and guard stations. Elisabeth parked near the entrance, and she and Lucy watched in spellbound silence, trying to take it all in.

"The plan is to just leave them on the beach?" Elisabeth wondered aloud.

"Seems like it."

"But it's cold. And the wind blows here like nowhere else. There are just a few tents and shacks here. The people will die without shelter in this cold."

Elisabeth turned the ignition. She was flustered by what she was seeing.

"You okay?" Lucy asked.

"We've got to find somewhere bigger and nicer."

"That won't be easy. Remember how much Pierre is charging us to rent the farm."

But Elisabeth was not listening. When she had a goal, no one and nothing could stand in her way.

Late for the market, they arrived in Elne, a small town with a certain charm. They hoped all the good produce had not already been snatched up. They parked Rocinante and walked to the market on foot. Elisabeth stopped to peer through a rusted fence at a yard. The grounds must have been beautiful at one time, but now they were run down and full of weeds and thistles. Then she looked up at the small palace beyond the yard.

"Lucy, have you seen this place?" She pointed to the moss-covered exterior blackened by time.

Lucy noticed a stagnant pond in the yard and counted three stories to the building. It was big enough but surely beyond their means.

"You're a dreamer, Elisabeth."

The young woman smiled, taking it as a compliment. Her father had always told her that life allows people to achieve what they can dream or imagine. Elisabeth had found that to be true on several occasions. If she could imagine it, surely she could achieve it, or at least try.

Peter

GERONA
January 31, 1939

Prime Minister Negrín was studying the map of Catalonia with vacant eyes. Franco's unstoppable advance had pushed the Republican forces into the Pyrenees in recent weeks. The government had not been in Gerona even a full week, and they needed to get out immediately. General Yagüe was outside the city with his bloodthirsty Moroccan and Italian soldiers as well as the Requeté militiamen from Navarre.

Peter stood in the office, having been summoned a few minutes earlier by the prime minister's secretary.

"My son, we've got to evacuate again, but first I want you to read me these letters from the British cabinet, in case some detail has escaped me. I don't have much faith that they'll do anything. They've already let Austria and Czechoslovakia fall, and we matter little to them. With his supposed 'peace for our time,' Neville will go to any length to avoid war."

Peter read the letters aloud. When he looked up, the prime minister's face was even more desolate than before.

"There's nothing to be done."

"Madrid is holding out," Peter countered, trying to lift his spirits.

"When it's fully surrounded, it will only be a matter of time."

"Surely there's something."

"If I weren't an atheist, I'd tell you we can always pray, but my recommendation is that you get out of here and try to find your wife. The only hope we've got now is to survive and, once war starts in Europe, try to reclaim our beloved land."

Peter walked away racked with ambivalence. He was deeply sad—it had all been a waste. Yet he also felt free. Now the only thing that mattered was finding Isabel.

As he walked away from the building to find a vehicle heading for the border, he could hear the bombs falling outside the city. That unmistakable smell of powder was always a presage to death.

He walked along the highway. For the first time he was traveling alone. There were crowds of civilians and soldiers also marching, but he was not with any of them. A few hours in, he opted for a secondary road to move faster. His mother always said it was better to take the path less traveled. Confused, disoriented masses tended to walk right off a cliff.

It was more peaceful away from the main road. The carefully tended fields and villages that were still in one piece helped him forget the war for a while. He found a suitable walking stick and, after several more hours of traveling, sat and ate his last provisions. He crossed a river, went into a forest, and was walking up and up, ever up toward the border. Then he heard the unmistakable sound of tanks. He hid behind some rocks and watched a column of Italian soldiers and vehicles pass. He was so focused on the combat vehicles that he did not note the light footfall behind him. But he did note the cold barrel of a gun against his neck. Instinctively, he raised his hands.

TEN

Isabel

We walked for hours without resting, stopping only to hide from soldiers and gendarmes and to beg food at the farms we came upon. Some pelted us with sticks and stones, but others gave us bread and cheese, *fuet* sausage, or milk. The cold was less intense the farther we went from the Pyrenees, but the nights were still freezing. We hid out in haylofts and stables, abandoned houses, or even under large trees. We were trying to put as much distance as possible between us and the border. As we traveled on our endless walks, I obsessed over whether or not I had killed the man who attacked América. The idea of having become a murderer tormented me, though my actions had been in defense of someone helpless. América and I did not speak of it. The poor girl was too famished and exhausted by trying to stay strong for what we were facing.

On the second day of our tireless escape, we arrived in Llauro, a small town with a beautiful monastery. We did not come upon a single soul as we walked the streets until we reached a small store.

There were jars of preserved fruits and vegetables out in the open. We were so hungry we almost grabbed them without thinking, but we held back and went inside the small establishment.

A very thin woman dressed all in black was knitting a wool scarf. She looked at us warily. Our clothes were dirty and torn after days of walking through fields.

"What do you want?" she asked in French. Seeing that we did not understand, she switched to Catalan.

"We are hungry," América said. Her blue eyes were shining in an unhealthy way in her pale, sunken face.

The woman waved us away, but then another woman appeared, heavier set than the first. Her white hair made a stark contrast with her black mourning dress. She said something to the thin woman and then smiled at us.

"Forgive my sister. She's naturally distrustful. Please, have these." She held out two sticky buns in a box, and we devoured them instantly.

"Poor dears. Come," she said, motioning us forward. "I'm Beatriu, and this is my sister, Dolors."

She led us to the back of the store, and we followed mutely. She guided us up a set of stairs and opened a door.

"Why don't you two take a nice bath. I'll find some clothes for you. I'm not sure we've got anything that will fit."

América and I studied ourselves in the bathroom mirror. We still could not believe what was happening. We got undressed and bathed in warm water. It was the first time we stopped shivering from the cold in days. Beatriu brought us a change of clothes, a brush, and toothpaste. When we left the bathroom, we looked like completely different people.

They looked up in surprise as we reentered the store.

"Well, incredible! Underneath all that dirt there were two beautiful young ladies! There's coffee and some cake here for you."

We ate and drank ravenously under their gaze.

"You aren't like what they describe in the newspaper and on the radio," Beatriu said. Her sister still eyed us with suspicion. "Dolors thinks you must be robbers and murderers. We hear that the Spaniards want to take our homes and our lands and that you're a bunch of Red demons."

"I imagine people say those things so no one will help us," I said, finishing the last delicious sip of coffee.

We told them a short version of our story and everything that had happened till we reached their store. Then we heard someone at the door. Beatriu hurried us to the back to hide.

"Ladies," a gendarme said.

"Sergeant," they answered.

"Someone in the area let us know they've seen two vagabonds passing through town. Have they bothered you?"

"Oh no, Sergeant," Beatriu answered.

"If you see them, it's best to denounce them immediately. The countryside is crawling with Spaniards now. They've all come in illegally and are potentially dangerous."

Dolors was about to speak, but Beatriu cut in, "We'll be sure to let you know."

"Thank you." He nodded and closed the door behind him.

As soon as he left, the sisters closed the store. It would soon be dark, and there were not likely to be any more customers.

"Thank you so much for everything," I said when Beatriu called us out. "We should be going. We don't want to get you in trouble."

"Trouble? Don't worry. We have an extra room. It was our father's, but he has passed on. Rest here for a few days before you continue your journey. The nights are too cold to be out and about, and you don't have good winter clothes. Where are you headed?"

"To Perpignan," I answered. "I'm hoping my husband will join me there."

"Well, then don't say another thing," Beatriu said, though Dolors seemed unconvinced.

We spent that night in a warm bed, safe from the cold. As we listened to the wind howling outside, it occurred to me that the world might still have a chance of being saved as long as there were women like Beatriu and Dolors who were willing to open their home to absolute strangers. I glanced at América and saw she was already in deep sleep. Her angelic, peaceful face stirred in me a maternal instinct I had never felt before. I had watched my mother suffer so much as she raised me by herself. It had stamped out any desire in me to bring new life into this world. And now, with all the suffering that was running rampant throughout the world . . . Yet in some way my mind and body were aching for a ray of hope, a new life that would make its own way and perhaps change the way things were.

Elisabeth

PERPIGNAN
January 31, 1939

Karl, Elisabeth, Lucy, and three other volunteers were in a sustained and heated debate. Mary, one of the youngest volunteers, appeared with a teakettle to try to calm things down.

"Don't you get it? Helping children is important, but so is helping families and expectant mothers," Elisabeth insisted in her passionate, vehement way.

"The mission has sent us to help children. That's why the sponsors are sending their money." Karl had retained his calm, conciliatory disposition.

"Then according to you, it's better to help the children but not do anything for pregnant mothers."

"They've got the French refugee camps. The French are responsible for them."

"Oh, Karl, I've seen one of those camps. It's a damp plot of sand completely hostile to actual human survival."

"For the time being, they're sending pregnant women to the hospital in Perpignan, and they're getting decent care there."

Elisabeth huffed. "Have you forgotten the way things were in that hospital? The doctors are overwhelmed, and there are no empty beds. When the tens of thousands of people from the border show up, they won't be able to do a thing for the pregnant women."

Karl crossed his arms. Lucy served the tea, and everyone else sipped at it edgily. They were used to the rousing debates between the two friends.

"You're absolutely right, but what do you think we can do for pregnant women if the French government can't even help them?"

"We can't help them all, but we can help some, just like we do with the children."

"For now, we have to stay focused on the children. The palace you found is way out of our reach, and we need all of our available teachers and nurses here with the kids."

Elisabeth stood up abruptly from the table and let the door smack shut on her way out. Lucy thought about following her but stayed to talk with Karl.

"I understand your position, Karl, but I think Elisabeth is right about this. You haven't seen the camps."

"It's short term. I'm sure the government will improve them soon."

"The only thing the French government wants is to get all those people to go back to the other side of the border."

Karl shook his head. "I don't think so. Nobody's going to willingly return to Spain unless Franco swears to respect their lives, and that's not going to happen. The guy's an inhumane megalomaniac."

"The Francoists are right at the border, and the people who are escaping are reporting terrible brutality. Executions, rapes, concentration camps for soldiers, children being stolen to send them to orphanages—it's pure horror."

"I know, but we have to stay focused on our mission. The authorities have given us permission to run small care centers for children, and that's what we need to do for now."

Lucy stood and went to find Elisabeth. She was stretched out facedown on her bed, crying.

"You all right?" Lucy asked.

"No, that hothead won't open his eyes and see what's going on. This is the biggest humanitarian crisis in Europe since the Great War. We have to do something."

"Right now the only thing we can do is pray for all those people. If God wants you to open a maternity hospital, he'll provide the way."

Elisabeth dried her tears, sat up, and looked at her friend.

"You're right. I get all tied up in knots about these things, but what I need to do is have faith."

The two friends hugged. They were far from home and were so concentrated on giving to others that they hardly had time or space to face their own fears and griefs. They went back down to the dining room. The children's rest time was over, and it was time to start taking care of everyone again.

———

Peter

FIGUERES

January 31, 1939

The Requeté militiaman led Peter to his corporal. Peter kept his hands raised. He was not afraid. For years he had intrinsically understood that death would only reach people when their time had truly come.

"For God's sake, Federico—another mouth to feed? Why didn't you blast his head off when you found him?"

"He's a Yankee. He's not from here," the soldier answered with a thick Navarre accent as he chewed a chunk of licorice root.

"Precisely, you numbskull. The foreign Reds are the worst kind. At least the ones here have Spanish blood."

The soldier shrugged and brought Peter before the captain, who ordered Peter's captors to take him to the legion at the concentration camp that had recently opened not far from where they were.

The corporal and the soldier left their regiment and had to

walk four hours in the rain with Peter back to Figueres. They were cursing their fate the whole time. Eventually Peter spoke up.

"At least you get out of combat for a day. It would be a shame to get killed now that the war is so close to being over."

"We're fighting for God, our country, and our king. We're not like you, Communists with no real country," the corporal said with a scoff.

"I'm neither of those things. I very much belong to my country, and I've never been part of the Communist Party."

"Then what are you doing here?" the soldier asked, scratching at his head beneath his helmet.

"I'm fighting for freedom, democracy, and the weakest members of society."

The corporal pursed his lips and jabbed his gun into Peter's back. "You're better off keeping your mouth shut, you disgusting atheist."

"I'm not an atheist either. My father is a Presbyterian minister."

They eventually got to the outskirts of the city and came upon a squad of soldiers that gave them directions to the concentration camp. A few minutes later, they were waiting in front of a barbed-wire fence. A sergeant came out to meet them.

"Sir, we've brought a prisoner from the International Brigades."

The sergeant's shirt was unbuttoned at the top despite the intense cold. He studied the Requeté soldiers in silence for a few moments. Finally, he spoke. "We're so full not even a needle could fit."

"Well, we can't take him back with us. We're on an offensive with the Italians."

The sergeant gave a disgusted look, then grabbed Peter and threw him through the gate. "He'd better not last long," he called back to the Requetés. "The ones who survive the hunger and the fleas usually die from exhaustion or beating. It's natural selection," he finished with a guffaw.

The Requetés shrugged and turned to go. They were soaked completely through and had hoped in vain for a bowl of soup and a place to rest before returning to their unit.

The sergeant pushed Peter through to the entrance of what had been a storage room for coal. Another soldier opened the door, and they went in. It was a large room empty of everything but coal remains and prisoners covered in dark dust.

"This is no Hotel Ritz. There are no beds or conveniences. Find yourself a corner and steal a plate and a spoon from someone. That won't be hard since a couple Reds die every day in here.

The sergeant turned to leave, and the soldier pushed Peter farther inside. Peter stumbled to his knees, then got back up and looked for an empty spot along the wall. There was not much room, but one prisoner scooted over to make a space for him.

"You're welcome here, comrade."

Peter sat beside the man. Only then did he feel how exhausted he was.

"Welcome to hell. The Francoists laugh in the face of the Geneva Conventions. I'm Josef, a volunteer fighter from Russia."

This took Peter by surprise. He had met many Russians, but most were army advisors, political commissars, or spies.

"A son of Stalin?"

The Russian shook his head. His hair was so blond it looked white. "Good God, no. I despise that tyrant as much as his predecessor. The Bolsheviks are like the plague. They destroy everything they touch."

Peter looked around him. Many of the combatants would be Communists, and he did not want to get in the middle of any problems. He leaned over and lowered his voice. "So is it true about the purges they've done throughout the country? In his *New York Times* articles, Walter Duranty said it was all bologna and that the famines had been exaggerated."

"That's the problem. In our world today, ideology has infected everything. You're either for something or against it, and nobody cares about the truth. Stalin wants to make his own Red empire. He doesn't care about the proletariat, poverty, or the fight against Fascism."

Peter nodded. He had debated these things with many of his comrades. He leaned forward again. "So how have you managed to survive so long in Spain? Haven't the political commissars been after you?"

"I was with an anarchist militia before they all got dissolved. Then I joined a tank unit. Most of them were trained fighters who didn't care much about politics. A few days ago we went up against some Italians. We were out of ammunition, and they destroyed all our combat vehicles. In the end, like always, the Soviets have betrayed us."

Two soldiers were handing out rock-hard bread and water and rushing the prisoners to eat fast. Soon lights would be out, and no one was allowed to make any noise.

"These guard dogs are worse than their masters," Josef said. "They starve us and beat us to death. The worst one is Fidel, the sergeant who brought you in. He's always looking for a reason to whip us. But I'm not afraid of his kind."

Peter nibbled his bread the best he could, then leaned back against the wall and tried to think about Isabel. He desperately hoped she was safe on the other side of the border. Soon enough he was deep into sleep. Only asleep did he feel truly free.

ELEVEN

Isabel

The Andavert sisters hid us for several days until we could put a little more flesh on our bones. América looked happy again. Her smile had come back, and her cheeks were rosy. Beatriu and Dolors told us about their father's recent death. He had raised them himself. Their mother had died when giving birth to Dolors. Life had not been easy, but they were not complainers. They had dedicated their adult lives to their father, as he had dedicated his to them when they were young.

"Death always betrays us. We knew Dad would die, and we watched him slowly fading away, but still, it's always hard to see someone you love go. Even though we're old ladies now, we feel like orphans."

Listening to Beatriu's words, I nodded and remembered all too well the pain of loss, my mother's illness, being sent away from our building, and trying to make a new life for myself.

"I'm so sorry," América said. She, too, knew what it was to be alone in the world.

Dolors started crying. Up to that point, she had not expressed much in our presence. I went up and hugged her. Between sobs, she spluttered out, "The last day, that night before he left us, it was the day before his birthday. I asked him what he wanted for his birthday, and with just a thin whisper of a voice he answered that we were the best present life had ever given him and that he could die a happy man. He died the next day on his birthday. He lived ninety-five years of goodness and wisdom."

"How hard it must be for you two," I said.

"Yes, Isabel," Beatriu said, her eyes full of tears, "but we have hope that we'll see him again one day. He's with our beloved mother now. He waited years for that moment. His heart and mind were always with her. They only had five years together as a couple, but they're finally together again."

That seemed like the right time to tell them that we would be continuing our journey. "We're so grateful for everything you two have done for us, and we feel like we should make our way to Perpignan tomorrow. I don't want Peter to get there and not be able to find me. I've written to a cousin of mine in Spain. Would you be willing to mail the letter for me?"

The sisters grew serious, and Beatriu begged us to stay longer. "The police are hunting down Spaniards in the streets. At least wait until things calm down some."

"Thank you, Beatriu, but we really must keep going." América looked at me in anguish. She hated to return to the cold, the uncertainty, and the constant fear of being captured. I added, "But América can stay if she wants."

She frowned and shook her head. "I'm not leaving you. I don't know what would've happened to me if we hadn't met."

I let out a long sigh. I had always hated goodbyes, but the only way to keep going and get out of our hellish situation was to find Peter.

"Tomorrow is another day," Dolors said to lighten the mood. Then she pulled out a bottle of champagne and opened it. "We've been saving this for years, but I think it's high time we shared it. Life has gifted us with two new friends. For Isabel and América!"

She poured three glasses of champagne and water for América, and we all toasted. We stayed awake the whole night playing cards and telling stories, soaking up every moment with one another until the light of dawn would separate our paths forever.

====

Peter

FIGUERES
February 5, 1939

After a few days, Peter began to lose all hope of getting out of the concentration camp alive. They were woken before dawn. After lukewarm, bitter coffee, they were marched an hour to a road they were supposed to repair. Their hands were numb with the cold, but if anyone paused or stopped working, the sergeant would fall on him with his rod. Josef became Peter's shadow, protecting him like an older brother and helping Peter learn what to do as quickly as possible. Josef even took more than one beating to spare Peter.

They were served lentils with worms floating in the broth or rotten horse meat. They were forced to work until night, when they marched back on foot and fell exhausted to the floor with just a thin blanket if they were lucky. They were never allowed to bathe, and they were disgusting. The stench in the coal storage room was unbearable. And every day was like the day before.

After the day's work, Peter and Josef slumped against the wall, gnawing their piece of hard bread before bedtime. A man named Francis came up to them. He had traveled from Louisiana to join the International Brigades and was an aviator throughout the war.

"Howdy, countryman. I heard you're from the United States." Francis plopped down beside Peter and handed him a piece of ham. "A farmer gave it to me yesterday. There are still decent people in this world, believe it or not."

Peter split it with Josef, and it tasted divine. "Thank you so much."

"I've got a plan to get out of here, but I need help."

Peter and Josef looked at him nervously. Josef checked to make sure no one was listening. "What did you say?"

Francis continued. "We're close to the border. We could cross it within two hours, but for that to happen, we'd need them to not notice we were gone till we were far enough away."

Peter shook his head, not believing escape was possible. "The camp is watched at all times, and they never take their eyes off us when we're out working. Sooner or later they'll let us out of here, or our government will demand they let us go."

"Nobody knows we're here, and those pigs will either starve or work us to death. After a month in here, we'll be taken out feet first."

Josef put his hand on Peter's shoulder. "Francis is right about that. I've seen too many people die in here. What do we have to lose?"

Francis started drawing on the floor. The coal was like graphite. "The main door is watched, and they never go in or out at night. Well, I've discovered a little trapdoor at the back of the room; probably it was for getting coal in and out. This morning as we were walking outside, I found where it leads to. We'll have to run about a hundred yards, climb the fence, and then head for the woods."

"That's crazy. They have spotlights," Josef said.

"But they don't use them at night so that they don't get detected by enemy planes," Peter explained. That much he had noticed.

"So the plan is simple. We wait till everyone's asleep, open the trapdoor, and escape."

"I don't understand what you need us for, Francis," Josef said.

"It's easier if we all three go at once. I've watched you two, and you seem like the strongest both in body and spirit. If we get discovered, we'll all run our separate ways, and they'll have to decide how to divide up their forces."

Peter and Josef looked at each other. Josef shrugged. "We've got nothing to lose."

"Well, I've got a wife waiting for me and family back home."

"I've also got somebody waiting for me back home," Francis said, "but if we stay here much longer, nobody's ever going to see any of us again."

They waited until the rest of the prisoners were asleep. Peter could not rest, but Josef nodded off occasionally. Peter tried to pray, and he thought about his parents on the other side of the world and about the sons his parents had already lost. He wanted to get home alive.

Francis stood up on the other side of the room, and Peter and Josef carefully made their way through the bodies covering the floor. Some were groaning, some were snoring, and more than one was at death's door. At the back of the room, Francis pointed out the trapdoor. Between the three of them they pried it open and lifted it to the side as silently as possible. Josef went down first. They had nothing to light up the way and had to pick their way in complete darkness through a basement smelling of mold and coal. They felt along the walls until they came to a kind of ladder. They pushed, and a door gave way. Francis peeked out and saw two soldiers not far away, smoking by a fire. Their backs were to the prisoners. Peter and Josef helped let him down. When he was on the ground, Francis reached up and helped them descend. When all three were outside, they carefully closed the door back. Then they dragged themselves through the muddy yard to the fence.

Francis took out a makeshift knife he had fashioned from a sharp rock and attached to a wooden handle. It took him a painfully long time to cut into the fence, but he managed to get a hole big enough for them to crawl through. He went first, then Peter, but Josef got stuck as he tried to wriggle through.

Just then a dog barked. The guards turned on their flashlights and started scanning the fence.

"Get lost!" Josef whispered.

"Are you crazy? Fidel will kill you," Peter said.

"That's better than all three of us getting caught," he said, struggling to free himself.

Francis took off running. Peter hesitated but finally joined him.

Josef tried to force his way through, but the light caught him, and he raised his hands. The soldiers started after him with their growling dogs.

Fidel arrived with two soldiers and, when he saw the Russian, ordered the dogs to be let loose. The mastiffs sank their jaws into him, and Josef howled.

The sergeant delayed calling off the dogs and then shouted, "Of course it's the Russian. Where are the others?"

"I was on my own," Josef panted.

"Nonsense! You and that Yankee are always together."

A searchlight beamed into the forest and showed two figures running. The machine guns started firing at once.

"You lying dog!" the sergeant growled and started beating Josef with his nightstick. As the blood poured out of him, Josef returned in his memory to his childhood. He was living in Russia with his parents during the summer before the revolution turned his world upside down. They were walking along the bank of a river. The sky was blue, and his parents were holding hands. That was his eternal moment, and he would never again feel afraid. He would be with his parents forever.

Yet his death in far-flung Spain would erase that scene forever. Not even memory could outlive him—only a silent, eternal void.

TWELVE

Isabel

We left before dawn to avoid raising suspicion. The Andavert sisters had prepared us a pack full of clothing and food. We said goodbye with a brief hug and without looking back. When I turned to América, her eyes were teary and her cheeks flushed.

"We never know when we'll see the people we love again. If fate allows it, we might run into them again," she said, swallowing back her tears.

"Oh, friend, you know we won't. We've already lost too many people along the way."

I felt a mixture of excitement and worry as we left the Andavert home behind. We were on our own again, and we were finally heading to Perpignan. The news coming from Spain was bleak. We came upon a few cars and one wagon loaded with hay, but we saw no other refugees or walkers. The road was muddy, and our shoes stuck in some places.

Two hours in, we sat to rest on some rocks. The sun had come out, and the glacial morning cold was starting to lift. We ate a couple of butter cookies and were about to start walking again when we saw a police car. We got off the road and ran for the woods, but the vehicle stopped, and two gendarmes got out running.

"Quick!" I hissed, heading for the thicket. América was following me but tripped after a few yards. I helped her up, and we ran toward a slope. It looked too steep to go down, but the police had nearly reached us. We went down as fast as we could, but we lost our footing on the loose ground. I looked up and saw the two gendarmes almost within arm's reach of América. The younger one leaped and landed on top of her. The poor girl was trapped beneath him.

I did not know what to do. I could not leave her alone; she was just a child. So I stopped, and the other gendarme grabbed my arm.

"Why were you running? Papers! Visa!" the older one barked dryly.

"We don't have a visa. We are Spanish political refugees," I answered in my poor French.

The gendarmes helped us go back up the slope, then put our pack into the car.

"Where are you taking us?" I asked in anguish. "I have to get to Perpignan to find my husband."

The gendarme shrugged as if he did not understand my words. "To the commissary," he said. They sat us in the back of the car and then got in front.

Terrified, América took my hand. I squeezed hers, then touched her face. "It'll be okay," I said.

The poor girl leaned against my shoulder, and that is how we stayed until the car approached a town. I caught a glimpse of the sign: Perpignan. One way or another, we had reached our goal.

The car stopped in front of the police station. The men opened the doors for us to get out and then led us into the white building to where a sergeant behind a counter took down our information. We handed over our IDs; then they took our photographs and showed us to a bench. The room was full of people like us. Beside me was a woman about thirty years old. Her head was bowed, and her blond hair covered her face. We took a small block of cheese out of our pack and started eating. I offered some to the woman.

For the first time she looked up. Her gray eyes were very sad. "No, thank you," she said.

"Are you all right?" I asked.

She shook her head. "My husband escaped from Barcelona a few days ago. I got a message that two bakers had hidden him in a town near Perpignan. I left my son with my mother in Spain and risked crossing the border. A sheep farmer helped me. He knew the paths very well, but he warned me that I would have to walk the part in France on my own. I managed to find my husband because he'd sent me a letter with clues to his whereabouts. But I couldn't convince him to come back with me. I had to get back to my family. I left very early in the morning and had been walking for a day without anyone seeing me. But this morning I went by a farm, and two men jumped out and grabbed me. They brought me here like I'm a criminal. Now I'm not with my husband or my family. I don't know how I got into this mess."

"I'm so sorry. I'm Isabel, and this is América."

"My name is María. My husband is a doctor. He fought for the Republic, and he's not guilty of any crimes, but Franco's savages are executing all the officers, and the ones they don't kill, they send to concentration camps. There's one near Barcelona, and the way they treat the prisoners is just barbaric."

The sergeant called out several names. We stood along with three other women. We were pointed to a door where two gendarmes were waiting for us. They handcuffed us and put us in a van.

"Where are you taking us?" María asked.

"Somewhere safe," the youngest policeman responded in perfect Spanish.

We sat inside. There were no windows, but light came in from the front part of the car. I peeked through and could tell we were heading for the coast.

"Where are you taking us?" I asked again.

The policeman who spoke our language turned and smiled. "I've already told you, to somewhere better. To a camp at Argelès-sur-Mer that the government has set up for the refugees. Don't worry. You'll get food there, and they'll process your visas, and if you find work you can leave as soon as you want."

"Thank you," I said. But I was worried that Peter would not be able to find me there. "My husband is looking for us."

"Your husband will probably be in the family camp or the military camp. Is he a soldier?"

"Yes."

"Then you can ask them to put you in contact with him there. This is just a temporary situation. Things will get better soon."

An hour later, the van stopped, and the gendarmes helped us get out. The sun was shining brightly. It was not as cold as in the Pyrenees, but the air was damp and disagreeable. They led us to the entry. All we saw was sand and a few barracks. Two Senegalese soldiers stopped us and spoke with the gendarmes.

"We'll leave you with them now. Best of luck to you!" the policeman said.

"What's your name?" I asked him.

"Martín García," he answered. "My grandfather was from Spain."

"Please, don't forget about us. We are Isabel, América, and María."

The policeman seemed touched. "I'll come by to visit you and see if you need anything. Don't worry; you'll be safe here. You're out of harm's reach now."

I would never forget his words. We never know what fate has in store for us. We can only grope blindly toward the future.

Elisabeth

BERN, SWITZERLAND
February 7, 1939

Elisabeth was not the kind of woman to accept no for an answer. She asked Lucy to go with her to Service Civil International's main headquarters. They needed to speak with Rodolfo Olgiati immediately. This was a very different trip back to Switzerland than their previous journey. Elisabeth was no longer half asleep due to extreme exhaustion. Now she was in full form and willing to try anything to get a maternity hospital opened. Karl and the rest of the group could not understand it, but the decision was not ultimately theirs to make.

France was getting ready for war. As the women made their

way through Lyon, they saw huge military contingencies head-ing for the front with Germany. Apparently no one wanted peace anymore, to the chagrin of Britain's prime minister, Neville Chamberlain. Peace was no longer possible.

They arrived in Bern after two long days in trains and buses, but they finally found themselves in one of the few Swiss cities that was not on the shore of a lake.

Rodolfo picked them up from the bus station. He was an attractive Italian in his midthirties, with curly hair, a wide fore-head, and a friendly smile. He and Elisabeth had met in Spain in 1937 and were very close. His wife, Irma Schneider, had overseen a maternity hospital in Madrid. Rodolfo had taught for several years at the Swiss school Escuela Suiza de Barcelona but had left Spain the previous year, and his wife was expecting.

"How was your trip?" he asked the two women while driving to the small villa where SCI had its offices. It was close to one of the camps where SCI held workshops on pacifism and cultural encounters. However, it seemed that their mission had been an abysmal failure in the face of the extreme violence and fanaticism that had spread throughout the world.

"Long and uncomfortable like they always are, but the impor-tant thing is that we got here. Do you know Lucy? She was with the Quaker mission but has been helping us out in the orphanage in France."

"No, we haven't had the pleasure of meeting before," Rodolfo said, smiling at Lucy.

"How is Irma?" Elisabeth asked.

Rodolfo sighed with worry. "She's two weeks past due, and apparently the baby is in no hurry. We've been hoping to avoid a C-section."

They arrived at the house. Rodolfo opened the gate and drove up to the front door. The snow was four or five inches deep, and it was colder there than in southern France.

He led them inside to the main parlor. The three work desks there were empty, and Irma was waiting for them on a couch by the hearth.

"My dear Elisabeth!" she exclaimed, struggling to her feet. The two women embraced.

"Oh, you're gorgeous!" Elisabeth said, taking a step back to eye her friend. "Pregnancy suits you."

"Well, I'd rather have the baby in my arms, though I get the feeling he prefers it in here." She patted her belly.

"It'll work out," Elisabeth said and then introduced Lucy. The three women sat on the couch while Rodolfo pulled up a chair.

"Rodolfo told me you're hoping to open a maternity hospital near the internment camp the French have set up."

"Yes, conditions there are terrible. I haven't seen anything that bad since we arrived in Spain. Entire families are literally just living on the beach with nothing. The mothers have no milk for their children—there isn't even enough drinkable water."

Irma's face clouded over. "That's terrible. People say that the postwar period is often worse than the war itself, but I'd never believed it before."

"Well, sweet Irma, the reality is that this situation is desperate. There's no way of knowing for sure how many people are fleeing Spain. Some say it's as high as one or two million. Just think of all those people crossing the Pyrenees in the dead of winter," Elisabeth said with a shudder.

The tone of the conversation concerned Rodolfo for Irma's

sake. He noticed that she kept her hand protectively over her womb. "Why don't we speak in private, Elisabeth?" he suggested.

Irma shot him a glance. "I'm pregnant, but I'm not an invalid."

"All right, let's keep talking then," Rodolfo conceded.

Elisabeth had been waiting for this moment for days, but now she was unsure how to proceed. "Well, I think we need to do something for the mothers. The way they have to raise their children is just horrible."

Rodolfo nodded but said, "It's not that simple. First we'd have to get permission from the French government. For some inexplicable reason, they seem convinced that most of these refugees are going to voluntarily return to Spain shortly, and the rest they don't mind leaving at the border. The French are preparing for war elsewhere."

"But that's absurd, Rodolfo. The Spaniards aren't going back to what would be certain death. The hatred runs very deep, and Franco's government doesn't seem too keen on amnesty or a plan for national reconciliation."

Irma butted in. "What I don't understand is how the general's wife and most of the government can call themselves Christians and still act that way."

Rodolfo extended a hand and nodded in support. "Yet it's not our job to judge anyone. What we have to decide is if we can take on the founding of a maternity hospital. That requires professional staff, funding, authorizations, and a new line of supplies. Our organization isn't that big, and I don't see how we can get everything we need in the time it's needed. By the time we can get it up and running, most of the refugees might have already moved on. The Red Cross is already offering aid to mothers and pregnant women in the camps."

Elisabeth crossed her arms. "I'm telling you, the refugees aren't going back to Spain, and if—when—the war starts in Europe, the situation is only going to get worse for them."

"Service Civil International was founded after the Great War to spread Christian pacifist teachings and practices. Civil service was an alternative to military service. Pierre Ceresole and Hubert Parris wanted to teach young people the dangers of militarism and ultranationalism—" Rodolfo began.

Elisabeth cut in. "I know the principals of our organization, Rodolfo, but this war can no longer be avoided. The only thing we can do is try to decrease the collateral damage."

Rodolfo knew that Elisabeth was right, but it would not be easy to convince the rest of the committee or get the necessary support. He sighed and shook his head. "I'll do what I can."

"And I'll be watching him," Irma said.

They all chuckled at that. There was always too much work to do and too few people willing to help, but somehow, miraculously, things usually got off the ground and support arrived from the least expected sources.

═══════

Peter

AT THE FRENCH BORDER
February 6, 1939

Peter and Francis ran the entire night, picturing Josef's death. But the only thing that mattered right then was surviving. The next day they met up with other soldiers trying to cross the border, but now all the known passages across were in Fascist hands. The only way to make it into France was through byways generally only used by shepherds. One of the Spaniards in their group was named Daniel Expósito. He was from Gerona, and though he had never lived near the border, he had heard about a way across: through a deep valley and then climbing the shaded side of a tall mountain with slippery slopes. They did not have the necessary equipment, but it was their only option at that point.

They reached the valley in the morning. They were fortunate to have avoided checkpoints and police patrols, but they had very little food, and their boots were worn so thin they slipped constantly on the ice.

Francis grew quiet and nervous when he saw the mountain. "We don't have things like that where I'm from."

"Don't worry," Daniel said. "It looks harder than it is, and we'll help you." He pulled out his ropes and started preparing the knots.

"Are you sure this is a good idea?" Peter asked.

Daniel shrugged in answer, and they started the ascent. Daniel went first, followed by Peter, then Francis, and then Manuel. They got through the first stretch, which was the easiest, without difficulty. After that, the path narrowed and grew steeper before becoming an almost vertical wall. Francis kept glancing behind as they ascended.

At the final stretch, Daniel climbed up with the rope tied around his waist. He tested each spot carefully, knowing that if any of them slipped, the rest might be dragged down. They made it past the first part of the wall without mishap, but just as they rounded a corner, Francis's foot gave way. He was dangling between his two comrades, who grabbed and pulled him up.

Clinging anew to the face of the rock, Francis whimpered, "I want to go back."

"You can't," Daniel said. "Just ten more minutes, and we'll be at the top, and then the only thing left is to walk across a field."

They convinced Francis to keep going, but just a few yards farther up, Francis slipped again. Manuel reached for him, but then they were both swinging back and forth over the abyss. Daniel and Peter could not support the weight of both men.

"Cut the rope!" Daniel shouted.

The men swinging above nothing put unbearable pressure on Peter's waist, and he was about to slip. Finally, he accepted the knife Daniel held out to him and sawed the rope. His comrades plunged down, and Peter looked away. When he glanced back, he could see their bodies sprawled at the base of the cliff.

Daniel and Peter resumed the climb. At the top, they tumbled down, exhausted, onto the grassy plain. They had both seen too many things during the war to be broken by what they had just experienced, but it horrified them nonetheless. And they had been so close to finishing the climb.

THIRTEEN

Isabel

The camp was a stretch of empty ground. When we arrived, they gave us two pieces of bread, some very hard sausage, an orange, and some potatoes, which we had no way of cooking. We walked down the long central row that began at the barracks where food was distributed, very sick individuals were kept, and new refugees were registered. Then we walked past shacks that people had built with sticks, straw, boxes, and blankets. It was a city of the destitute, I thought while taking it all in. People stared eagerly at new arrivals, hoping to find their friends or relatives. Our section of the camp was for women only. Next to us was the family camp and, beyond a creek, the military camp that looked better kept. At the end of the main row, we sat down on the sand. There was nothing else to do. It was not raining at that moment, but the air was still damp and cold from the night before. There was no way to get out of the elements.

"I guess I'll go look for some sticks or reeds," I told América. She was completely withdrawn in shock. María went with me while América stayed with our few belongings. We walked the nearly two miles of the camp but found almost nothing of use. We saw people huddled under the trucks parked at the entrance and others who buried themselves in the sand and covered up with blankets.

"Well, we won't be the only ones sleeping out in the open tonight," María observed, but her comment failed to cheer me. If not for the hope of finding Peter and protecting América, I would have given up completely.

We went to the supplies barrack and were given a few cans of tuna, sardines, and beans.

Back at our plot of sand, we found that others had settled beside us.

"How many do you think there are?" I asked my friends as we watched the disoriented crowd. It was slowly dawning on us all that we were locked into this place like criminals.

A woman in a small hut nearby looked out and handed us a couple of sugar cubes. América downed hers in one bite.

"The other day," the woman began, "in the registration barrack I heard that there are seventy-five thousand of us and that soon the number will grow to one hundred thousand refugees come over from Spain."

"That's unbelievable!" María exclaimed.

"The Fascists are already at the border, so that will keep more people from leaving, but there are thousands wandering all about. When the police find them, they promise them shelter and food, and once they get us inside these fences, we have no country or rights." The woman plopped down, and we sat around her. We needed to learn how things worked in the camp.

"I haven't introduced myself yet. It seems we forget our

manners in difficult situations. My name is Clotilde, and I was a teacher in Aragon, but I got out before Franco's troops surrounded us. I knew that as soon as the Fascists arrived, I'd end up in front of a firing squad. One of the wealthy families in the area was out to get me."

"I'm so sorry," María said, her face contorted with empathy.

Clotilde nodded. "I still remember the day the Republic came into being. We all thought things were going to change. Our poor country has always been governed by a bunch of incompetent freeloaders. For over fifty years two parties have gone back and forth in power, just swapping out methods of corruption, not to mention the dictatorship of Miguel Primo de Rivera or the immorality and ineptness of King Alfonso XIII. My family has always been promonarchic, but why couldn't we have had kings like the British or the Dutch? Well, anyhow, the Roviras were a wine family like my family. My father lost everything when I was in Zaragoza finishing my degree. The poor wretch had taken to drinking. The year before, we'd lost my sister and my mom to tuberculosis. The Roviras took advantage of him and convinced him to sell everything to them. When I got back home, I refused to accept their conditions. Their lawyers won, and we were left with nothing. I was able to find work as a teacher and take care of my dad, but he got sick after the war had been going for about a year. A mob went after the oldest Rovira, Francisco. They executed him and took over his land. I denounced it to the socialist mayor, but he called it popular justice. Even so, the Roviras have always believed I was part of that mob. Ironic, isn't it?"

I shrugged.

"Small-town fights are worse than in the big cities. A lot of people are using the war as an excuse to settle old scores. I thought it would be wiser for me to escape to France, and there was nothing tying me to Spain anymore. I know a bit of French, and I hope to stay and live here. I don't see any way forward for our beloved country. I wrote an old friend who's a teacher in Paris, and when she shows up, I'll get out of this hellhole. Don't you know anybody in France?"

We all three shook our heads.

María said, "I want to go back home, but I came here to find my husband. But there's no way he can go back to Spain right now."

I told them my story, and América talked about wanting to study in Paris.

"You're lucky," Clotilde told me, pulling her hair back in a bun. "Your husband is from the USA, and surely he can get you out of here soon."

"I hope so," I said without conviction. As time went on, I had less and less hope that Peter was still alive and had managed to escape before the Fascists took control of the border.

Clotilde glanced at our thin blankets and then at her little shack. "There's room inside for one of you. I wish I could fit you all."

"América should sleep inside with you. María and I can make do with blankets," I said. We had slept in worse places before, or at least that is what I thought at the time.

"In the mornings, men come by selling sticks and reeds. If you buy some, you could at least make a roof."

"We don't have any money," I said, eyeing the surrounding huts with envy. Compared to bare ground, they looked like palaces.

"Republic money's not worth anything in here," Clotilde said.

"Besides, Franco outlawed it. A lot of people brought suitcases worth of money, and now they use it as kindling."

"So what do we pay with?" I asked.

"With food or clothing. That's the new currency here."

We lit a fire with a few sticks that Clotilde shared with us. As the sun went down, the humidity crept deeper into my bones. I went to the shore and looked out on the endless ocean. I had always loved the beach. My mother used to take me in the summer. Those had been rare, happy moments of leaving behind the dark, musty room we rented, the school where the other girls looked at me like an impoverished pest, and everything about our difficult life. Yet now the sea had become our jail cell. The waves crashing just a few yards from the shacks were nothing but threatening.

Peter

COLLIURE
February 10, 1939

Peter and Daniel walked for four days. Sometimes a truck driver would allow them to ride in the back, but they had to hide every time they came upon military officers or the police. The authorities were methodically rounding up the refugees and sending them to camps, but Peter and Daniel were trying to get to Perpignan to find Isabel. They never mentioned the harrowing accident with their comrades on the mountain. Forgetting was better.

The last truck driver they came across offered to take them as far as Colliure, which had them driving along the border quite a way. They figured it would be simple enough to find transportation from Colliure to Perpignan.

Marcel, the driver, was good-natured and friendly. He transported pigs around the country and was the only driver who let the men sit up front with him. It was the first time they had gotten warm and had something decent to eat in days.

"You like Iberian spicy sausage? It's not like the Italian, but they make it at the slaughterhouse where I'm headed with these pigs."

"It's delicious," Daniel said, and Peter translated since Daniel did not speak any French.

"In Perpignan there are lots of checkpoints. You'd better stay in the countryside till things calm down. It's such a shame what all has happened in Spain. I went there once with my wife, to Gerona. We had a grand time and had simply the best food, especially the fish on the coast."

"That country doesn't exist anymore," Peter said, a deep sadness filling his gut. He remembered Barcelona in 1936 full of light and color, happy people spilling out of cafes and bars, children playing along Las Ramblas and La Barceloneta, and the bright blue sea.

"War is terrible. I didn't fight in 1914, but my older brother did. The poor guy came home injured, and his mind was gone. He's never been the same. He was in Verdun, which was apparently one of the worst of the war. Where were you two fighting?"

Daniel hung his head. He preferred not to think about the years of pain and suffering. He hadn't spoken of his past to Peter.

Peter spoke up. "Well, the war found me in Barcelona when I was there for the People's Olympiad, to protest the Berlin Olympics. A friend and I both joined the International Brigades. From there we were sent to Madrid because the city was under siege. If it had fallen then, the war would've been over right away. The Fascists were already in the towns south of the capital, and the fight was bloody starting in November 1936, though the worst part came in the winter of 1937. We were out of ammunition and were completely disorganized. It was like the Tower of Babel, dozens of languages spoken. That's how I learned French, from my friend Pierre."

"Were there many Frenchmen in the brigades?"

"Actually, yes. They were brave and disciplined, way more than us from the States. Many had fought in 1914 or in the colonies. Our approach to battles was always a bit disorganized, though several of my countrymen got medals for bravery."

As they arrived in Colliure, Marcel let them out at the entry to the slaughterhouse. "I've got to leave you here. The problem is, you're wearing military garb and you'll get arrested as soon as you poke your noses out. You'd better put these on. They're old jackets I use when I'm unloading the trucks, but at least they'll cover your uniforms."

Peter and Daniel put on the jackets blackened by dirt and grime. While they no longer looked like military men, they could have passed for beggars. Marcel gave them a few francs for their bus ride to Perpignan.

The two comrades wandered down the semideserted streets of the town. In summer, Colliure was packed with vacationers, but it was nearly abandoned in the winter. They asked the way to the bus station and were on their way when Daniel stopped suddenly. He approached an old gentleman with a light felt hat and a black ribbon. He wore round glasses, and his cheeks were sunken from malnutrition.

"Maestro, good God! What are you doing here?"

The man glanced at them with a lost look. "Just out for a bit of sun, though here it's nothing like in Spain."

Daniel beamed at Peter. "I can tell my children and grand-children that I met Antonio Machado in person!"

"Or what's left of him," the poet said with a sigh.

"Don't you know who this is?" Daniel asked Peter.

"I've read some of his work, but I didn't know what he looked like."

"He's the greatest poet in Spain!"

"Federico García Lorca was a great master until those barbarians murdered him," Machado said.

Daniel noticed the pen and paper in Machado's hand. "Oh, you were writing. I'm so sorry we interrupted you."

"It's all I know to do. I've only begun a line about blue days and the sun of childhood. When a man gets old, all he can think about is being young again. It's like we want to get back to our mothers' wombs and save ourselves all the pain and heartache that started when we left them. I've been here since January 28. We found a room for my brother and my sister-in-law, and I'm with my mother in another room. The poor woman will never recover from this trip. We left Viladasens and got to the border by car but had to leave the vehicle a little before we crossed. It was hard getting over the summit, especially for my mother, Ana. She's nearly eighty-five."

Daniel was shaking his head in disgust as Machado spoke. "What a disgrace. This is how Spain treats its great men."

"SERE has promised to get us to Paris, but who knows when that will be. At least here we're close to our country."

The famous Spanish Republicans Emigration Service was overwhelmed with the onslaught of refugees.

"I hope they find you a better place soon," Daniel said.

"I've run out of steam, my boy. The only thing keeping me on this earth is my mother. My brother Manuel will be fine without me."

"No, don't say that. Life is a wonderful thing, and you've got so many more poems left to write."

"Death is always our final poem."

Peter and Daniel moved on in quiet sadness. If one of the greatest men of Spain was in that state, there seemed to be little hope for them.

They had never allowed themselves to fully imagine defeat. Yet as they walked the lonely streets of France, it now seemed inevitable. An entire generation had been killed for naught: anonymous heroes on both sides, idealists attracted by the siren songs of their leaders, who stayed safe in the rear guard. The only hope was to erase those painful years from their lives and try to start over from scratch.

FOURTEEN

Isabel

We could feel our strength draining. Along with poor nutrition and the cold, we did not have clean water to drink. We were not allowed to leave the camp to look for water, and we had to bathe in the sea. Mothers from the family camp next to us begged us for food because they could not produce milk for their babies, but we had nothing to give them.

We managed to fashion together a shack for the three of us. It was not very big, and the wooden floor was just as damp as the sand, but at least it helped us keep in the heat at night as María, América, and I slept huddled together.

"We should go get some soap," I told my friends. Our neighbor Clotilde had told us there was soap in the supplies barrack.

"What good is soap without water?" María asked. She was feeling sick and more discouraged than usual.

"At least it'll help get a bit of the dirt off," América said. Her youth helped her not wear down as quickly as María and me.

I took América's hand, and we walked the long street to the

supplies barrack. It was crowded, and there was a lot of commotion. Soldiers were handing out canned tomatoes, and the women were fighting over them. They had been giving us canned cod for several days without anything to go along with it. América managed to slip between the women and catch a can that a soldier tossed. A woman tried to grab it out of her hand, but she held on tight.

"Let go, please!" América said. But the woman was willing to fight for it. I came up and pushed her away.

"But I'm hungry!" she growled.

"We all are, but we aren't going to act like animals."

"I've had diarrhea for two days straight now and haven't had anything to eat," she said, dissolving into tears. Diarrhea was an epidemic in the camp. Out of desperation, many people drank the infested water we were given.

"You should go to the doctor."

"I did, but they didn't do anything for me."

I looked in the pockets of my dress. I still had one can of cod. I held it out to her. The woman looked at me and started crying again.

"I'm so sorry. This damned war has driven us all mad," she said.

We left her and went to the other barrack. Manolo was one of the workers there. He had small eyes and a black beard and was as ugly as he was mean. It always felt like he was undressing us with his eyes, especially the way he looked at América.

"Hello, Manolo." I forced myself to greet him politely. "I've heard there's soap now."

He frowned. "Not for everyone."

"Why not for everyone? The soap and everything the Red Cross gives is for handing out. It's one thing for you to steal, but you can't be unfair in the way you give out their supplies."

Just then Ismael, the one in charge of distribution, showed up. "Is there a problem?" he asked.

"Yes, sir," Manolo said. "These rabble-rousers are complaining about distribution."

"That's not true," I said. "Everyone knows that Manolo steals from the supplies and gives more to his friends and sells things on the black market."

Manolo stepped forward and brought out a club. Those who worked with distribution were allowed to carry clubs to keep people from stealing supplies.

"Manolo, step back! Have you lost your mind?"

"This woman makes my blood boil," he growled.

"Go on, then. I'll see to what they need," Ismael said, not taking his eyes off me.

"I just came to get a couple bars of soap. I know a shipment arrived."

Ismael looked in the boxes and handed me three bars. "Next time you need something, ask for me, Ismael Lapiedra."

"I will," I said.

"We're not all a bunch of brutes like Manolo. Hitting a woman—what a dog he is."

"Why don't you hire someone else?" I asked.

"I can't. He's a member of the party, and SERE appointed him."

"Don't tell me we're dealing in here with the same racket as back home! Doesn't anyone care that this kind of corruption and partisanship is what led us into this mess in the first place?"

Ismael shrugged. "I just follow orders."

I frowned. "That's what everyone says."

We headed back for our shack. We had gotten used to chatting in the afternoons with our neighbors, even singing together sometimes. Camp life was hard and full of disappointment, but it helped a little to know we were not alone in that city of losers.

———

Elisabeth

Elisabeth and Lucy started wondering if their trip had been in vain. Irma spent a lot of time with them. She was more peeved as the days went by, but she was still good company. Rodolfo was indecisive. Besides problems with financing and getting permissions to start a maternity hospital, he knew that Elisabeth did not have the necessary experience. She was not a trained nurse. When he had met her in Madrid in 1937, he was immediately struck by her work ethic, her strength, and her inexhaustible spirits. A great woman was housed within her small frame, and above all, she had heart. She wept with those who wept and laughed with those who laughed. Elisabeth already embodied the essence of a nurse: a person full of compassion, patience, empathy, care, and understanding. Perhaps being a nurse meant more than being able to suture stitches and ward off infection.

Elisabeth knocked at the door to Rodolfo's office. He seemed stressed. His desk was covered with papers, reports, and requests for all sorts of aid.

"May I?" Elisabeth asked.

"Come in, come in. I'd love a break. I have to balance the accounts and fill out several requests."

"That's the part people never hear about—all the bureaucracy and paperwork that every little thing requires."

Rodolfo nodded and smiled wryly, then leaned back and looked at his friend. "So things are really as bad as all that?"

Elisabeth sat and hung her head. She preferred to hide her tears. "You all right?" he asked.

She swallowed hard. "It's terrible, Rodolfo: all of those desperate people fleeing, the border jam-packed, children moaning from the hunger and cold. Besides losing the war, they are defeated, without hope, and there's nothing worse for a people than to lose hope."

"I get it."

"But the worst was seeing the camps where they've been taken. There's not enough of anything. It's just barbed wire and a few shacks the refugees themselves have built. The French government hasn't even given them tents. I've never seen anything like it, not even during the war."

"I see."

"If we don't do something, dozens or hundreds of children will die. The beach is no place for a baby to be born. You know I don't have the necessary experience, but mothers will have a better chance bringing their children into the world with me in a dry, safe place than they will cast out on that infernal beach. It feels like the powers of hell have conspired against those poor women."

For the first time since Elisabeth arrived, Rodolfo stopped thinking in terms of numbers, memorandums, and paperwork. He had been away from the front lines for too long and was starting to forget the look of a starving child's eyes, the fear of an orphan who no longer has a mother to hug, and the iron clutch of a man unwilling to let go of his wife's dead body. He stood up and gave Elisabeth a hug.

"I'll do everything in my power to get a maternity hospital opened."

Just then they heard someone cry out in pain. They ran to the living room. Irma's water had broken. They called the midwife and helped Irma get up to her bedroom. While Lucy gathered towels and hot water, Elisabeth held Irma's hand. "It's all right," she cooed. "Just breathe. The midwife will be here soon."

But the snow made it hard to travel. Irma's pains were getting stronger, and Lucy and Elisabeth stared at each other, not knowing what to do. Rodolfo was pacing up and down the hallway, listening to his wife's groans.

"We just have to start," Elisabeth said, rolling up her sleeves.

"But have you ever done this before?" Lucy whispered.

"Children have been coming into this world for thousands of years, and the only help women have had is themselves."

They put a pillow at Irma's lower back. Lucy squeezed her hand, and Elisabeth encouraged her to push. Irma was sweating and huffing and screaming, her face nearly purple with the exertion. Then Elisabeth saw a head.

She felt queasy as the baby's body started to emerge, but she nestled the creature gently. Trying to stay calm, she wondered how it was possible for the baby's body to come out of such a small space. After the head, the rest of the body came out so quickly Elisabeth could not hold it, and the baby rested gently on the bed. Lucy had found scissors and cut the umbilical cord. Elisabeth cleaned off the blood with a towel and looked at the tiny, wrinkled face. The baby's eyes were still closed as if refusing to wake up to the waiting world, and then he began to cry.

"Let me see him," Irma said with tears in her eyes. She had been waiting so long for that moment. She could not speak for all the things she was feeling. That creature had been growing inside of her for nine months, sharing her blood and her food. They had been one flesh, and now he had a new, independent life.

Elisabeth handed him over carefully, and Irma cradled the child so tenderly that both Lucy and Elisabeth teared up. They had helped bring this child into the world, and now they wondered: Why did the children of the poor mothers on the beach have to die? Their only crime was to have been on the losing side of the war.

Rodolfo came in and embraced his family. Just a few hours ago they had been two, and now, miraculously, they were three. The mystery of life, love, and passion had overcome death once again.

Peter

Peter sensed that he was near to his beloved. He felt like he could even hear her heartbeat as he and Daniel got off the bus. Everyone in the station was staring at their clothes, but they walked straight ahead. First they went to the Casa de España, the local place where expatriates had gathered for generations, to see if they could find any trace of Isabel.

It was a two-story building with a wide, open room on the first floor, filled with tables for playing *mus* and dominoes. Everyone turned to look at them when they entered. Peter and Daniel were dismayed by the looks of disdain thrown their way.

They went up to the bar, and Peter spoke to the waiter. "Good day, we're looking for a woman . . ."

The man interrupted. "We don't know anything about any refugees. You're all painting a shameful picture of Spain."

Daniel straightened up and was about to punch the man in the face, but Peter held him back. "Stay calm," he said.

An elegantly dressed man came up to them. "What's this foreigner doing here?" he asked the waiter.

Daniel spat out, "This *foreigner*, as you call him, has shed his blood for our country while you're sitting here sipping wine. He's more Spaniard than you are."

The man glared at him. "We don't let Red scum into this place. If you were so brave, you should've stayed in Spain to own up to your crimes, you Communists."

Daniel grabbed the man by his lapels and pushed him against the bar. Four other men rushed up.

"Everybody calm down! We're going now. Daniel, leave him be," Peter said, pulling at his comrade's shoulder. Daniel dropped the man, and they left without glancing back.

Out on the street, they looked at each other. "What is wrong with those people?" Daniel asked.

"Well, I think they're just scared. They've spent decades trying to gain acceptance in French society, and now a massive wave of refugees puts them in the predicament of having to choose: Do they identify with their former country or with the country where they've started a new life? We might act the same way if we were in their situation."

They walked along the town walls, and just as they were passing by the tower gate, they ran right into two gendarmes. The four of them looked at one another for a silent second, no one making a move, but then Daniel and Peter started running. Then the gendarmes blew their whistles and went after them. Daniel and Peter were soon surrounded. Daniel pulled out his knife, but Peter told him to throw it down. Daniel hesitated but finally did so. As soon as they were unarmed, the gendarmes tackled them to the ground, handcuffed them, and took them to the commissary. An hour later, they were in a truck on the way to the camp at Argelès-sur-Mer.

The truck stopped in front of the military camp. Getting down from the truck, Daniel shoved a policeman and took off running. Peter stayed quiet. He knew that escape was futile, especially when handcuffed. Plus, he wondered if he might find Isabel there. If he had been captured so easily, surely she had met the same fate.

Senegalese soldiers yelled, "*¡Allez, allez!*" as they pushed him inside the barbed-wire fence. They lined Peter up together with a group of soldiers, removed their handcuffs, and moved them forward to receive a ration of bread.

"Peter!" he heard someone behind him call. Turning, he saw Fabián. They had met in Madrid in 1937 but had not seen each other since.

"Good God, is that you, Fabián?" The men embraced, but the Senegalese soldiers pushed them apart. After the bread was passed out, the men were allowed out of line, and the two friends sought each other out. Fabián did not look like the young, flag-waving idealist Peter had met. He looked decades older now, with rings around his eyes and wrinkles creasing his face. The spark had gone out of him.

"You'll get used to it here; it's not as bad as it looks," Fabián assured him. "We even have a philosophy group for debates."

Peter looked out at the sea and sniffed the unmistakable smell of the winter ocean. He followed Fabián in a daze. The wooden barracks stretched out on all sides. They were really just cabins with no true floor, but the straight streets gave the place a small-town feel.

"There's room for you in my barrack. We've got two university professors, a famous lawyer, a doctor, two notaries, and a carpenter."

"What a crew," Peter said, coming to himself a bit. They went up to the fence but not so close that the Senegalese reprimanded them.

"What's over there?" Peter asked.

Fabián pointed. "That's the women's camp, and over there is the family camp. We're closed up in here like rats, and truthfully, the damned frogs treat us worse than animals."

Peter stopped listening after Fabián's first words. He stared into the women's camp, hoping to catch a glimpse of Isabel.

===

Isabel

ARGELÈS-SUR-MER WOMEN'S CAMP
February 11, 1939

As I sat at the edge of the sea, my thoughts drifted to Peter, as they always did. I was afraid of never seeing him again, afraid of always being alone, afraid of never having hope or peace again. The pink clouds in the slowly darkening sky seemed to say that spring would eventually come, but this had been the longest winter any of us had ever lived through, and we thought it would never end. We had the shattered dreams and broken hearts of a defeated people. We were stuck on a strip of land and belonged nowhere.

I could hear the strains of a song coming from the military camp. Dozens of men were singing, and the song grew as it spread across the barracks. The song wound its way through our shacks as well and pricked at something pulsing in our hearts.

Peaceful, happy, brave and daring,
Let us sing, soldiers, our battle hymn.
The world will admire our voices come together
And see that we are the sons of the Cid.
Soldiers, our homeland demands that we fight.

Part II

FENCES

FIFTEEN

Isabel

We went up to the fence. Sometimes French citizens from the surrounding areas would come and hand things out. Plus, we liked to see when new people were brought in, not to scoff at their misfortune or celebrate that they were joining our purgatory but to see if we found anyone we knew. Clotilde, our neighbor, had been sick the past few days, and there was nothing at the medical barrack to lower her fever. So when we saw the young policeman who had brought us to the camp, Martín García, we called out to him. At first he did not recognize us. Surely we were skinnier and dirtier than when he had seen us last. Our dresses looked very old by then, despite our efforts to keep them clean.

"Oh, ladies, I hadn't expected to see you again. I had hoped you would've been able to move on from here."

"Unfortunately not. We need your help."

He cast a glance behind. "I can't get you out of here."

"No, it's not that," I said. "We have a friend who's sick. Her fever is really high, and she needs medicine."

"But you should get what you need at the infirmary. The government stocks it every week."

"It isn't enough for everyone, and there are plenty of conniving people who siphon off supplies to resell on the black market."

He shook his head in disbelief. It was nice to see someone upset about our situation.

"Wait here for a moment. The Quakers have a van and hand things out. I might have luck there."

We waited patiently at the fence. Seeing Officer García had made our day. An old couple showed up at the camp gate, and they had a donkey with them. The Senegalese tried to take it from the man. Animals were not allowed. The man pulled the reins, but the soldiers pulled harder. Eventually one of them smacked the animal with the butt of his gun, and the beast crumpled to the ground, bleeding. The woman threw her arms around the donkey and tried to stop the bleeding, but it just lay there, limp.

"You're a bunch of brutes!" I screamed.

One of them came up and yelled, "Get back inside, you Spanish sluts. You've no business being out here!"

"You're not my boss, little soldier," I spat back. América pulled at my arm, but I was furious.

"Get out of here now!" the soldier roared.

"You're supposed to be here to take care of us, not to abuse us."

Just then Martín García walked back up and spoke in French to the soldier, who went away grumbling. "This is all I could get," he said, handing us the medicine through the fence.

"Thank you so much," I said.

"Next week I'll come back and see what you need. I hope to

God all of this ends soon. People are saying the war in Spain won't last much longer and then you can go back to your country."

"We don't have a country anymore," I answered.

"Well, things will get better."

I shook my head, unconvinced. All I wanted was to get out of the camp that was going to kill us little by little.

We headed back to our shack, which we had managed to improve a bit. The French had handed out more wood as well as kitchen utensils and blankets. First we went to see Clotilde and give her the medicine. She was shivering, and María held her hand tightly.

"How are you, Clotilde?" She opened her eyes and looked at me in fear.

"I won't be leaving this place alive. So much for my dreams of seeing Paris."

"No, no, you'll see it. You'll sail down the Seine and climb the Eiffel Tower," María promised her.

Clotilde shook her head. "I'll die on this beach, and they'll bury me out front with the legion of wretches who thought the French would help us out."

"Don't say that," América said, starting to cry.

"Don't cry, my child. Life is short, and I already knew that. I don't believe anything happens after it, but at least I'll be able to rest. Sometimes it's good to take a step back."

We tried to get the medicine in her, but she coughed and vomited it all out. We cleaned her up and wrapped her in blankets. She was shaking almost uncontrollably and was delirious by nightfall. We took turns watching her, fearing the end. On my watch, her labored breathing stopped. I leaned over and put my hand on her chest. She was cold, and I knew Clotilde had left us forever.

I did not wake my friends. There was no need to disturb their sleep. The next morning we looked for the men who carried away dead bodies, and they came with their wooden cart. They put Clotilde alongside three others, and we covered her with a blanket even though we knew the gravediggers kept everything they could find on the corpses. María insisted on saying a prayer for Clotilde's soul, but I could not believe in anything right then. I felt such a deep pit inside me that I almost envied Clotilde. I was so tired. I had lost all hope of finding Peter alive. A pleasant idea entered my head: I could walk into the freezing sea and just keep walking toward the horizon and never look back.

═══════

Elisabeth

ELNE
February 13, 1939

Elisabeth stood looking at the house such a long time that eventually a woman came up to her. The woman's graying blond hair was pulled back under an elegant hat, and her blue-framed glasses declared her spunk.

"The Château d'en Bardou—that's what we call it," the woman stated.

"Oh, I didn't know," Elisabeth replied.

"It's seen better days. It was built by a businessman named Eugène Bardou, and it's a pity to see it in this state. It's only been around thirty-seven years. But it's undoubtedly a monument to human vanity. We build castles and mansions but can't take them with us. The owner died with no heirs, and his wife followed soon after."

"What a sad story."

"The bank owns it now."

"The bank?"

"Yes, the only one in town. What makes you so interested?"

Elisabeth wondered how to answer. Most French were not eager to have immigrants wandering through their towns and fields.

"Well, to open a maternity hospital."

"A maternity hospital?" The woman smiled at the bizarre idea. "For the Spanish women," she guessed.

"For women. Who cares where they come from?" Elisabeth added.

"You're right about that. It's quite un-Christian to treat foreigners poorly   at least that's what Father Antuane says "

"The village priest?"

"Yes. He's a bit of a revolutionary, or so people say. I think it's pure Christian love. I've read the Bible, mind you."

Now it was Elisabeth's turn to smile. "And God might still be working miracles here on earth!" she said happily.

"Do you think?"

"Well, you're my little miracle for today."

The woman cocked an eyebrow and pointed toward the church. "Well, go get your miracle, then."

Elisabeth headed for the rectory. She knew that she was not alone in this venture. She stood up straight before the door, took a deep breath, and then knocked on the old wood and waited for her miracle. She did not need a chariot of fire to fall from the sky. All she needed was for a few hard hearts to be softened by love.

Peter

ARGELÈS-SUR-MER MILITARY CAMP
February 14, 1939

Peter had moved into the philosophers' barrack. Every day they chose a subject for debate. Fabián had introduced him to the group, and they would spend several enjoyable hours in friendly discussion, though sometimes opinions would get heated, especially between the Communists and the more moderate socialists.

Several small restaurants had opened up in the camp, though Peter never understood how they managed to find food. The French government was hardly providing enough for basic survival. If not for the Red Cross, other organizations, and anonymous donors, the refugees would have starved to death.

They arrived at "La Tierruca," widely held to be the nicest shack. It looked like an actual house from the outside. The owners had covered the bottom part with sand to secure the construction and then painted the wooden planks with different colors. The place belonged to Joselito Lavarde, a metalworker turned chef. La Tierruca was the gathering place for Fabián and several friends, and there they made the best of life at camp.

As they entered, Peter was surprised to see several old comrades he knew from his time in Madrid: Abelardo, Aguado, Noreña, and the Ramos brothers. They all sat around the table, and Zabaleta brought out a huge pot of paella. The group cheered. They could not remember the last time they had seen something so delicious.

"Oh God, this is what I miss most from back home!" Santiago

Ramos exclaimed. "How terrible the food has been since the start of the war!"

They divvied out the rations on metal plates, and for several minutes the only sound was the clinking forks and the busy jaws of the soldiers. Then Mariñas, his mouth still full, said, "Don't worry, comrades. Soon enough we'll be back in Spain and we'll kick all the Fascists back to Africa. We'll reconquer our country. Right now the French are treating us like dogs, but when they need us for their war, everything will change. They think it won't happen to them, but Hitler's an old fox and at any minute will drag the Old World into a war."

"Don't kid yourself," Fabián said.

"Kid myself? I've heard that in a few weeks they're going to be recruiting volunteers to dig the trenches at the front with Germany. It's just a matter of time."

"Well, I'm not so sure I want to get involved in another war," Luis Rodríguez added in his Catalonian accent.

"We have to get back to fighting. They've stolen our country, and without Spain, we're just a bunch of vagabonds with no future," Mariñas declared.

Just then Serapio Ibáñez entered with a cake made with sweetened condensed milk. Everyone cheered and applauded.

"Now that is something I never expected to find here!" Fabián exclaimed. He turned to Peter in happy disbelief, but Peter's gaze was lost in the distance. "What's got you?" Fabián asked.

"I can't stop thinking about Isabel. We're here eating and drinking, and maybe she's out there somewhere starving to death."

"Have you asked at the registration barrack if she's in the women's camp?"

"Registration barrack?"

"Yeah, at the front office. They can tell you there."

Peter jumped up from the table without touching his dessert, which the comrade beside him quickly claimed for his own.

"Hang on. I'll come with you," Fabián called, stuffing the last of the cake into his mouth as Peter left the restaurant.

Peter was walking with large, quick strides, but Fabián caught up to him.

"I don't know if they're open in the afternoon," he warned Peter, but Peter was already banging on the door.

"What in the world? What is going on? What are you making such a racket for?" A bald man with glasses opened the door and stared at Peter.

"I need to know if my wife is in the women's camp."

"Well, we're closed for the day, and this is where I sleep. Come back tomorrow."

Peter grabbed the man by his shirt, and the man lifted his hands. "All right, all right, no need to get pushy. I'll look for her records," he said.

They went inside the barrack, which had a solid wooden floor. The man opened the drawer of a filing cabinet and searched for Isabel's last name. It took him five minutes, but then he said, "Yes, she's here. She hasn't been here long. Her number is 17,456. You'll need that number to find her. You can't get into the women's camp on your own."

Peter grabbed the card from the man's hand and shot out of the barrack toward the camp gate. Two French soldiers stopped him.

"Halt! Where do you think you're going?" they demanded.

"I have to find my wife," he said, trying to get free.

"You can't leave without permission, and certainly not at this time of day," a soldier explained in poor Spanish.

"You don't understand!" Peter cried.

"If you don't calm down, we'll have to send you to correction camp."

Peter had heard that soldiers who tried to flee or fight back were sent to another camp that was much worse. He calmed down immediately.

Seeing the commotion, an officer came over. "What's going on?"

The soldiers explained the situation. The officer looked at Peter and asked where he was from.

"I'm a citizen of the United States, and you have no right to hold me here."

"You've entered France illegally. Of course we have the right to retain you."

"I want you to call the consul immediately. I demand it!" Peter was desperate.

The officer turned on his heel and walked away without another word.

"Come back tomorrow," the soldier explained more politely. "If we take you there now, you won't have hardly any time at all with your wife."

Peter turned and started walking along the fence. Fabián followed him.

"Please tell me you aren't thinking about jumping the fence. A lot of guys have tried it, but no one's successfully escaped yet."

"Do you think I have any alternative?" Peter demanded.

"Of course you do. Tomorrow they can tell you exactly where to find Isabel."

"They're not going to let us be together. I can't wait any longer."

"This is madness." Fabián sighed. He looked toward the soldiers in the distance. They would not hesitate to shoot anyone who tried to escape. The fence separating the camps was lower than the fence to the outside, but even so, it would be nearly impossible to jump it without getting terribly cut up.

Peter looked at his friend, then looked all around. Before Fabián could stop him, he was up and over the fence and running into the darkness.

SIXTEEN

Isabel

Sometimes destiny shows up in a surprising way and saves our lives. The night after we watched Clotilde's body be taken away, I had decided that, once everyone was asleep, I would sneak away. I would slowly walk into the huge darkness of the sea until the cold froze my body, and I would disappear forever from that world that was too much for me. I had never thought of myself as weak or cowardly, but I no longer had any desire to live. One friend after another had died in the past few weeks. I had seen the horrors of the bombing and had survived the desperate flight to France. But what I could not bear any longer was being separated from Peter. I was walking to the shore when I heard a noise. I thought América was following me, but when I turned I saw the figure of a man jumping the fence and going toward the shacks.

There was not enough light to see who it was, but my heart

leaped instinctively, and I stopped short. Then I heard a man's voice calling with quiet insistence, "Isabel! Isabel!"

At first I could not move. I had waited for this moment for so long. I started moving toward him, but my stiff legs were not working right. I tried to speak, but no sound came out. Finally, with a superhuman effort, I managed to whisper. Something inside me broke open, and a floodgate of tears came out. "Peter! Peter! I'm here!"

The man turned and saw me in the darkness. Then he was running and beside me within seconds. He hugged me and threw me into the sky, and we were laughing and crying all at once.

"I thought I'd never see you again," I exclaimed as he swung round and round with me. Then he took my hand and led me away from the shacks. "How did you get in here?" I asked, worried. Men were not allowed inside the women's camp at night, though we had heard of rapes. And some women sold their bodies in exchange for food or a pass to leave the camp and work as a maid in French homes.

"I'm in the military camp. Tomorrow I'll ask them to move us to the family camp and to call the consul. We have to get back to the States as soon as possible. I don't want to spend any more time in this country."

"Do you think they'll let us leave?"

"Of course they will. I'm a US citizen."

We hugged again and then found a spot among the dunes. Our bodies were electric. His caresses had never felt so sweet. Afterward, we held each other as the hours passed slowly by and we waited for dawn.

Elisabeth

Elisabeth had not been back to the camp since her trip to Switzerland. She parked Rocinante and glanced at the barbed-wire fence as Karl got out of the van.

"You all right?" her friend asked as he opened the door for her.

"I thought I saw something behind the dunes over there."

They went up to the fence, and Elisabeth could just make out the figure of a woman holding a child. The woman was wailing and screaming.

"Something's going on with that woman!" she exclaimed.

She and Karl ran to the gate and showed their passes to the soldiers, who took their time examining them. Elisabeth kept her eyes on the dunes. Exasperated, she cried out, "Can you please go faster?"

The soldier with the long, messy mustache frowned at her. "Who do you think you are? We're doing our duty. Imagine what would happen if all this riffraff got out and wandered all over France. The robberies, the attacks, the rapes!"

Elisabeth held her tongue, took their documents, and hurried Karl toward the dunes. The woman was on her knees in the sand, holding her baby.

"What's going on?" Elisabeth asked, sitting beside her.

"She's got a fever and hasn't had anything to eat or drink

since yesterday." The woman's swollen eyes were pleading for Elisabeth to do something.

"Let me examine her," Karl said, but the woman would not release the child.

"He just needs to check her over," Elisabeth said, gently reaching for the baby. Unwillingly, the woman let go of her daughter. Karl laid her out on the wet, compact sand. He checked the child's pulse, breathing, and temperature. Then he shook his head.

"But she was warm . . . ," Elisabeth said.

"She was pressing her so tightly to her chest that it seemed like the baby almost had a fever, but she's not breathing."

The mother seemed removed from the conversation. She just stared at the baby dressed in pink rags and covered with a blanket. Turning to the mother, Elisabeth took her hands and tried to control her voice.

"Your daughter isn't here anymore," she said. "She's gone to heaven."

For the first time the woman looked directly into Elisabeth's eyes, finally seeming to understand what was happening.

"That's not true!" she yelled. She lunged for the child and pressed her to her chest.

"She's not alive anymore," Karl explained.

"Liars! You just want to keep my baby, but I'll never sell her!"

Elisabeth tried to hug the woman but was pushed away brusquely.

"She's my daughter! My only daughter! I came here for her, so she would have a better future, so she wouldn't have to grow up in the land where her father and grandparents were murdered." The woman dissolved into tears, overcome with the pain of it all. Elisabeth was able to embrace her then, and they stayed like that for a long time, without speaking, until Karl came with the grave-diggers. The two unkempt men with muddy shoes took the baby and put her on their cart. The woman pushed Elisabeth away and made to grab for her daughter, but Karl held her back.

"They need to take her."

"I can't even keep watch over her? I'll never see her again."

The gravediggers shook their heads no. The woman's cries followed them as the men rolled the cart away. Elisabeth and Karl stayed with her until she was calmer; then they walked her back to her shack and left her to rest.

As they walked away through the camp, Elisabeth started speaking. "Now do you see what's going on here? We're in the heart of Europe, and the world looks on, apathetic to such suffering."

"You know you've got my support. I need most of the care-takers in the orphanage, but as long as the volunteers show up, we'll help you all we can."

But Elisabeth's mind was elsewhere. "How many children have been lost along the way? How many women have died dur-ing these desperate days?"

Karl put a hand on her shoulder, and they stared at the jam-packed camp before them. More and more people arrived by the day. Elisabeth marveled at how an entire generation was being lost there. The hopes and dreams of thousands of young people were buried forever beneath the sand of that beach in the middle of nowhere. She felt so helpless, and all she could do was weep.

SEVENTEEN

Isabel

Sometimes I wondered if that night with Peter had been a dream. At dawn, the French police had entered the camp and searched everywhere for Peter. They eventually spotted us together on the beach and surrounded us. One of the soldiers had a gun trained on us.

"You, come with us!" the sergeant ordered, coming up slowly.

"Peter, we'd better not try to fight."

"Can you please tell me what I'm being accused of? I've done nothing wrong. Isabel is my wife."

"You ran away from the military camp and entered this camp illegally," the officer said.

"That's absurd! If I had tried to escape, I wouldn't still be here. I'm a US American citizen, and I demand—"

But the soldiers tackled him, and even though I tried to stop it, it was useless. I kicked and swatted with my fists, but they threw me aside.

"*Ma'am, you're lucky we're not arresting you as well,*" the sergeant said and then ordered his men to lift Peter.

"*Where are you taking him?*"

"*To the correction facility. He needs to spend a while there.*"

I went up to my husband, and the sergeant made a motion to his men to let me through. I kissed Peter and said, "*Don't worry. I'll be all right. Now that I know you're alive, I can keep waiting. I'll write to you.*"

"*I'll get in touch with my father in the States and with the ambassador here. They can't treat us like criminals.*" Peter twisted again, but the soldiers held him tight.

A month had gone by, and we had barely had any contact. They allowed us to write one letter a week, and I knew that Peter had gotten in touch with his father and with the consul. Surely it would not be long before they let him go.

Not long after that, the French opened the camps, and we were allowed to roam freely between them. América, who was thinner than ever because of our scant diet and frequent diarrhea, would go to what we all called the Barrio Chino. That is where we could get supplies the French did not provide.

That morning, after several weeks of very low spirits, I decided to go with her. We walked a long way to the northern part of the camp to where there were about fifty shacks decorated with ribbons and vibrant colors. The Barcelona mafia had claimed that section of the camp. They, too, had fled from the Francoists and were now managing all sorts of businesses inside the camp, including exploiting women they had brought with them from Spain. It was a disgusting place, but América was used to seeing it by then. The prostitutes were outside washing their clothes and fixing their hair.

América had become friends with one named Jacinta, who was around América's age and had curly red hair, brown eyes, and a girlish face full of freckles. We passed by Jacinta's shack. Usually she would have been washing clothes or making coffee, so América was surprised that she was not there.

"I'm going to check inside," she said nervously. She stuck her head through the blankets that served as a doorway but saw no one.

"Maybe she just went out to run an errand," I suggested.

"That's really odd. I doubt it. She's never away from her shack in the morning. She's afraid of everything and everyone. The only one she trusts is her pimp. Stupidly, she thinks he loves her and that this situation is temporary. She thinks he's going to get her out of here soon so they can settle down and start a family. But he's a complete bum, a social parasite who lives off women."

"We should go on and sell our books." That is what we had started doing in the Barrio Chino, bartering books. It did not bring in much but was just enough to buy a few extra things on the black market.

"Let's look for her just a bit," América said.

We went along La Rambla, which is what everyone called the main street of the camp. As we picked our way through the miserable shacks, I came to see that others had it worse off than we did. Wandering farther away from the hustle and bustle, we heard shouting. América took off running, and I followed as fast as I could, but I was carrying a dozen heavy books and did not have energy to spare.

When we got to the shack where the shouts were coming from, we saw naked feet poking out from the doorway blankets.

"Jacinta!" América cried and started pulling at the girl. I helped her, and we got her out. Then a man thrust his head out of the shack. It was Manolo, the man we had argued with over soap in the supplies barrack a few weeks before.

"What do you think you're doing? This whore owes me money. She won't pay, so I'm settling the debt."

"You're raping her, you nasty pig, and we're going to report you to the captain."

Though overseen by the French army, each camp had a representative of the Spanish government, so refugees resolved internal affairs on their own.

"Who's going to believe a slut?"

Jacinta got to her feet and straightened her dress. She had one black eye and bruises all over her body. América hugged her and tried to steady her. She was shaking all over. I grabbed a stick from the ground and shook it at Manolo.

"Stay away from us! You understand?"

He came out of the shack and spat at the ground beside me. "I'll get you one by one, and then we'll see who's making the threats."

We all sighed in relief when he walked off.

"Isabel, we have to bring her back with us to our camp," América said.

"No!" Jacinta protested. "I have to stay with Luis, my boyfriend."

"He's not your boyfriend, Jacinta. He's using you," América said.

"He protects me. The soldiers took him away for stabbing a gypsy, but he'll be back soon."

I knew that the Spaniards sent to the correction camp often stayed for quite a while. I went up and touched Jacinta's cheeks gently and said, "Why don't you come back with us, just until Luis returns?"

She shook her head adamantly. "I'm saving up money for when we get married, and I can't take time off from work."

We escorted her back to her shack and then went on to the improvised market at the back of the Barrio Chino. We laid our books out on a blanket, and América called out the prices. I hung my head and thought about Peter. I missed him more with each passing day.

======

Elisabeth

BROUILLA MATERNITY HOSPITAL

March 17, 1939

Elisabeth was not satisfied, though Lucy tried to convince her otherwise. Not enough money had come in to buy the building in Elne, so they had opened the maternity hospital in a town just a few miles from Perpignan. It was not ideal. Money from donors trickled in slowly. Everyone seemed to be preparing for war, and no one was eager to part with resources. Elisabeth sent memorandums, news, and photographs of camp life to Bern in hopes of softening donors' hearts, but it seemed to be in vain.

She looked at the fruit crates they had repurposed as cribs and covered her eyes. "The poor babies won't even have a proper cradle."

"Just think of Moses, floating in that basket among the crocodiles," Lucy said brightly.

"That was thousands of years ago. Europe is a rich continent but doesn't have enough money for these poor children."

"You can get by with this for now," Karl said, bringing in a box of baby sheets and blankets. "It'll work fine as crib linens."

"Besides, anywhere is better than those beaches. It's been two months, and the conditions are no better. The only thing the government has done is open more camps, each one worse than the last. I hear there are over half a million refugees in southern France right now," Lucy said. The British consul she had just gone to see with a request for aid had filled her in.

Elisabeth looked at the recently painted room. They had worked hard for weeks, but the place still was not what it needed to be. "I just keep thinking about that castle in Elne. I'm not going to give up on it."

Her friends knew she could be hardheaded, but that kind of persistence made change happen. Elisabeth had managed to start a small infirmary in the camp. Pregnant women who were healthy enough could stay there until it was no longer safe for them to be out on the beaches. Then they would be brought to the maternity hospital and could stay for the first few months of the baby's life, until the baby was strong and healthy.

Ruth von Wild, one of the volunteers, came running into the room, wringing her hands.

"What's going on?" Elisabeth asked, trying to calm her down.

"A woman has gone into labor, and we don't know what to do! The nurse is getting ready for her to deliver there at the camp."

"What? Have they gone crazy? Let's go get her!"

Elisabeth and Ruth ran downstairs to Rocinante and drove as fast as they could to Argelès-sur-Mer. On several occasions Ruth was worried that Elisabeth would drive off the road, but they arrived safe and sound. They stopped at the gate and requested permission to enter.

"You can't bring that piece of junk in here," the soldier replied.

"There's a woman in labor, and we need to transport her," Elisabeth said, not covering up her impatience.

"Transport her? To where? This isn't a boarding house—it's a refugee camp."

"Well, is it a prison? We need to get to her now!"

The soldier hesitated but finally asked his companion to raise the barrier. They parked right outside the infirmary, jumped out, and ran inside. The woman in labor was screaming in pain as the nurse tried to make her comfortable.

"We've come for her."

The nurse frowned and shook her head. "She's almost ready; you can't move her."

"I know, but she can't give birth here. There aren't enough resources for her or for the baby. The water is contaminated. Most people have lice, fleas, and mange. The child won't last a week."

"Well, they both might die if you transport her," the nurse warned.

Elisabeth went up to the woman on the bed, put her hand on her forehead, and asked, "Do you want us to get you out of here?"

"Yes, please! I don't want my baby to be born in this camp."

Elisabeth glared at the nurse. She and Ruth got on either side of the woman and steadied her under her arms. They settled her carefully into the back of the van. Elisabeth drove as quickly and gently as she could. The woman's cries grew increasingly louder the closer they got. Lucy and Karl were outside waiting with a cot and took her to what had become the delivery room. Everything was ready.

Ruth, who had graduated from nursing school a few months before, looked at the pregnant woman and then at Elisabeth.

"Don't you know what to do?" Elisabeth asked her.

"In theory, yes."

"Well, I've done it once, and I figure it happens the same way each time." Elisabeth rolled up her sleeves and asked Lucy for clean towels. Karl left them to it, feeling the satisfaction of having helped get the maternity ward up and running. Saving the life of just one child would make it all worth it.

═══

Peter

ARGELÈS-SUR-MER CORRECTION CAMP
March 18, 1939

Peter learned at least one thing at the correction camp. hatred ruins hope. He watched with interest as his hatred toward the French grew over the weeks. He hated them for locking him up in that place. He hated the consul, who seemed to care little about getting him out and helping Isabel. And he hated himself. The only thing that kept him sane was reading. He had found an old copy of *Don Quixote* and had read it cover to cover four times. Most of the prisoners around him were true criminals, but he had found one who seemed to be trustworthy. Mauricio was a brigade soldier like Peter and was from Mexico.

"Reading Cervantes again?" Mauricio asked.

"Is there anything better to do with my time here? Books calm me down. The wait is unbearable."

"I've been here two weeks longer than you have," Mauricio quipped.

"You've never said what got you in here."

Mauricio fiddled with his brown mustache before answering. "I'm a loser, and that has always been my fate. I thought that things in my country would change after the revolution. My family was poor. For generations we've worked for a landowner in Tijuana. He managed to survive the revolution, and it turned out there was no land distribution after all. The rich guys even came out ahead, gobbling up some of the common land. So we were worse off than before. One day I saw him beating my father with a rod. I was only about fifteen years old. I snuck up on him from behind, grabbed the rod, and beat him senseless. I didn't stick around to see if he was dead or alive. I headed for the capital and showed up in the DF without a peso to my name. I shined shoes, swept the streets, did carpentry work—anything and everything. Then I met Roberto. He was the salt of the earth. He talked about equality, about class struggle and Marx. It fascinated me. It was what I'd been struggling for my whole life without knowing it. But they killed him like a dog during a strike. Then the war broke out in Spain, and I enlisted. I dreamed about utopia starting in at least one place on earth. I fought in lots of places, but finally my superiors noticed I was good with motors, so they had me working as a mechanic. We were pulling back farther and farther as the Fascists kept advancing. We crossed over into France, and they took me to the camp. One morning I saw a Senegalese soldier beating an old man. That was it. I couldn't take it anymore. I grabbed his club and went after him. I wasn't even thinking; it was just automatic. When they got me off him, the guy was halfway dead. So they sent me here, and that's that. It's a common enough story, just like millions of needy wretches all over the world."

"Why didn't you tell me any of that before?"

Mauricio shrugged, then lit a cigarette and started smoking. After a few puffs, he started coughing and spitting up blood.

"You okay?" Peter asked.

Mauricio nodded but kept coughing. Peter called for the soldier guarding them. Unlike the other overcrowded camps, there were only about a hundred prisoners in total.

"Mauricio is sick," Peter said.

The soldier looked at him in boredom. "There's no doctor today. He'll have to wait for tomorrow."

"But he's bad off. Call a doctor, please."

From the other side of the fence, the soldier shook his head. "The doctor comes in the morning, and he's a volunteer. You should be grateful."

Peter shook the gate in frustration, but the only result was that the solder pointed his gun at Peter and other guards came running. Peter backed away and returned to Mauricio. He tried to help him breathe calmly, but the coughing was choking him. Peter held him for five long hours until Mauricio stopped breathing for good.

EIGHTEEN

Isabel

Some dates are impossible to forget. April 1, the day I officially
lost my country, was one of those for me. The commotion started
early that morning in the camp. Some had heard that the Republic
had surrendered. No one was surprised, but we had all been hoping war would start in Europe and save us.

María, América, and I went to the mail barrack once night had
fallen. There was a radio there. It was hard to get close enough to
hear with all the people around. Everyone had turned out for the
final war dispatch.

"Have they said anything yet?" I asked a woman.

"No. I've been here for four hours, but there's been nothing
yet."

"Maybe it was all a mistake. I heard that Cartagena is still
holding out, as well as parts of Alicante," María said.

"It's hard to know what's really going on. There's so much
propaganda with the war," the woman answered.

Just then we heard the music that was always the precursor

180

to the Francoist dispatches. There was absolute silence in our camp. The voice of Fernando Fernández de Córdoba, a second-rate actor turned radio announcer, started reading the war dispatch with his triumphalist tone, and people started weeping.

> Official war dispatch, from the headquarters of the general, corresponding to today, April 1, 1939, the third Year of Triumph. Today, with the Red army captive and disarmed, the Nationalist troops have achieved their final military objectives. The war has ended.
>
> Burgos, April 1, 1939, Year of Victory
>
> General Franco

The camp erupted in a cry of desperation. Some were shaking their heads in denial, refusing to believe their ears. Women were wailing, and children mimicked them without comprehending why.

"Oh dear God, I can never return to Spain with my baby!" María moaned in desperation.

América and I were calmer than the others. We had never hoped to return. We just wanted to get out of the camp and get on with our lives.

"It's all right, María. The war is over, and things will eventually calm down."

María was five months pregnant, though she had only recently realized it. At first she had thought her symptoms were a result of the stress of fleeing from the war, combined with the inadequate food. But eventually she figured out that she was expecting, thanks to the brief time she had spent with her husband before the gendarmes captured her.

"Damn it all!" she cried out. We tried to make our way out of the crowd and get to the infirmary, but it was hard to maneuver in the crowd. When we finally made it there, the place was overrun with people having panic attacks.

"My friend needs help," I told the nurse.

"Go to the station set up by the Swiss Aid to Spanish Children organization. They'll have room for her."

We went as quickly as we could. María had started bleeding, and we feared she would lose the baby. She could barely stand on her own by the time we got there. A woman in a white uniform motioned for us to come in. She examined María and had her lie down.

"She just needs to rest. She can stay here tonight. I can look after her and make sure she gets enough food to recover her strength."

"Is one night enough?" I asked.

The nurse shrugged. "She's got a long way to go until she gives birth, and we can't take women out of the camp until they're close to going into labor. If we filled up all the beds, what would we do when women are in labor?"

"That's fine. We'll come see you tomorrow, María," I told her. She seemed calmer and drowsy.

"Thank you, Isabel and América. I don't know what I'd do without you two."

We left the little building and walked in silence down La Rambla toward our shack. The entire place was in mourning. People were walking with their heads down, and hardly a sound was heard in that city of losers. América and I both hesitated at the doorway of our shack. Instead of going inside, we went to the sea and watched the reflection of the moon dancing on the dark waters.

Just then a man in a fancy suit came up to us. He tipped his bowler hat in salute, then continued walking. He walked directly into the waves without altering his gait. We did not know what to do. América jumped to her feet and started yelling for him. The man turned and waved calmly while continuing his progression into the waves. A minute later he was gone. He was not the only one that day. Many refugees no longer had anywhere to return to, and life lacked any meaning. The only thing they could do was end it all and disappear.

Elisabeth

BROUILLA MATERNITY HOSPITAL
April 1, 1939

Rumors were spreading that the French wanted to close the camp at Argelès-sur-Mer. The French authorities were pressuring the Spaniards to return to the country now that the war was over. Yet they failed to understand that, for many, returning to Spain meant certain death. The wave of violence unleashed within the country was staggering. As General Franco had announced, there was victory, but no peace, and the losers were paying a very high price. The death sentences grew by the thousands each day, and firing squads could hardly keep up.

"How are they going to close Argelès?" Lucy asked the woman who had brought the news.

"Since the war ended, a lot of people will go home of their own accord. But I don't think the rest will be allowed to roam freely about France."

"So what will be done with them?" Elisabeth was looking at the two women while also glancing every so often at the crib. They had already helped many children come into the world, but it was never enough. So many mothers were still left with no option but to give birth on the beaches of the camps scattered throughout southern France.

"I think they'll send them somewhere else while they improve conditions at the camp."

"Well, that would be a welcome result," Lucy said.

"But why haven't they done that before now?" Elisabeth huffed.

"Who knows?" Lucy answered.

"They thought the war would be over right away and so if they made the camps livable, the refugees wouldn't want to go back home," Elisabeth opined. She was disgusted by the French government's policy toward the Spanish refugees. The French and the British had supported a noninterventionist plan and had even held back on sending weapons to the Republic; meanwhile, the Germans and Italians had sent troops and all sorts of aid.

They heard voices, and Elisabeth hurried to one of the rooms. A young woman who had arrived a few days ago, Clara, had gone into labor.

"Let's get her to the delivery room," Lucy said as Elisabeth soothed and encouraged Clara.

Between the three of them they lifted Clara and helped her to the delivery room. They called for Ruth, but she was not in the building.

Elisabeth realized soon enough that this birth would be complicated.

"Please, go find the doctor," Elisabeth said to the others.

Clara began to cry. "Is something wrong?"

"Don't worry; we're right here with you," Elisabeth said, but she could not fully mask her worry.

In time, Clara began to push, but the baby would not come out. Elisabeth and Lucy tried to help her stay calm. Elisabeth felt around with her hand and sensed that something was wrapped around the baby's neck.

They tried to get the baby out for ten minutes, but nothing happened. The doctor rushed in and pushed up his sleeves but could only confirm what they all feared.

"The cord is wrapped around the child's neck. The more the mother pushes, the more it strangles the baby, and he can't breathe."

The doctor's explanation shook Elisabeth to the core. Lucy stepped aside to pray while Elisabeth helped the doctor. They attempted an emergency C-section and got the baby out, but he was already purple. The doctor tried to resuscitate him, but it was of no use.

The young mother began screaming for her baby. The doctor gently placed the child in his mother's arms. She needed to see his face in order to say goodbye and somehow overcome the tragedy.

Elisabeth calmed Clara as best she could, stroking her hair and speaking gently to her, but the tears did not stop. There was no comfort possible for a mother holding her baby's corpse.

Elisabeth and Lucy wept together. They had opened the maternity hospital to save lives, but they had not been able to do anything for Clara's son. They understood they could not save everyone from the jaws of death, but that did not make it hurt any less. Elisabeth stroked Clara's hair again and told herself that no mother should have to hold her baby's dead body.

Peter

ARGELÈS-SUR-MER CORRECTION CAMP

April 1, 1939

After Mauricio's death, Peter attempted to file a complaint with the overseeing officer, but the only result was two weeks in solitary confinement. In the two-by-two-yard cell with no light source, Peter thought he would go insane. The only thing that held him together was thinking about Isabel and his family and praying. He had no notion of the passage of time. He tried to stay as active as possible, but his strength waned by the day.

Finally he was allowed out of that hole. He was in shock when they gave him clean clothes and allowed him to bathe with cold water.

"Yankee, you'd better clean up. The consul's secretary is coming to see you today."

Suddenly, Peter's mood lifted. He would get out soon and get back to his country.

An hour later, Peter was seated in a barrack, drumming his fingers on the desk and humming. A man with a gray striped suit entered, took off his hat, and sat down.

"Mr. Peter Davis, is that correct?" he asked.

"Yes, I'm Peter Davis. I've been writing the consul for months and trying to get in touch with someone in your office."

"Mr. Davis, you have to understand we are overwhelmed with work at the moment. You're not the only US citizen requesting repatriation. To make matters worse, with the tensions in Europe right now, many citizens are trying to return before war breaks out."

Peter tried to stay calm. It was not a good idea to lash out against the consul's secretary now that his request was finally receiving attention.

"The first thing is to wait until you're set free. You've been arrested for misbehavior, and you've got two weeks left."

"Is that a joke? I'm a political refugee. My only crime was trying to see my wife, whom I haven't seen in months, and then asking for a doctor to see a sick comrade. Those are crimes?"

The secretary crossed his arms and studied Peter in silence for several moments.

"The reasons don't matter. The fact is that you've been arrested. We might be able to process your exit from the country by May, but I can assure you that you're not at the top of the list. No one asked you to get involved in the war and support the Communists."

Peter counted to three before answering.

"I'm not a Communist. I was only trying to defend a democratically elected government, but it doesn't matter what you think about it all as long as you do your job. I've also requested a visa for my wife."

The secretary took a document out of his briefcase and put it on the desk.

"Your marriage isn't valid. There's no proof of it."

"We have our marriage certificate and the family registry," Peter said.

"The registries of the government of the Republic ceased to be legitimate once the war began, which means it's as if your wedding didn't happen. You can't travel with your . . . friend."

"Friend? She's my wife, and I won't go anywhere without her!"

"That's your problem," the man said. He picked up the document sent by Franco's government to the world's embassies and returned it to his briefcase.

"If I were to get married in the consulate, the document would be valid, right?"

"According to our laws, you'll have to be officially married for at least a year before your wife can get a visa. But the processes are slow and always take longer."

Peter could not believe what he was hearing. "This is madness. You're telling me we have to stay in this hellhole at least another year. Have you lost your mind?"

The secretary stood and put on his hat. "I can see you're displeased with the regulations, but these are the rules I must follow. I will request your repatriation, but you will have to travel alone. Your wife can join you once the wedding which you will have to repeat has been authorized and she is granted a visa. Good day."

The secretary left without another word. Peter covered his face with his hands and wept, wondering how on earth his country could leave them stranded in a place that was preparing for war. If the Nazis attacked France, they would go after citizens of the United States right away.

NINETEEN

Isabel

Misery is a crushing force that empties the heart and makes one lose all faith. Peter's letters came ever more slowly and further apart. He had promised we would be together again soon, but the weeks came and went, and things only got worse. A few days before, a storm had blown most of the shacks away. There was water everywhere, and a rushing torrent had formed between the family camp and the women's camp. Many people had died. For the first time since our arrival, people had rebelled and stood up to the French. It had not done us any good, though a few days later the regional prefect visited and promised that conditions in the camp would soon be improved.

The day after the big storm, I started feeling very bad. It started with diarrhea, then with vomiting and soreness all over my body. I stayed in bed for five days straight. I lost even more weight and was growing weaker and weaker.

María's pregnancy seemed to be going better, but she had not gained much weight. We did not receive enough food for a regular diet, much less for a pregnant woman. The Swiss infirmary gave her extra food, but sometimes we sold it to buy other things we needed.

That morning I was really bad off. Everything looked blurry to me, and I felt my life slowly slipping away. América did not leave my side. Hour after hour she put cool rags on my forehead to bring my fever down, and she made chicken soup to help stop the diarrhea.

"We've got to get her to the infirmary," she told María. They looked at each other and then at me. They fashioned a cot with a blanket and two long sticks, settled me in the middle of it, and headed for the camp infirmary. The two nurses there told them they had no medicines to give me. They had not received supplies for several days, and they recommended we try the hospital in Perpignan. América and María spoke with the camp authorities, but they refused the request. The hospital was already over capacity.

"Let's try with the Swiss infirmary," María said. They picked me up again, but when the Swiss nurse saw them, she shook her head. She did not speak Spanish well.

"We don't treat sick people, only pregnant women and infants," she stammered.

"My friend is dying, and if no one sees her, she won't see the end of this week," María said.

The nurse seemed indifferent. Then another young woman appeared and came up to us. She asked what was going on and then asked the nurse to let me lie in the bed.

The woman examined me and turned to my friends. "She's pregnant."

América and María looked at each other in surprise. The words reached me from a great distance.

"We can give her an IV and antibiotics," the woman said and then turned to the nurse and gave some instructions.

"Thank you for everything," María said.

"You're pregnant as well, aren't you?" she asked.

"Yes, I've been coming here for extra food for several weeks now."

"Well, you still look too thin. Why don't you stay here a few days? Your baby needs to grow and put on some weight."

"What's your name?" María asked.

The young woman smiled and answered, "Elisabeth Eidenbenz."

That name stayed with me. What I did not know then was that our paths would cross again and that fate would bind us together in the most important work of our lives.

TWENTY

Isabel

Time does not turn tragedies into blessings, and problems do not solve themselves. Often the wait for healing is so terrible that a person becomes someone else, usually bitter and resentful. Even so, I did start to feel better after about three days. María did not leave my side the entire time, and América came by to visit at first. Then two days passed, and we had not seen her. That worried me. I did not want her to be alone. There were too many dangers lurking about, and she was safer if she stayed close to me and María. I was worrying about all of this when María stood up with a huge smile. She was looking greatly improved and was already six and a half months into her pregnancy.

"I have a surprise! Close your eyes."

I obeyed and opened them a minute later to behold the face of my beloved Peter. At first I was paralyzed with the shock and could not breathe. Then we were kissing and hugging.

"Oh God, I can't believe it!" I said, touching his arms to assure myself that he was real.

"How are you? I asked all over the camp for you and learned you'd been taken to the infirmary in a bad state. But I didn't find you there, and I was worried."

"I'm getting better but am still weak. I have some news for you."

Peter's big blue eyes grew wide.

"We're going to be parents! This is not the best time or place, but we're going to have a baby."

"That's amazing! Things are finally starting to look up!" he said, dancing around.

María stepped into another room, and Peter told me all about his time at the correction camp. He was notably gaunter than the last time I had seen him.

"I haven't been able to get a visa to go to the States, and we have to do our wedding over again," he said, his head sunk deep into his chest.

I cradled his chin in my hands and said, "None of that matters. We're together now, and nothing is going to keep us apart. You're my country. Your home will be my home."

We wept like two babies. I thought back to the day we had met, the day that changed our lives completely.

Peter came to see me every morning and stayed beside my side until night, despite the nurse's complaints. I had asked him to look after América, but he said he could not find any trace of her.

"I have to go look for her."

"Things out there are pretty wild. They closed the Barrio Chino because of all the crime, but the prostitution ring just started up somewhere else. They're going to close this camp soon and move everyone somewhere else," Peter said.

I stood up and got dressed. I was feeling much better. I put my shoes on and was ready to leave.

"You can't leave yet. You're still too weak," he protested.

"América is still just a child. She's young and innocent and shouldn't be on her own. I promised her we'd take her with us. I don't understand why she's just disappeared."

María, Peter, and I left the infirmary and looked far and wide for América. I grew increasingly nervous as the hours ticked by but felt sure we would eventually find her.

TWENTY-ONE

Elisabeth

Money had finally come from Switzerland, but it still was not enough to purchase the house in Elne and remodel it. Sickness only increased in the camp as summer approached. The hospital in Brouilla was too small and not adequately equipped for treating all the women who needed care.

"There's got to be another solution," Elisabeth said after counting all the money.

"Sometimes things just happen a certain way. It may be that God doesn't want us to have a different place," Lucy said, glancing around. Yet no one seemed willing to give up on the idea.

"God is on the side of the daring, and that's what we're missing. We need to talk with Swiss Aid and the prefect and get the local councils in Perpignan and Elne involved."

"SAS is out of money. You know that Swiss Aid depends on

SCI," Karl said. Everyone stared at Elisabeth, knowing she would not give in.

"Rodolfo will have to send us more money. A lot of refugees have returned to Spain, but there are still hundreds of thousands here, and we have to offer them long-term support."

Elisabeth walked out of the room, and Lucy followed. They put on their jackets and got into Rocinante.

"Where are we headed?" Lucy asked.

"We need help, so we're going to go find it. We'll call Rodolfo. In Perpignan we can put a call through to Switzerland. Then we'll visit the prefect and will threaten to denounce the situation to the international media if they don't contribute money for the maternity hospital."

"You wouldn't do that."

Elisabeth smiled. She knew she was capable of that and much more. As a young girl, she had been shy and withdrawn, but now she found a strength inside that surprised even her. She remembered a winter afternoon when she was fourteen. She had been helping her father get the church ready for a prayer meeting, and one of the older women in the congregation came up to her. The woman's name was Úrsula, and many people thought she was crazy. Úrsula claimed that God was so close to her when she prayed that she could smell his perfume. The old woman took Elisabeth's soft young hand and said in a sweet voice, "Be strong and courageous. Do everything you can in your strength, but remember that someone bigger than you is supporting you. Start praying from a young age. He'll do all the work. Though you think you're small and unimportant, he sees you as very great." Elisabeth had always remembered those words. Though she was often racked with doubts, she was convinced that good would somehow triumph over evil.

At the phone booth in Perpignan, Elisabeth called Rodolfo. At first no one in Switzerland picked up, and the operator advised her to try again later.

"Please keep trying," Elisabeth asked.

Finally, someone picked up.

"Rodolfo?"

"Good day. With whom am I speaking?" the man asked, though he knew perfectly well that the only person who would call him unannounced from Perpignan was Elisabeth.

"Good day, Rodolfo; we need to talk. The place where we're currently operating is not sufficient for a maternity hospital. I'm going to ask the prefect to intervene so we can get the house in Elne, but we need more money."

"We've sent you all that we can."

"I don't think you understand. It's not enough. Children are still dying on the benches, and we can only treat a very small number of mothers."

"I understand where you're coming from."

"No, I don't think you do. Every day I see mothers and babies die. I need you to get more money. Cancel the summer camps if you have to. The money is needed down here."

Rodolfo sighed and huffed at the other end of the line. "If the committee approves it, I promise we'll send the majority of our funding this year to the maternity hospital."

"Don't make promises. Do it, please."

"Fine, fine, we'll do it. Good Lord, you're stubborn, Elisabeth; worse than Balaam's ass."

Elisabeth smiled and hung up. That was satisfying, but there was more to be done. Lucy looked at her with raised eyebrows. She had never known anyone like Elisabeth.

"And now let's go visit the prefect and the mayor."

"We don't have an appointment," Lucy pointed out.

"Well, we'll just show up," Elisabeth said as they headed back to Rocinante.

TWENTY-TWO

Isabel

ARGELÈS-SUR-MER CAMP
May 23, 1939

We looked for América for three days, but it seemed like the earth had swallowed her up. More and more people were leaving for Spain. The formerly overcrowded La Rambla street was starting to empty out. Even so, many families remained in France out of fear of reprisals.

On the third day of our search, we came upon América's friend Jacinta, the prostitute we had saved from being raped by Manolo. She was in a terrible state, living in a remote section of shacks where women still practiced prostitution despite it being against camp rules.

"Jacinta, have you seen América? We've been looking for her for days."

Jacinta was in a stupor. It was clear that she had been drinking, and from the looks of her place, that seemed to be the norm. In desperation I grabbed her by the shirt and shook her awake. I had to know what had happened to my friend.

Jacinta finally looked up and tried to focus on my eyes. "I saw her a few days ago with a guy named Javier. That surprised me. He's a thief and a pimp."

"Where? Where did you see her?" I demanded. Every minute counted.

"In the shacks near the military camp."

That did not make sense. Someone should have denounced that a girl was in that section, but many times the Spanish authorities in the camp looked the other way.

Peter and I went to that section. He knew of the place Jacinta had described. While I had been in the infirmary, he had been sleeping in the philosophers' barrack again.

We got to the shacks and looked in one after the other. From one, the most disgusting and abandoned of them, a nauseating smell was emanating. There we found a half-naked body covered with a dirty sheet. I was shaking at the mere thought that that bruised body might be América. I turned the figure over carefully and saw my friend's face. Her eyes were swollen, her lips cracked, and bruises distorted her lovely face. Her eyes opened just a slit, and she struggled to speak.

"Isabel?"

"América! What have they done to you? How did you get here?"

She tried to speak but did not have the strength. Tears dripped down the dirt on her face. Peter scooped her up and we took her to the infirmary. People turned to watch us as we passed. The nurse instinctively pulled back in horror when she saw América. María started crying and stroked the girl's cheek.

"My child, what have they done to you?" she whispered.

We cleaned her gently with damp cloths. Her whole body was covered with sores and bruises. The nurse shook her head after examining her. "Who did this to you?" she asked.

There was no answer. Peter, María, and I watched over her the rest of that day and into the night until her breathing stopped.

I went out and sat on the stoop of the medical barrack. I could not stop crying. All my friends had died. María was a good woman, but she could not fill the space that América had left in my heart.

Peter came up and kissed the tears on my cheeks like they were a treasure to him.

"Are you all right?" he asked.

I shook my head and then instinctively touched my belly, which was starting to grow.

"Do you think it's a good idea to bring a new life into a world like this?" I asked.

He leaned his head on my shoulder. He was a dreamer and always had been, but even he seemed spent. "We're all going to stop breathing someday. We came into the world with the seal of death engraved on our foreheads. We'll return to the land we came from. The only thing that's truly certain is that we will die."

"But not like this, Peter. She was a young girl full of dreams with her whole life ahead of her. She had lost her family and had no one left in the world. Other people would have thrown in the towel, but América wasn't one to give up on her dreams."

Peter took my cold hands and warmed them in his. He looked out to the sea, and his blue eyes lit up again.

"I have hope that someday the world will leave behind the dark valleys of hatred and violence, that it will rise up and walk down a path of justice and love. We may not be able to see it yet, but the only way to reach it is by renouncing our own sense of justice."

"Who's going to do justice for us then?"

Peter was trembling. It looked like he could break down at any second, yet at the same time he had a confidence I had not seen in him before.

"We shouldn't fear the people who can harm our bodies as long as we keep our souls intact. We're going through really difficult, terrible times, Isabel, but I want to keep dreaming. I dream about my house and my family, knowing that I'll always have a place to go back to, a place where we can raise a family. I haven't lived the way my parents raised me, but after this war, I've realized that my father wasn't wrong about everything. Violence never leads to a better world. Just the opposite. It destroys the good that's already here in this one. I've seen my best friends bleed to death beside me. Young men full of dreams who no longer exist—I sense them whispering to me from somewhere that we can't lie down and die, that we have to keep living, that being happy is the best way to rebel against all the suffering and darkness."

"I wish I could believe like you do," I mumbled between my tears. His words did me good, but they also pointed out the chasm between us. I felt so much hatred, so much fear, and so little hope that the only thing I wanted to do was run away. Yet I knew the feelings were inside of me and I could not escape them.

"We can't lose our liberty, our freedom. Freedom is not just the absence of chains. It's overcoming the brutality of reality and, despite it all, daring to be happy," Peter said.

That night was so long. I remember it as the most bitter moment of my life. I felt so lonely that not even Peter's company brought consolation. I still had not yet grasped that, at the core, each soul is fundamentally alone and that there is a void that no one and nothing can fill. I had not yet understood that one reality supersedes the rest: one day we will have to face our own death—cross that mysterious, inscrutable threshold that separates the living from the dead—as naked and alone as the day we entered the world.

Part III

THE ELNE MATERNITY HOSPITAL

TWENTY-THREE

Elisabeth

ELNE MATERNITY HOSPITAL
May 30, 1939

Elisabeth studied the building. It was not overly attractive, but the glass tower crowning the roof set it apart. The red brick made a pleasing contrast to the yellowed stone and the coffered facade. It was flanked on both sides by balconies accessible by curving stone staircases that lent a palatial feel. To Elisabeth's eyes, it was a worthy place for new lives to be brought into the world. The building in Brouilla was falling to pieces. She was eager to transfer the women to Elne, but there was much work to be done first. The work crews supplied by the Perpignan town council were far from efficient. The only ones getting anything done were the Spaniards she had recruited to restore the building.

Elisabeth went inside, tied on an apron, and started painting the walls in one of the rooms. Karl walked in and was surprised to see her. He marveled at her endless energy.

"So besides getting a priest's help to convince the mayor and prefect of Perpignan to help you get the building, and squeezing more money out of Switzerland, you're also going to paint the place."

"The workers aren't going fast enough," she said with a sigh.

"All the best workers are already out on the front, reinforcing the trenches. Only old men or lazy bums are left in town," Karl said, grabbing a brush and starting to work beside her.

"Well, it doesn't look like it's going too badly for you," Elisabeth quipped and then purposely dabbed a splotch of paint on his jacket.

"Hey, this is my best suit!"

"Who in the world would start painting in nice clothes? You're clearly bourgeoise."

"Said the pastor's daughter," Karl volleyed back.

They started flicking paint at each other and lost themselves in uproarious play. For a few moments they were the two carefree young adults they would have been if the world had not gone mad a few years before. Then Elisabeth slipped on the paint, and Karl stumbled on top of her.

"Oh, sorry," he said, turning beet red.

"Don't worry about it," she said, getting back to her feet.

They stared at each other for a suspended moment. Karl reached out his hand and brushed paint away from Elisabeth's face. Her cheek quivered at his light touch.

"Well, I'd best be going," he said, taking off his paint-covered jacket.

When she was alone again, Elisabeth slumped onto a bucket and let out a long sigh. She had given up so much for her mission. Sometimes the loneliness crushed her. She covered her face with her apron and wept like a child in need of a parent's embrace. She missed her family so much.

TWENTY-FOUR

Isabel

The week after América's death was one of my hardest weeks in the camp. To top it all off, María got sick. She had to stay in bed for several days, and I was afraid for her life as well. I tried to find out how América had ended up like she had, but nobody was willing to talk. They seemed to be afraid of what would happen if they did.

I searched for Javier, presumably América's pimp, but he, too, had mysteriously disappeared. Then one day I ran into the gendarme who had brought us to the camp several months before. Perhaps because of my physical deterioration or my pregnancy, he did not recognize me at first.

"Martín!" I called when I saw him walking by. He stopped and studied me from the other side of the fence.

"Oh, hello! I'm here to help with the evacuation of the camp. How are you and your friends getting along?"

He must have seen the pain in my eyes. He looked at me closely and tried to touch my shoulder through the fence.

"América died a few days ago. That is, she was murdered. And María is very ill."

"I'm so sorry to hear that. I never dreamed things would turn out the way they have. If I had known, I would have let you escape."

"I'm trying to find a man named Javier Royo. He's a small-time criminal, a thief. I've come to learn that he got América into prostitution while I was sick. He might be responsible for her death."

The gendarme asked some of the policemen standing around and then came back to me. "Javier Royo turned up dead ten days ago."

"That can't be," I said, perplexed. That meant that Javier had died before we found América.

"He was found badly beaten, and nothing could be done to save him."

"Who found him?"

After speaking with the other police officers again, Martín said, "A Spanish official named Ismael, but nothing more is known about the crime."

"Ismael Lapiedra? The distribution manager?" I knew him well. He was Manolo's boss.

Martín nodded, and I thanked him and said goodbye. I went to the supplies barrack. All the workers were packing things up in preparation for the move, and Ismael was taking inventory.

"Please, sir, may I speak with you a moment?"

He laid a folder down on top of a box and came up to me. "I'm very busy right now."

"Did you find Javier Royo's body?"

He stared at me for a moment, scratched at his ear, and then shook his head.

"But the police said you did."

"It wasn't me. It was Manolo."

My blood froze when I heard that. I turned and spotted the vile man. I went up to him from behind.

"It was you, wasn't it?" I hissed.

He turned. When he saw me, he lifted his lip and spat at the ground.

"Lady, I don't have time for you. I've got work to do."

"You raped América and killed Javier. You're responsible for the death of two people."

He put his hands on his hips and eyed me up and down. "I was just getting my dues. She wouldn't play along, and we can't allow that. Then her little pimp came along saying I had damaged his merchandise, but I hadn't been that rough."

I threw myself at him and tried to scratch out his eyes, but he was much stronger. He had me on the ground, pressing his knee into my belly, when Ismael smacked him hard on the head with a nightstick.

"What's that for?" Manolo bellowed.

"Let that woman go, you scoundrel. I've put up with you long enough."

Manolo stood and went to attack his boss, but Ismael laid him out flat with two hard blows from the club.

He turned to me and said, "Don't worry about him anymore. I'm turning him over to the French police today."

Ismael's words were not enough to calm my rage. That scum deserved to die a painful death. I held myself back but did spit in Manolo's face before stomping off.

People were gathering their things. Some were eager to get out of there while others were reticent to leave the only place they had known since coming to France.

I watched a man standing at the shore. He had come to be a fixture in the camp. He was dressed in the same sea captain's uniform he had worn since leaving Spain. Every day he would stand on the beach, waiting for a ship to come take him away. In the evening, he would return, disappointed, to his shack. Yet the next morning he would be back on the beach, dressed and waiting. That day it occurred to me that this was precisely what life consisted of: standing on the immense shore of nothingness and waiting for Charon to come take us to the other side of death.

Peter

ARGELÈS-SUR-MER CAMP
May 30, 1939

Fabián stood up in front of the whole group. The next day the camp would be evacuated, so this was their last philosophical chat. In recent weeks, many of their comrades had decided to return to Spain. Some called them deserters for going back, though returning to Spain was perhaps just as painful as staying in a country that wanted them to leave. Fabián spoke.

"Many of us started this journey thinking it would be short, that war would break out in Europe, that the French would want our help, and that then we'd take our beloved Spain back. Now, several months later, I want to express my gratitude that the journey has not been short. I have learned so much from all of you. The hardships and experiences we've faced in this camp have made me wiser, or at least I hope they have," he clarified as some in the group chuckled. "Some of our comrades are no longer with us, whether devoured by misery, hunger, or disgrace, but those of us who have survived have learned one of life's great lessons. We've learned that it's wiser to wait than to rush in with haste; we've learned that the journey is more important than the destination; we've learned that what makes us strong is knowing that Spain will always be waiting for us. We may feel like orphans, but we still have a mother on the other side of the Pyrenees. Now that spring is turning into summer, if hope withers with the heat, I want to leave you with our immortal Antonio Machado. Though he has left us in the flesh, his spirit will always remain."

Peter studied Fabián's face as he began reciting the poem and was impressed by his composure and courage. Everyone listened attentively.

The spellbound crowd broke out in applause as Fabián finished. Then came the sounds of whistles and the voices of gendarmes. The men filed out of the barrack and were asked to line up in rows. The head police officer stepped forward and began a rousing speech.

"You're all aware that tomorrow we'll be evacuating all of the camps here at Argelès. Before that, we want to encourage everyone who so desires to be repatriated. We will provide transportation to the border along with money. There is peace in Spain now, and it makes no sense for you to suffer here far away from your families and friends."

"We're only suffering because of how you treat us!" a voice called out. The officer tried to see who had spoken but waved it off and continued.

"Returning to your homeland is neither betrayal nor an abandonment of your principals. It is simply the way to get on with life. Those who are willing, please step forward." The officer stepped back and waited for the group to respond.

Eventually, a few Spanish soldiers took a tentative step forward.

There were calls of "Traitors! Cowards! Bastards!" Yet all of those standing out front had a reason to go back: families waiting for them or simply the accumulated exhaustion of camp life. The number of soldiers willing to return grew slowly. One who stepped forward was Fabián. Peter smiled at him and nodded in approval.

"You're a traitor like Judas!" one of their comrades yelled.

Peter turned and glared at him. "Fabián is no traitor. He's one of the bravest men I've ever met, and he has every right to try to get on with his life."

The man hung his head while the line of soldiers repatriating started marching away. One of the refugees started up a familiar war song, and the rest joined in. Peter longed to get out of there, but he and Isabel had not yet even been able to make their marriage official under the new laws. Peter had neither seen nor heard from the consul's secretary since their last meeting.

TWENTY-FIVE

Isabel

The walk to the new camp was long. Supposedly they were going to transport the children, older adults, and pregnant women in vans, but there were not enough vehicles, and María and I had to walk. The way was mostly flat, but it was two hours north for a strong walker, and María was very weak. Argelès-sur-Mer had been both refuge and jail. It had stamped out of us the hope of recovering our lives one day. We were now flea-infested riffraff with bones aching from damp nights spent on hard sand with thin blankets. The starry sky had been our prison roof.

We paused to rest beside a cemetery, hoping to find room on one of the transport trucks. Every now and then a refugee would attempt to escape en route, but most of us trudged mutely on and now observed the graveyard in silence. I thought of all who had died at Argelès-sur-Mer: our kind neighbor Clotilde and, above all, my beloved América. Her dreams of seeing Paris and becoming a journalist or a dressmaker were buried with her.

A truck stopped, and Peter helped María get up. When he tried to help me in, I said, "I'm not leaving your side." So he hopped on as well. Several older adults scoffed when they saw him, but no one said anything aloud.

The caravan wound through a narrow stretch surrounded by vineyards. The slow journey dragged on. Townspeople came out to see us as if we were a parade. When we filed out of Argelès, some of the residents cried quietly for us, but most cheered to see us go.

We had to walk the last few miles on foot but finally made it to the new camp. It was another beach. Small, floorless wooden barracks were laid out in a grid pattern, as if to mimic villages. They were better than our homemade shacks at Argelès, but it looked like another prison.

We went to one of the barracks, but a gendarme did not let Peter through.

"She's my wife," Peter explained. But the gendarme checked his list and pointed Peter to another barrack close by.

María slumped down on the bottom bunk. I would have to climb to the top every night. My belly made me less agile than usual, but I did not mind being farther away from the sand.

Still weak, María stayed in bed to rest while Peter and I took a walk around the camp, our new home. It was not very different from Argelès. There were little huts with toilets set back from the main area, and someone started calling them "Federico." Other than that, we had simply been moved from one beach to another, with no apparent improvement in living conditions. At least there was a tree that provided some shelter when it started raining. Eventually we headed back to the barrack. I found María still in bed, but now she was bleeding. We had to get her to the infirmary immediately.

Elisabeth

BROUILLA MATERNITY HOSPITAL
June 20, 1939

They had started moving some of the maternity hospital's supplies to Elne. Time was running out for the building in Brouilla. Even if Elne was not yet ready, they could no longer adequately tend to women in Brouilla. Besides, the French government had moved the refugees to a town closer to the new building, which would help things.

Elisabeth and Ruth were arranging things in what would become the delivery room in Elne when Lucy ran in.

"What is it?" Elisabeth asked. Lucy generally meant bad news.

"There's a pregnant woman at the new camp who has started bleeding. We cared for her for several weeks when they were at Argelès. Her name is María."

"Well, why didn't you bring her here or to Brouilla?"

"The new officer in charge wouldn't let me. He said the camp had the necessary health services to deal with women in labor."

"Oh, why do they always put idiots in charge? We have permission from the prefect and the mayor!" Elisabeth left everything, and she and Lucy jumped into Rocinante. The van spluttered. It was harder and harder to get Rocinante to start up. But fifteen minutes later, they were at the gate of the refugee camp at Saint-Cyprien. It was Elisabeth's first time to see the place. It was a step up from Argelès, but barely.

She requested to see the officer in charge, Captain Pierre Mercier. A soldier led them to a cabin. Unlike most of the others they passed on the way, it had a wood floor, a wood-burning stove, and windows.

"Good afternoon. How can I help you, madame?"

"We need to transfer a pregnant woman to our maternity hospital, but your men have not allowed it. The case is urgent, and the woman is at risk of losing the baby."

The officer fiddled with his mustache. The gel on his dark hair shone in the lamplight. "We have an infirmary here with Spanish doctors and nurses and a French director. The medical barrack is equipped and supplied with everything a pregnant woman could need."

Elisabeth was starting to lose patience. "We don't have much time. If the woman keeps bleeding, she'll probably lose the baby. The prefect has authorized our maternity hospital and given us full permission to take pregnant women there from the camp and care for them and their babies."

"I have my doubts about that permission," the officer said. "It is my job to look after not only the Spanish refugees but also the French residents. Surely you've heard how the Spaniards are robbing and threatening our citizens?"

"A sick, weak woman who is eight and a half months pregnant does not pose a serious threat to the state of France," Elisabeth said conclusively.

The officer thought for a moment and finally signed a transfer letter. "You can only take women who are at risk of dying or of losing their babies. Is that understood?"

"Yes, Captain."

Elisabeth took the paper and ran with Lucy to the infirmary. They found María weak and pale after losing so much blood.

"Please, take her with you," Isabel pleaded.

"Do you know her blood type?" Lucy asked, getting María onto a stretcher.

"The same as mine, A negative."

"Come with us."

While aids from the infirmary carried María to the van, Isabel said goodbye to her husband and ran after the two nurses. Elisabeth tore out of the camp and drove Rocinante as fast as the van would allow to the maternity hospital in Brouilla. The three of them got María up to the delivery room. A newer nurse, Laure, was waiting with everything ready.

"She's lost so much blood," Laure confirmed. "She's got to have a transfusion."

When they settled Isabel into the chair beside María, they realized she, too, was pregnant.

"Oh!" Elisabeth said, looking more carefully at Isabel. "You're the young woman we took care of last month. I hadn't recognized you."

Laure shook her head. "But we can't take blood out of a pregnant woman!"

"It's fine. I'll recover quickly," Isabel insisted.

Elisabeth nodded. "We have to. María is too weak already."

After the transfusion, they helped Isabel into a bed.

"You'll need to stay here a day or two for us to watch you. I wish we could keep both of you here until you deliver, but until we open the new building in Elne, we just don't have room for more women," Elisabeth said, covering Isabel with a blanket.

"Thank you for everything you're doing for us," Isabel murmured.

"You may not believe it, but I love your country. It pained me greatly to leave it. I've never known people like the Spanish—so generous and joyful despite hardship. When I arrived in Alicante, it made me remember Leo Tolstoy's story about the king and the shirt."

Isabel was starting to feel the effects of the blood loss. Elisabeth's melodious, angelic voice reached her as from a great distance. The sheets were clean, and there was a real roof over her head. The combination of sensations produced a peace Isabel was at a loss to describe.

"A king fell gravely ill, though what really happened was that nothing made him happy. He was dissatisfied with life. The doctors were worried and searched high and low for a cure, but nothing was working. A troubadour who had spent his life cheering up the sad king announced that if the king found the happiest subject in the entire kingdom and exchanged shirts with him, the king would immediately be cured. The king's messengers spread out across the kingdom, yet it seemed that there was not a totally happy man to be found. Some had great wealth but were embittered because of ill health. Others were strong and healthy but grieved all the suffering their poverty inflicted. One day, the king's son passed by the simplest, humblest hut in the land. It was just a shack. He heard a man inside expressing gratitude for how happy he was because that day he had eaten and was in good health. The prince went into the hovel and offered the man half the kingdom in exchange for his shirt. But the peasant answered that he had none. The happiness I witnessed in your country is like that of the man with no shirt. I was born in a rich country, but the people are plagued with melancholy. In your country, there's a light shining that's brighter than the sun in the sky—it's the love of life."

Elisabeth's last words were lost on Isabel, who had fallen into a deep and blissful sleep. It was the most restorative rest she had enjoyed since before the war in Spain.

TWENTY-SIX

Isabel

SAINT-CYPRIEN CAMP

July 14, 1939

During my short stay at the maternity hospital run by Elisabeth, I had felt for the first time in years like I was home. María and I had not stayed there long. María had less than a month left until her baby would be born, but I was four months out. Peter found a Spanish farmer who by some miracle had managed to keep his cow, and every day he brought us fresh milk. It was an unthinkable luxury in the camp.

A week before, a swarm of flies had settled on the camp and attacked us mercilessly. Sometimes it felt like we were going through the ten Egyptian plagues. We wondered if we would ever be set free and led home like the Israelites.

On July 14, the day France celebrated their independence, we were awoken by bugle. Bastille Day meant liberty for the French, while we had nothing to celebrate but continued slavery. It was terribly hot. Even so, the refugees put on the best clothes they had, whatever had not been thoroughly worn out by overuse and the harsh conditions of the camp. We filed out to the camp's plazas

and were made to line up before the French flag. A band was playing "La Marseillaise," and despite ourselves, we choked up hearing
their national anthem. It could have been our own. The Spanish
refugees also longed for brotherhood among all people, equality,
and the liberty we had lost long ago. The soldiers and gendarmes
were decked out in dress uniform—yet their ceremonial uniforms
symbolized our oppression. We were the shirtless revolutionaries
but had failed to change the course of human history that July 14.

We walked all together to where the parade was going to pass.
From the other side of the fence, the townspeople stared at us
with both curiosity and distrust.

"Long live liberty! Long live France!" rang out from all sides.
The tricolored flags flapped back and forth against the hot summer sky. Then a Frenchman beyond the fence pulled out our flag,
the Spanish Republic's flag. He and the people around him cried
out, "Long live the Republic!" We followed suit, and the air rang
with our proud voices. For a moment we forgot our troubles, and
the dream of returning to our own Spain felt real.

Peter was beside me. The day seemed blessed with good news.
The secretary to the consul would be coming to formalize our
marriage. That was the first step toward getting out of there and
going to the United States. Then the gendarmes announced we
would have a special meal that day.

The meal was a disappointment: meatballs made with oxen
meat in a yellowish sauce, a few slices of peach, and cigarettes. We
left the supposed feast and went to the barrack where the consul's
secretary was expecting us. I had never met him, but Peter had
described him perfectly as a heartless bureaucrat. The man was
sitting at a desk and did not even look up as we entered. He took
a dark brown piece of paper out of his briefcase. We signed our

marriage certificate, he handed us a copy, put another in his case, and that was that.

"When can we get out of here?" Peter asked impatiently. The secretary looked up, raised his eyebrows, and gestured sharply at me with his nose.

"Well, I didn't know your wife was pregnant. If the baby comes before you get your visa, you'll have to request another one for the child, which will delay your departure."

Peter jumped up ready to attack the man, but I held him back.

"Thank you very much," I said with my recently learned English.

He answered me in English as well. "I hope delivery goes well. Good day."

We were left sitting there holding the precious piece of paper bearing the seal of the United States of America. But that piece of paper meant nothing to us. Our real wedding had occurred years ago. We had not had much money, the war had started, and Peter had to rent a suit. I was wearing a white dress I had borrowed from a cousin and altered myself. We had gotten married at a small church on the outskirts of town. Peter had left the money for the reception with an old friend, but he turned out not to be so friendly after all. He disappeared with the money, and we had no reception. We went with a few friends to a bar for a drink and then spent the night in a hotel. At least that part had already been paid for. I still remember the joy of being together for the first time. I had never been with a man and had no idea what sex would be like. Peter was so tender toward me, and I felt like the queen of the world.

We left the barrack with our marriage certificate just as the fireworks were starting. They lit up the darkening sky. Peter kissed me, and I had my hand over my belly. We were a family now and had to stay together no matter what happened. He and I no longer belonged just to each other. The life that was forming inside me, the union of all that was good about us, would determine the course of our lives forever.

=====

Elisabeth

ELNE MATERNITY HOSPITAL
September 1, 1939

It was a special day. The work on the new Elne building had finally been completed, and they had moved all the remaining supplies and equipment from Brouilla. The prefect and the mayor were at the inauguration. Elisabeth was exultant. Beside her, Lucy and the rest of the volunteers wore bright new nurse uniforms. The prefect gave a short speech as the guests stood and munched on canapés. Elisabeth felt out of her element among such high-profile people. She preferred the company of simpler folk. Karl observed her slip away to lean against the banister of the stone steps.

"You've done it," he said, coming up beside her.

She smiled. "Done what?"

"Opened the maternity hospital, got all of this going." He waved a hand to take in the grounds, the well-tended garden, and the building that still smelled of paint and varnish.

"I haven't done anything. You know we're mere mortals. What I want now is to see this place full of pregnant women."

Just then a man entered the grounds and ran up to the stairs. "Where is the prefect?" he cried.

"At the reception, in the garden behind the house," Karl answered. "What's going on?"

The man ran up the stairs and stopped in front of them. "Germany invaded Poland."

The announcement left them speechless. There had been rumors for months about Hitler wanting to recover East Prussia, but no one expected a full-scale invasion.

"Are you sure?" Karl stammered.

"They just announced it on the radio, and we've received a telegram at the prefect's office. France and the United Kingdom will surely declare war against Germany, and we all know what that means."

Elisabeth looked at Karl with true fear in her eyes. What they had all been dreading was finally happening. "Has the world truly gone mad?" she asked. "Did we learn nothing from the Great War? Has SCI been teaching peace for years just for this?"

Karl's only answer was to hug his friend. He was tempted to tell her what he felt for her, but it was not the right moment. He merely offered comfort. A few months before they had escaped one war unscathed. They knew what bombing raids against civilians meant. They had seen dozens of children dead after a bomb hit their school; had seen mothers wailing over the bodies of their sons and daughters; had witnessed the hunger, the misery, and the fear. All of this would now be unleashed upon Europe with unprecedented fury. Elisabeth and Karl knew what the future would hold, and they were terrified. But they also knew that small lamps shine bright in deep darkness. Their mission was to stay calm and keep doing their work.

TWENTY-SEVEN

Isabel

The hunt for volunteers to serve at the front got serious a few days after the war officially started. The French government promised freedom, good wages, and residency papers to any man who enlisted. Many Spanish refugees volunteered, but there were still not enough men to prepare the long, well-known Maginot Line. The tone changed to forcing men to enlist or else face expulsion. At first, men with families and those advanced in age were exempted, but the authorities were desperate. I was more and more worried about Peter and terrified that we would be separated again. María had gone to the Elne hospital to have her baby and had remained there ever since, and Peter and I were finally allowed to stay in the same barrack together since our marriage had been formally recognized.

I was with Peter at a meeting organized by several Spanish groups to deal with an argument that had broken out the day before. When people learned that the Soviets had started the invasion of Poland and had signed a treaty with the Nazis, the political arguments in the camp had turned violent, from words to hands. The French officials had instituted a curfew and had forbidden political gatherings.

"We can't let them push us around anymore. Life here is hard enough as it is without them taking away our right to political debate," César, one of the Communist leaders in the camp, said.

"Political discourse is one thing, but aggression is something else," the anarchist representative said.

"Comrade, yesterday you all were insulting us by comparing us with the Nazis," César said.

"What we were saying was that it is a shame and disgrace for all the members of the Socialist International that Stalin has signed an agreement with Adolf Hitler. The Nazi dictator has persecuted our German, Czech, and Austrian comrades. He's outlawed our parties and syndicates just like Mussolini did. How can Stalin make a pact with the devil?"

A murmur ran throughout the barrack, and some of those in attendance started mouthing off at one another.

"Let's stay calm, comrades. Let's use our voices and not violence," one of the older members pleaded.

"You Communists are a bunch of traitors! After what you did to us in Barcelona and in Madrid at the end of the war . . . ," one of the younger anarchists spouted off.

Peter stood, and I was proud that he wanted to speak in the midst of the disgruntlement.

"Comrades, please, a word . . ."

"What does the Yankee have to say? He just wants to get out

of here and get back to his capitalist country," the young anarchist snapped.

"Let him speak!" the others said.

"Don't you think we're all responsible for what's going on in the world right now? Some ninety-one years ago, in 1848, Friedrich Engels published Karl Marx's *Communist Manifesto*. The working class thought it was the new gospel that would bring peace and prosperity to all humanity, that the chains of oppression would fall off, and that the class struggle would lead to the rule of the proletariat, which would prepare humanity for the next stage: harmony and the creation of the new man. In 1917, the Bolsheviks came to power in Russia. Lenin tried to apply Marx's ideas but failed . . ."

Several in the crowd roared at that, but others quieted them down so Peter could finish.

"Lenin had to step back. He allowed private property and for small producers to follow the rules of the market. The economy improved, and the country started to prosper. But after his death, Joseph Stalin imposed a reign of terror. His calculated, heartless economy led to terrible famine in Ukraine and other regions. The Soviets covered this over, and the world turned a blind eye."

Again there were interruptions, but Peter continued.

"We're all responsible for the lack of values that currently prevails in this world created by Marxism, Fascism, and Nazism. We've all embraced Nietzsche's ideas as if they were gospel truth. By getting rid of God, we thought we were freeing ourselves from divine tyranny. But all we did was turn men into gods and our ideologies into the new religion. Nihilism and historical realism erased everything that was once sacred and of value in our world. We destroyed moral values and erected the most atrocious relativism in their place. The only new beginning we can reach for is to destroy all the tyrants and lay a foundation of hope for a world that is truly fraternal and is ruled by love for others and respect for human life and dignity."

The men could not hold back any longer. The Communists jumped to their feet and started throwing punches at the anarchists and socialists. Then someone shouted, "The gendarmes and the military! It's a raid!"

Everyone started running. Peter and I went out the back door, but two gendarmes caught and started hitting us.

"My wife is pregnant!" Peter said, throwing himself between me and their nightsticks.

Just then my water broke. Peter begged them to call for a doctor.

"She's telling the truth—look at her!" one of the gendarmes said to the other.

"Take the whore to the infirmary. I'll take this one to the camp for undesirables."

They separated us. I kicked and screamed, but the gendarme carried me to the infirmary. One of the nurses from Elne was there. When she saw me bleeding, she asked the gendarme to call for an ambulance.

"For this Communist rat?"

"Babies are not responsible for whatever their parents may believe," the nurse said.

Ten minutes later, I was in an ambulance being taken to the Elne maternity hospital. But I could not stop thinking about Peter. Now that we finally had the chance to get a visa, we were separated again.

Elisabeth

An ambulance parked in front of the door and two men brought Isabel in on a stretcher. Soon she was on a bed in the delivery room. The midwife, Louise, was ready. Despite her rough appearance, Louise was gentle with Isabel.

Elisabeth came in a short time later. She remembered Isabel from the last time they had seen each other and greeted her warmly. She got ready to help the midwife.

As she moved about the room, Louise kept asking Isabel questions. "Is this your first time?"

"Yes, but it shouldn't be happening now; it's too soon."

"Don't worry. It'll be all right. This happens sometimes."

Isabel was crying. She was terrified about losing the baby. She had never dreamed she could have such fierce love for someone she had never met, but she could feel the child inside her. The baby was part of her very being. And now that this mysterious being was about to show its face, it might become one more victim of the horror of their times.

Isabel nodded at Louise's comforting words and then screamed in pain. She was sweating all over and felt like something was wringing her out from the inside.

"Shh, shh, steady now. You can be calm. I think this will be quick. I've examined you, and you're already dilated quite a bit.

Just follow my instructions, and before you know it, you'll meet your baby."

Isabel started breathing in and blowing out the way Louise explained. That did help the pain, but as soon as she got distracted and stopped, the contractions grew so strong she could not breathe.

Elisabeth stood at the head of the bed and took Isabel's hand. "Calm and steady. Women from the dawn of time have gone through this. It's what our bodies are made to do. You can get this baby out just fine."

Elisabeth's voice calmed Isabel greatly just like it had the day she gave her blood to María.

"Your friend María is doing great. Soon you'll get to see her and meet her baby."

Isabel groaned and writhed with the force of a new contraction.

"You're doing great," Louise said.

Isabel took a deep breath, and then Louise told her to push. Isabel did it with all her strength and noticed how the lump in her abdomen lowered a bit.

Louise beamed. "That's it! Now do it again!"

With each push, Isabel thought her body would split open and that she could not take it anymore. Yet she kept at it. Finally, the midwife uttered wonderful words. "Here comes the head! Push just a bit more!"

Isabel made a last herculean effort and felt an enormous release of pressure. Louise caught a tiny, bloody body and put it facedown.

"Come on, sweetie. Cry for me," she cooed, giving the body a gentle little slap.

The child let out a gusty wail, and suddenly Isabel's pain disappeared. She looked at her baby and wept.

"She's a beautiful little girl," Louise said, giving the child to her mother.

Elisabeth smiled at the baby lying on her mother's chest. Isabel studied the eyes that were shut tight, the soft fuzz, the tiny arms and legs, the red little body. She was a mother. She said it over and over through her tears. She was crying with joy and with sadness. She was holding the daughter who had come early but was miraculously healthy. But where was Peter?

Elisabeth and Louise took Isabel and the baby to a quiet room and left them to rest. Completely exhausted, Isabel fell into a deep sleep.

———

Isabel

ELNE MATERNITY HOSPITAL
September 17, 1939

I was awakened by the sound of my baby crying. Somehow I knew immediately that it was her. Then I saw María lean over the crib and lift my baby out. I had heard that her delivery had gone well, but we had not seen each other in a long time. She held up the child and looked at me in surprise.

"Well, this wasn't supposed to happen for a few more weeks!"

"Oh, María! It's so good to see you. How are you?" She looked good, even happy.

"I'm very, very well. I've practically forgotten camp life.

Congratulations, your daughter is beautiful. Elisabeth told me about the birth. I'm so happy for you!"

We embraced. Now something more than misfortune united us: hope for our children to survive and grow strong.

"Thank you!"

"Later you'll meet my daughter. With our love and care, the lives of these little girls can make up for so much of the death and pain we've witnessed," María said, handing me my daughter. "Do you want me to nurse her, or do you feel strong enough for it?"

"I want to try."

My baby rooted around, found my nipple, and latched on.

María raised her eyebrows in surprise. "This is amazing for a first-time mother!"

I shrugged. "I've never even held a baby. I was the only child of a single mother." My eyes filled with tears at the thought of my mother. How much she would have loved to see her grand-daughter. Then I realized something. "Wait—what day is it?"

"It's September 17. Why?"

I caught my breath. It was too much. "This is my mother's birthday."

María smiled at me and pulled up a chair. "Let me tell you about life here in Elne. It's wonderful. They've helped me get in touch with my husband. You remember that he's a doctor? He's going to start working here so the French will give us work and residency permits. Now that the war has started, they're not so eager to kick us out of the country. They need us to help in the war effort."

"They only want us for what we can give them," I said, not taking my eyes off my daughter. She exuded an inexplicable peace.

"My delivery went well, and they treat us like queens here. I

can't believe that just a few miles away everyone is still living in
that hellhole of a camp."

"Let's not talk about the camp," I said.

"How is Peter?"

My face clouded over. Haltingly, I explained what had happened. And now, besides having to request a visa for the baby, we
would have to wait until they released him from the disciplinary
camp.

She shook her head in compassion but said, "You've already
come through so much. You'll get through this. I know you will."

I looked out the window to the garden full of flowers. That
was another thing I had not seen in a long time. Flowers could
not grow where sand devoured everything.

María looked out and saw the mountains in the distance.
Surely she was thinking about what lay on the other side: Spain,
her son, and her mother. I knew she was wondering if she could
ever go back and if her family would ever be together again.

"Do you remember the day we met?" I asked.

"Yes. So much has happened it feels like eons ago, but really
it's just been a few months. Sometimes life balls up and squeezes
out the last drop of blood," she said, turning back to me.

"Do you think we'll ever go back home?"

My question floated in the air between us. We resisted giving an answer, brushing away the weight of words for the airy
perfume wafting up from the babe in my arms. The smell of tal-
cum powder and flowers held within it the levity of existence.
Hell would break out over Europe, but the Elne maternity hospital
was a garden of Eden for us.

TWENTY-EIGHT

Isabel

ELNE MATERNITY HOSPITAL
October 15, 1939

Everything would have been perfect if Peter had been with us. Our daughter, Lisa, grew bigger and more beautiful every day. He was itching to see her, and telling him about her through letters was not enough. Her eyes were big and blue like her father's. She had my lips and the shape of my face, but the rest of her was pure Peter. María and I spent most of our time together. Our daughters were just over a month apart, and we would walk together on the hospital grounds or even through town if a volunteer went with us. People still looked askance at us, and sometimes we overheard mothers warning their children to stay away from the "Red devils." But we paid them no heed. We were too happy to mind insults. María's husband lived in the town, and they hoped to be fully reunited soon. I could not deny my jealousy. I longed to be with Peter again, even if it meant returning to the camp. I would rather be with him in hell than comfortable but apart.

"You've heard the rumors about how Mexico is setting up a town for the Spanish Republicans?"

"What?" I asked in surprise.

"President Cárdenas thinks that Spaniards have a lot to offer his country. Go figure: Franco wants to kill us in cold blood, and other countries are inviting us to settle there. We're considering it. I've heard people talk about all the opportunities there."

"When Peter gets out, I hope we can go to his country. There's nothing keeping me in Spain anymore," I said. Yet I also wondered how I would handle being in a country so different from everything I had ever known.

"Surely it can't be that much longer," María said.

"But I will miss the maternity hospital. They've treated us so well."

Next week I'll be allowed to move in with my husband. But I miss our son so much. If we weren't in the middle of another war, I would try to bring him here."

We arrived back at the house and went into the living room. A fire was burning in the chimney, and several women were keeping warm by the soft flames. After we'd endured so much cold and exposure to the elements, nothing was more pleasant than sitting and listening to the crackling of a warm fire.

Every morning, all the women in the house tended to our duties. I helped wash clothes, though Elisabeth also often asked me to help out in the nursery, especially with the newborns. It was delightful to feed and play with them.

There were three main nurses on the team. All of them were Swiss and had been sent by a Swiss nursing school. Ruth was the nicest. Then there was a doctor and a Swiss midwife, Madame Ida.

Most of the women did not seem to like Madame Ida, but she had always been kind to me. The gardener, the cook, the carpenter, and the driver were all Spaniards.

All the rooms were named after places in Spain. At first I slept with María and a few others in the room called Spain.

"Oh, how nice it is to sit by the fire!" I sighed contentedly to María. She smiled, nodded, and started nursing her baby.

Then we heard voices and steps coming from the kitchen. Elisabeth, Ruth, and Lucy appeared in the doorway with a cake. The flickering candles lit up the smiles on their faces. They were looking at me.

I looked around in surprise. I had not told anyone that it was my birthday. It was sad for me to celebrate it without Peter.

"Isabel, happy birthday!" they said, placing the chocolate cake on the table. No one had made me a cake since my mother's death. I started crying and kissed them all. I could not believe anyone would care about me like that—I was nobody special.

"Thank you, thank you," I said, handing Lisa to María.

"Before you blow out the candles, you have to make a wish!" Ruth said, clapping happily.

I closed my eyes. I knew exactly what I wanted: to see Peter as soon as possible. Having him far away again was eating at me.

I blew out the candles, and everyone started singing "Happy Birthday" in Spanish. They hugged and kissed me, and I was overwhelmed as I watched them set the table with all sorts of special foods. It was like a dream. I had put on weight since being in Elne and no longer had a gaunt, pale, haggard face. My cheeks had started to be rosy again.

Peter

Peter had been locked up for weeks in that disgusting place. It was much worse than the correction camp he had been sent to months before. The only good thing was that, since there were not many prisoners, they were allowed to eat more food.

That morning a recruitment officer had showed up. When they saw him, the prisoners presumed that all the volunteers had already been used and that they were now going to be forced to go to the front. Spaniards were not usually sent to fight but to do manual labor on the trenches and run supplies.

"At one time, most of you were soldiers fighting for a cause you believed to be just. Now, the country that welcomed you needs you. The Nazis are preparing to attack, and we are expanding our defenses along the Maginot Line. We need all available hands to help protect France. If you enlist, in exchange for three months' service you will be granted your freedom, a visa, and payment. If you prefer to stay here, supported by the state, your sentences will be prolonged by a year."

The men protested loudly, but the French officers knew that the only way to recruit people was to give them no choice. "Those who are ready to enlist, please step forward!"

Half of the men stepped over the line the officer had traced with his toe. Peter hesitated. He could not stand being shut up any longer. He had no idea when his request for a visa for his family would be approved. Finally, he stepped forward into the line of volunteers.

"Sergeant, may I make a request?"

"You already have, Yankee."

"My daughter was born a few weeks ago, and I still haven't been able to see her. Could I visit her before going to the front?"

The sergeant pursed his lips in thought.

"The army isn't a beneficence club. I'll allow it this one time, but you'll be escorted by two soldiers at all times."

Several hours went by after the volunteers were transferred to the recruitment center. Peter was starting to lose hope of seeing Isabel and Lisa before he was sent north.

Just then he heard the officer. "Yankee! The truck is ready for you. You've got one hour, and my men will bring you back."

Peter could not hide his joy. The two soldiers led him to the vehicle, and fifteen minutes later he was standing at the door of the Elne maternity hospital.

"We'll wait for you here. Don't even think about pulling any stunts," one of the soldiers said, opening the gate for him.

"I'm a man of my word," Peter said and went into the front lawn. The sound of leaves crunching underfoot pleased him. He was glad his daughter had been born in a place with trees and plants. He went up the stairway and spoke to a woman in an office near the front.

"Hello. I'm Peter Davis, Isabel's husband. I've been granted permission to visit her."

"Oh, come in, come in! I'm Elisabeth. Right now Isabel is hanging out the laundry in the back. Do you want to surprise her?"

Peter smiled and followed Elisabeth to the back of the house. Isabel was tossing a white sheet over the line. Peter came up from behind and put his hands over her eyes. When she felt his hands in hers, she knew immediately.

"Peter! Oh God! You're free!"

She turned, and they kissed among the billowing sheets.

"Come meet your daughter."

They ran up the stairs and through the house to the nursery on the first floor. They entered quietly, and Peter peered into the crib that Isabel pointed to. He was smitten at the first glimpse of his daughter. Her face reminded him of his mother.

"Can I pick her up?"

"Of course. She's yours!"

Peter picked up Lisa so gently that Isabel could not keep from giggling. Then he nestled her onto his lap and studied her closely.

"She's beautiful," he said.

Isabel stroked Lisa's cheeks and watched her husband's exultant face. He looked so happy.

"Peter, are you crying?"

Tears were streaming down his face and soaking the neck of his shirt. The small family embraced for the first time. Isabel led Peter, still holding Lisa, out of the nursery to her room, where they could talk more comfortably.

Peter did not want to give Isabel false hope. He finally got out the words that he had been dreading to say. "I've been recruited to go to the front."

"Recruited? To the front? Why? This war has nothing to do with us."

"It's in exchange for shortening my stay at the camp for undesirables. They'll pay us and transmit our visa. Now you won't have to go back to the camp on the beach while we're waiting on permission to enter the USA."

Isabel started crying. "No, no, not another war. I can't take it."

"I'll only be working on the trenches. I won't have to fight. I won't even see a German. I promise."

They hugged again, and Isabel clung to him like she was drowning.

"I can't bear it any longer—the uncertainty, the constant fear of getting news of your death. You have a daughter now, Peter."

"This isn't going to be like it was in Spain. It's different."

The three of them went downstairs to where the soldiers were waiting impatiently at the gate. When they saw Peter at the door, they stamped out their cigarettes and got into the car.

"I have to go, sweetie." They kissed again. Then Peter pressed his face into Lisa's and stroked her soft forehead. "Behave yourself, young lady. I'll see you soon."

Peter dragged himself down the stairs and through the yard. Passing through the gate, he turned again and waved to Isabel.

It started sprinkling as he got into the car. Isabel watched him until the car disappeared down the road and then went back inside. María saw her crying and asked what was going on. Isabel poured out her heart to her friend. María was already packed to move with her husband into a house near the maternity hospital.

"You and Lisa can come live with us," she offered.

"I don't think the authorities would allow it," Isabel answered. Her mind was swirling.

"I'll hire you as a maid. Then they'd grant you permission."

"Thank you, but don't worry about me. I'll be all right. Just enjoy your husband and your new home."

Isabel went back out to the garden to pull in the sheets before they were totally soaked. As she gathered them up, her tears mingled with the raindrops wetting her face. She thought she had exhausted the fountain of grief and that things would only get better after Lisa's birth. But grief was one fountain that never went dry.

TWENTY-NINE

Isabel

ELNE MATERNITY HOSPITAL
December 24, 1939

Every day I got the chance to try out life for the first time. The chance to wake up, open my eyes, and see what life had in store. Having a healthy, happy daughter was the best news in my world. Meanwhile, the rumors about an impending Nazi invasion of France had me terribly nervous. I had received a few letters from Peter. He said he was fine, that he was working ten hours a day and fell asleep as soon as he lay down on his cot. His only day off was Sunday, and he went with a few comrades to a church where a military chaplain held services. Supposedly he would be home in two months, but I did not put much stock in the promises of military authorities.

Elisabeth had called me to her office at the beginning of December. I had already stayed in Elne much longer than the eight weeks customarily allowed, and I presumed she would tell me I would have to return to the camp. The situation at Saint-Cyprien was bleak. After massive flooding, they faced an infestation of rats. Yet to my surprise, Elisabeth asked me to stay on as a volunteer. There was more and more work to be done and not enough nurses to do it. I moved with Lisa up to the second floor, where the staff rooms were located, and shared a room with the cook.

Lucy, Ruth, and Elisabeth had been decorating the house for Christmas over the past several days. We had not celebrated Christmas since the start of the war. The Republican authorities had said it was a Catholic holiday, and the Catholic Church had betrayed the Republic. I was not very religious, but Christmas had always been special to me. I remembered the presents my mother gave me on Epiphany, Three Kings Day. The memories of the city lit up by special lights, of fudge, of marzipan, and of shortbread cookies were all sweet to me.

"Isabel, would you help us set the table?" Ruth asked. She and I had become close since María moved out.

Together we unfolded and spread out the fancy tablecloth. We did not have many luxuries at Elne, but Elisabeth and her colleagues celebrated every birthday and made each one of us feel like we were in a real home.

We placed the silverware, the plates, and the glasses and then set out candles and small decorations.

"Oh, it looks so nice now," Ruth said, stepping back. "Everything will be ready within the hour!"

"Do you need help in the kitchen?"

"Why don't you see if Carmen needs help? She's up to her neck down there."

We went down to the basement to where the pantries and kitchen were. A little while later everyone was upstairs, and Elisabeth stood blocking the door to the dining room. She had not let anyone enter until we could all go in at once and experience the sight. She opened the door, and joy spread across the faces of the women, many of whom had not had a celebration of any sort for years.

"Come on in!" Elisabeth exclaimed.

Giddy with excitement, we were all hugging one another. Juani, one of the mothers who had been there the longest, started singing a Christmas carol.

> *Silent night, holy night!*
> *All is calm, all is bright*
> *round yon virgin mother and child.*
> *Holy Infant, so tender and mild,*
> *sleep in heavenly peace,*
> *sleep in heavenly peace.*

> *Silent night, holy night!*
> *Shepherds quake at the sight.*
> *Glories stream from heaven afar,*
> *heav'nly hosts sing, Alleluia!*
> *Christ the Savior is born!*
> *Christ the Savior is born!*

> *Silent night, holy night!*
> *Son of God, love's pure light*
> *radiant beams from thy holy face*
> *with the dawn of redeeming grace,*
> *Jesus, Lord, at thy birth,*
> *Jesus, Lord, at thy birth.*

In hushed joy, we all observed the Christmas tree and the nativity scene by candlelight until Ruth announced, "Please, take your seats! Tonight, we're serving you."

We sat around the table as the volunteers brought out trays

of food. The roasted chicken smelled heavenly. Each plate had a name card on it as well as a small gift.

"It's a special night, and we're going to have a special blessing," Elisabeth said. All the women closed their eyes, but I kept mine open. I had not prayed since I was very young. Elisabeth started, "Our good God, thank you for keeping each of us safe. Thank you for all of these healthy, strong babies. Today we are celebrating how you also came as a babe wrapped in swaddling clothes, how you came to this world and became a man to fulfill a mission. Bless the food we are about to eat. Thank you for your provision."

We all began to eat with relish, but I kept thinking about the thousands of refugees who were still in the camps, out in the cold and with little food. Christmas would mean nothing to them.

"Are you all right, Isabel?" Ruth asked.

"Yes, I'm just thinking about Peter and everyone at the refugee camps."

"You're right—not everyone is as fortunate as we are. Just think about the people in Poland and the invaded countries. We can only hope that doesn't happen to us and that the war ends soon."

The food was so good we licked our fingers clean, not to mention the fabulous cake for dessert.

"Now let's open the packages!" Elisabeth said with glee.

We tore into the colored paper like young children. Each of us received a gown for our babies and a change of clothes for ourselves, as well as chocolates, biscuits, and sweets. Most of us had not seen luxuries like this since before the war.

After dinner, we sang Christmas carols until midnight. That night we went to bed full and happy. Yet deep melancholy seeped through me when I lay down. I thought about Peter and wondered how he was spending Christmas. I wished with all my heart for this to be our last Christmas apart.

As sleep stole over me, I thought about my mother. She had given everything for me. She had given up her dreams so I could reach my own. I looked at the crib beside me, where Lisa was sleeping peacefully.

"I will always love you, my baby. No matter what you do or who you become, my love for you is unconditional," I whispered, kissing her forehead. Then I fell back into bed and kept thinking about Peter, about the day we met, and about all the happy moments we had shared.

THIRTY

Elisabeth

ELNE MATERNITY HOSPITAL
February 18, 1940

Elisabeth went up to Rubén, one of the youngest babies, and put her hand on his forehead. He was hot with fever on top of being congested.

"We need to isolate him," she told his mother, Remedios.

Remedios frowned and said defensively, "Other babies are sick too."

"Yes, we're going to isolate them, too, and call the doctor."

Isabel helped the mothers, and a few minutes later all the feverish babies were in the Madrid room.

"Isabel, please go get the doctor."

Isabel put on her coat. After the holidays, winter was dragging on and on. She had no news of her husband and now was starting to worry about their daughter.

Fifteen minutes later, she was at María's door. Despite María's invitations, Isabel had never gone to visit her. She always had too much work in the maternity hospital, and when she was not working, she was too tired to leave.

"Isabel! How wonderful to see you!" María cried. She ushered in her old friend, and they embraced.

"I've come for something urgent. Your husband is needed at the hospital. Several of the babies have a high fever."

"Is Lisa sick too?"

"Yes, her fever started last night."

"Wait here just a minute. I'll go get Carlos."

María called out, and a moment later Carlos ran down the stairs with his shirt untucked. He kissed his wife and went out with Isabel.

They walked as quickly as possible to the maternity hospital, and Elisabeth explained the situation. Carlos went up to the first floor and examined the sick babies one by one.

All the mothers were waiting at the door, cringing with worry. Carlos came out and looked at them gravely.

"I wish I could give you good news, but the truth is that three babies are in a very precarious condition. Nicolás, Marcelo, and Lisa."

Isabel felt the floor give way beneath her. "Lisa is in a bad way?" she asked as if not understanding the doctor's words.

"At this point the only thing to do is pray."

The three mothers spent that night seated at the door, jumping to ask the doctor how their babies were every time he went in or out.

At dawn, Carlos came out to the hallway again, exhausted and with circles around his gray eyes.

He got straight to the point. "I have bad news."

"What is it?" they all jumped in.

"Most of the children are recovering well, but the three who are the sickest grew worse during the night."

The mothers started crying.

The doctor took a deep breath and continued. "Two of them have passed away. I'm so sorry. There's still a chance that the third might pull through."

The mothers stared at one another in shock, not knowing whose baby had lived.

"Who . . ." was all that Isabel could get out.

"Lisa is the one who survived. She's stable at the moment, but it's too early to tell if she'll recover."

The other two mothers, Anita and Susi, broke down weeping. They begged the doctor to let them see their children.

"The nurse is preparing them and will bring them out in a moment."

Isabel tried to comfort the other mothers, but Anita and Susi wailed inconsolably. After enduring so much hardship, when they finally thought things were going well, they had lost their babies.

That afternoon, the gardener dug two small graves at the back of the garden next to the grave of the stillborn child.

The mothers carried the bodies of their babies in small boxes. All the hospital's residents walked behind the weeping mothers. When it was time to place the tiny coffins in the graves, Anita screamed out, "Oh God! Why, why, why? Why did you take him?"

Susi kneeled down, placed the coffin in the grave, and started throwing dirt on her own head. Elisabeth consoled her while Lucy tried to help Anita let go of the box. Before the gardener started burying them, Elisabeth stood to speak and pray.

"I have no words to express my grief. I am so, so sorry for Anita and Susi's losses. Nothing is more painful than losing a child. I would like to say a prayer for them."

All heads were bowed, and Carlos took off his hat.

"Eternal God, receive the lives of these two innocent children into your bosom. They are angels you sent to us for a short time, and now they are in your presence. Console our sisters, and fill their hearts with peace. Amen."

When the first shovelfuls of dirt hit the coffins, the two mothers started screaming with grief. Ruth and Lucy led them inside, and the procession quickly disbanded. Only Elisabeth and Isabel remained at the graves.

"Do you really think those babies are in heaven?" Isabel asked.

Elisabeth nodded firmly. "We're used to thinking that this life is all there is. When I was in Spain and I saw all those people suffering—mothers who lost their sons, children who were left orphans—I had a crisis of faith. Why would God allow so much suffering? I wrote to my father and asked him about the pain and death of so many innocent people. He answered me a few days later. He said that he didn't have all the answers, but that one day we will see all of our loved ones, and there will be no more pain."

Isabel started crying. The only thing she saw were two small graves: two dead babies. She had witnessed so much suffering in the past few years that it was impossible to believe a god would stand by, undaunted by the pain.

"I hope you're right. I'm tired of all the injustices. Life doesn't make sense."

Elisabeth embraced Isabel and then looked straight into her eyes.

"Sometimes we have to feel our way in the dark in order to find the path, but beyond the fog the sky is still blue, and the sun is still shining."

THIRTY-ONE

Isabel

ELNE MATERNITY HOSPITAL
March 2, 1940

My work as a volunteer in the maternity hospital increased as the months went by. There were more and more mothers and babies, and more and more hands were needed to keep things running. The refugees had returned to the camp at Argelès-sur-Mer, which had been improved significantly.

Elisabeth entrusted to me the work of supporting the nurse in the camp infirmary barrack. There we tended to mothers who were at risk of miscarriage and those who were just a few weeks away from giving birth. Some of the women would fake being worse off than they were to get permission to stay in our barrack. Spanish guile was not restricted to the other side of the border.

The first time I went back to the camp, I was furious seeing the starving, dirty children clinging to their mothers' skirts. They had not chosen the war, but they were its victims.

The barrack that Elisabeth and her volunteers had built was in two sections, one for mothers and the other for babies. At least it had a floor, which could not be said of most of the other barracks for the refugees.

The new camp was more like Saint-Cyprien than like the original camp at Argelès-sur-Mer. The barracks were arranged as in small towns, and there were specific barracks for the mail, a school, and other services.

Most of the remaining refugees were women, children, and older adults. All the young men had been recruited by the army to dig trenches, though the "Phony War," as everyone called it, seemed like it would never end.

There was also a barrack for children over six years old. It was hard to see them separated from their mothers, but at least they got more food in that barrack. They were also receiving basic lessons. Most of the children had stopped attending school after leaving Spain, and the youngest ones had never even seen a school building.

One of the youngest pregnant women, Remei, seemed to have no maternal instinct. She had tried to kill herself several times.

"Why are you so angry all the time?" I asked her. "You're going to be a mother."

The young woman frowned beneath her brown hair. She was so thin her cheeks were sunken. "That's exactly why I'm mad. I don't want this baby. It's the baby's fault that my boyfriend left me, and now I'm locked up in here. I want to get this pregnancy over with so I can get out of here."

"What about the child?"

"That's not my problem," she snapped.

"But I think it is. You're the one who's going to birth him."

"It was an accident."

"Children aren't accidents. They are gifts," I heard myself say. I was starting to lose my patience.

"You think so? Who would want to have a baby in a place like this? Don't get mad, Doña Isabel, but the only thing I want is to get out of here."

Part of me understood her completely. She was too young for such a big responsibility, but she had to accept the consequences of her actions.

Just then one of the women started having painful contractions. It was Lucia, a blond-haired woman in her forties. I called the ambulance, and we transported her right away to the maternity hospital.

We arrived at Elne as quickly as possible, and within minutes Lucia was ready to give birth. Afterward, I helped her clean up, and I held the baby so she could rest.

"Thank you for everything, Isabel."

"You're welcome. We're here to give one another a hand. In the maternity hospital we're one big family."

"It's a lovely place, nothing like the camps. I haven't been in France as long as most other people. My husband and I decided to stay in Spain. He was a musician and hadn't committed any crimes. We're from a town near the city of Alicante. But a few months after the Francoists showed up, the purges started. Every night they would take a dozen or so people out and execute them in open fields or against a cemetery wall. One night they took my neighbor Pilar. The poor woman was pregnant. She was a Protestant and was a teacher in the town. Some of the townsfolk hated her for being a Red and a heretic, as they said, but she was a good person. That very night we got out of there. Our province had been the last to surrender, and the Francoists were by no means lenient. It was terribly difficult to get to the border. We had to spend three nights and three days on the mountain. We got here a couple months ago."

"That's quite an adventure," I said.

"I figure there are hundreds if not thousands of stories like mine. My Pascual is at the front now. They recruited him against his will last week, though he tried everything to get out of it. These froggies just want us as cannon fodder."

"My husband is at the front too. They took him for what was supposed to be three months, and it's been over four. You can't trust a word they say."

Just then I heard a commotion from downstairs. I looked out the window and saw a group of women around a thin, bald man.

"Who is that?" I asked one of the volunteers close to the window.

"You don't know him? That's Pablo Casals, the famous musician."

"Oh? Did he come to give a concert?"

"No, even better: a donation."

I went down to the yard just as Elisabeth was greeting the man.

"It's a great honor for us to have you come to the house."

"I've wanted to see this place for a while now. I've heard such good things about your work. Thank you for helping the Spanish mothers," he said kindly.

"Please, come into the living room."

Casals climbed the stairs and nodded at me as he passed. He seemed to be such a nice man. In the living room, there was a cello waiting for him.

"Now, who put this here?" he asked with a smile. Then he sat and started tuning the instrument.

Everyone in the house who could get to the living room formed a tight circle around the man, and Elisabeth introduced our guest.

"Pablo Casals is one of the greatest composers, musicians, and orchestra directors in the world!" she said, beaming.

Casals closed his eyes and started playing the cello. None of us breathed for a few minutes. The music lifted us up and carried us far away from there to the happy world we had all left behind. The air rang with the emotion of the song after he finished. His face had changed while he played, but when he looked up we burst out in applause.

"Everyone who knows me knows that I'm proud to be both Catalonian and Spanish. My friends, I suffer deeply to see my compatriots in these dire situations. I wish I could do more for this maternity hospital; that is what I desire, for there is no greater deed than saving the life of a child. Children are our future. I ask one thing of you as mothers: Don't raise them to be full of hatred and resentment. One day may all Spaniards come together and be reconciled, and may this war be nothing more than a forgotten nightmare."

Moved by his words, we applauded again.

"Thank you so much, Mr. Casals," Elisabeth said.

That short, common-looking man was much more than a music virtuoso. He was a great and humble soul, someone who thought we mattered. He took his leave of us one by one and asked about our children. When he came to me, he asked, "From Catalonia, no? We're siblings twice over then." When he hugged me, tears sprang to my eyes again.

It was a surreal day for us all, as if life had gifted us a bit of peace and calm before the storm of war unfurled.

Elisabeth

The news could not have been less uplifting. After conquering the Netherlands and Belgium in record time, the Germans had entered France where they were least expected, through the thick and majestic Ardennes Forest. The French papers professed an optimism that was not matched on the streets. In the best possible scenario, even if France was victorious, it was now clear that the war would be long and difficult. Elisabeth wondered if the maternity hospital would be able to keep functioning. The number of sponsors supporting the institution was on the decline. Aid from the Netherlands had disappeared immediately, and support from within France was waning. The only ones staying faithful to the mission were her fellow Swiss, who still believed the war was something that would stay in other lands.

The other volunteers noted Elisabeth's crestfallen face and how she barely touched her food.

"Are you all right, Elisabeth?" María Sardà, one of the cooks, asked. The staff often ate in the kitchen together after all the mothers had been served.

Madame Ida, the Swiss midwife who came off gruff, looked around and said in broken Spanish, "Everyone keeps giving Elisabeth grief. She's too soft, but if you all understood what she goes through to keep food in your bellies, you'd work more and gossip less." She had never understood why the Spaniards felt the need to talk so much. People in her country were not such chatty busybodies, as she understood them.

"No, no, that's not it. I'm delighted with our volunteers, and they're doing wonderful work. It's just that the German invasion of France has me worried. While Pablo Casals is still providing a lot of funding, we no longer have many donors. Since January, many of our sponsors have stopped sending money."

"Oh, I'm sorry," María García, one of the other mothers who had joined the staff, said.

"I don't mean to worry you all."

After the meal, Elisabeth went with Lucy to Perpignan. They had been expecting a large shipment of food, but it had not come yet. For the time being, supplies were being sent over the Alps to avoid the war, but if the Germans occupied that area, the supply line would be cut off.

In Perpignan, people talked about the war and only the war. Some said the Maginot Line could not hold as it had in the Great War. Germany had already conquered five countries in a matter of months. Though those nations were smaller and weaker than France, everyone feared the German lightning strikes.

The women arrived at the large distribution warehouse and sought out the manager, Pierre. They were puzzled as to why they had not yet been notified about the shipment.

"Good afternoon, ladies. To what do I owe this honor?"

"You know, monsieur. Our shipment hasn't arrived," Elisabeth said. She was quite familiar with Pierre's tricks.

"Ah, I'm so sorry, but I'm following the prefect's orders. All available food is to be kept in storage. Surely you're aware that the Germans are already here in France?" the Frenchman explained patronizingly.

"That food belongs to us, and the prefect can't commandeer it on a whim!" Elisabeth snapped.

"We're at war, madame. What is in France belongs to France." Pierre's tone was losing its ingratiating lilt.

"Pack up our food and medicines and send them to the hospital at once. I'll speak with the prefect."

Pierre gave her a patronizing smile, knowing the futility of challenging the man who had the power to shut down the hospital.

"Well, get to it. Start loading up! We'll be back in an hour." Elisabeth turned and stormed out, Lucy following her. There was a good chance the prefect had finished for the day, but they went to his office regardless. The secretary confirmed that he had gone home after lunch.

"Where does he live?" Elisabeth asked.

The man shrugged. "I can't give out that information."

"This is a life-and-death situation!" Elisabeth said in exasperation.

The secretary hesitated but in the end gave them the address. It was not far, and the two women hurried there on foot. At the gate, they rang the bell insistently. A servant came out to meet them.

"How can I help you?"

"Is the prefect home?"

The servant looked them up and down. They were dressed well enough, but she had never seen them before. "The prefect does not tend to matters of business in his home."

"Ma'am, we have to see him immediately. We're the directors of the maternity hospital in Elne. He knows us very well and won't hesitate to receive us. Do you want us to tell him later you refused to show us in?"

Elisabeth's voice was so firm and commanding that the

woman had no choice but to open the gate and let them in. She took them through the front door and asked them to wait in a small parlor.

The prefect came down from the second floor in gray pants and a silk robe. He had a sort of net over his hair. With his elegant manners he asked them to have a seat, but he was clearly displeased by this invasion of his privacy.

"You have the floor, ladies."

"We've just come from the central warehouse," Elisabeth began. "Pierre told us you've ordered the requisition of all food and medicine that comes into the city. Because of this, he's withholding our supplies from Switzerland."

"We're at war, as you are surely aware."

"Of course we're aware of that. But those supplies are Swiss, not French, and you have no jurisdiction over them." Elisabeth was getting riled up. Lucy put her hand on Elisabeth's arm to rein her in.

"That is not the case. The French government has the final word over what occurs in our country. This is not Switzerland." The prefect crossed his legs as if to leave no doubt about his authority.

"We're only here because your government has refused to do what needs to be done for the refugees. Those supplies are from the Swiss Red Cross. We've recently started working with them directly. Therefore, sir, you are stealing from the Red Cross. Furthermore, since these are Swiss supplies, you are starting a diplomatic conflict and are in effect in breach of the Geneva Conventions. We will ask the Swiss ambassador to inform your government, and we will complain to the press. Just imagine the headlines: 'Perpignan Prefect Steals Food from Starving Babies.'"

The prefect turned aggressively red and leaned forward. "You will do no such thing," he said, waving his finger in Elisabeth's face.

"We need you to sign a document authorizing us to pick up our supplies and assuring that this will never happen again. We will say it has all been a misunderstanding."

"You know I can close the maternity hospital."

"Yes, sir, that is within your power to do; yet you will also have to explain to the press why you turned thirty-three mothers and their infants out on the streets in the middle of a war. I can't imagine that would sit well with you."

The prefect stood, went for paper and pen, scribbled a few lines, and then stamped the paper with his seal. He held the paper out as if it was rotten.

"Thank you very much. You've been so accommodating, as usual," Elisabeth jabbed.

The man merely nodded toward the door.

"Please give your wife our greetings!" Lucy called from the threshold.

When they were a few paces down the street, they looked at each other and burst out laughing. "Are you crazy?" Lucy asked, wiping a tear off her face. "You could have gotten us shut down."

"Oh, honey, you don't understand politicians. They'll do just about anything to maintain public opinion. Even that wretched Hitler wouldn't last a week in power if people stood up to him. But right now most Germans *want* him as their leader."

They returned to the warehouse. Pierre was astounded when he read the document. "Do your wiles have no limits?" he said with a snort.

"I have the most powerful boss in the universe," Elisabeth said, raising her eyebrows to the sky.

They returned to Rocinante and were about to head back to the hospital when they saw a pregnant woman sitting along the side of the road. They went up to ask if she was all right.

"I can't understand you," the woman struggled to say in French. Her accent indicated she was from Germany, so Lucy pulled out what she knew of the language to repeat her question.

The woman started crying. Her hunger and exhaustion were evident. "I'm from Munich," she began. "Before the war I crossed the border and was living in Lorraine, but the Nazis will be there soon."

"How do you know?"

"I know what my countrymen are capable of. When they started going after the Jews in Munich, I went into hiding. Munich is the heart of National Socialism. But a neighbor gave me away and told the authorities that my papers were falsified. That's why I escaped to France. Now I don't know where to go. I had thought maybe to Spain, but this baby will come any day now."

"What about your husband?" Elisabeth asked.

The woman's tears started flowing again. "He died of TB six weeks ago."

They helped the woman get to her feet and took her to the van. She lay down in the back and immediately fell asleep.

"What do you think?" Lucy asked Elisabeth.

"I think this is just the beginning. There's going to be a diaspora all throughout France as soon as people know the Nazis are coming to their town. We have to get ready for the avalanche of humanity that's headed our way."

THIRTY-TWO

Isabel

The German troops had been in Paris for six days, and all the major thoroughfares were packed with refugees fleeing south. The French government had relocated to Bordeaux, but everyone said that they would soon be signing an armistice with Germany. I was afraid the Nazis would show up at any minute in Perpignan and send us back to the camps, or worse.

Peter's letters had stopped. I had no idea where he was after the front fell, and I could only hope he had escaped. The possibility of moving to the United States with him and Lisa was less and less likely. Lisa was growing up without her father, and I saved all my crying for nighttime, when no one would see and get worried.

That hot June night I decided to go out to the backyard to clear my head. I took a cigarette, though I had not smoked in years. I just needed something to help calm my nerves. I had only been outside a few minutes when I heard footsteps behind me. Elisabeth put her hand on my shoulder, and we sat together on the stairs.

"It's a beautiful night," I said.

"Yes. It's such a pity that there's so much hatred here beneath those stars." She sighed.

"The war in Spain ended. This one will too."

"Yes, but at what cost? Hitler seems to me to be the absolute worst possible leader of the world. At the core he's a prototype of the antichrist."

I looked at her puzzled, unfamiliar with the term.

"Antichrists are people who oppose Christ—they preach hatred instead of love, violence instead of peace, death instead of life."

I took a long drag on the cigarette and let the smoke out slowly. "That description reminds me of a number of Spanish priests I've known. They're always pressuring people to confess and filling them with fear."

Elisabeth took a deep breath and sat quietly looking out at the sky.

"There's something special about you. You've got a love I don't see in most people, a peace inside you, except"—I jabbed her playfully with my elbow—"when you're mad at the suppliers."

She graced the garden with her light laughter. "I've been very blessed. But I can understand how people resent the church. I myself don't understand why evil is allowed to continue."

"The crusades were waged in the name of religion, and the conquest of the Americas. Where was God during all that?" I asked.

Elisabeth smiled. My arguments were not new to her.

"Do you know the poet John Donne? He was a famous British poet who refused over and over the priest position that the king of England offered him. But finally he accepted it for financial reasons. After his wife died, and after the plague that lambasted London in 1623, he wrote a series of poems about death. Every day, while his life was dangling by a thread, he would hear the church bells ringing the number of deaths. He wrote some of the most beautiful lines in the English language after Shakespeare:

"'Who casts not up his eye to the sun when it rises? But who takes off his eye from a comet when that breaks out? Who bends not his ear to any bell which upon any occasion rings? But who can remove it from that bell which is passing a piece of himself out of this world? No man is an island, entire of itself; every man is a piece of the continent, a part of the main. If a clod be washed away by the sea, Europe is the less, as well as if a promontory were, as well as if a manor of thy friend's or of thine own were: any man's death diminishes me, because I am involved in mankind, and therefore never send to know for whom the bells tolls; it tolls for thee.'"

"It's beautiful, but what does it mean?" I asked.

"That even if we aren't paying attention, the death that bells announce will one day be our own. To take life seriously, we have to think about what eternity will hold."

Elisabeth trailed off just as the first rays of sun announced the arrival of a new day. Side by side we watched the dawn.

Peter

Peter and four comrades had been running from the German troops for days. They feared the Germans would not treat American and Spanish soldiers with the same leniency—if leniency there could be—as the French soldiers and would send them to work camps in northern Germany. As they got close to the Swiss border, they hoped to cross and beg for asylum, though the rumor was that the Swiss sent most refugees back and handed them over to the German authorities.

The five men approached a village just as the sun was beginning to rise. They were very hungry and hoped a villager would give them something to eat.

"We'd better go up one or two at a time. It could be a trap," Lieutenant Gutiérrez said. Though he held no official rank in the French army, he still exercised his previous authority in the group.

"I'll go with Emmanuel. If we see anything suspicious, we'll run the other way, and that will be your cue to get out of here," Peter said.

Gutiérrez nodded, and the two of them approached the village carefully. They came to an open stable and looked inside. A farmer and his wife were milking their cows. They screamed when they saw the soldiers, and Peter spoke in French to reassure them.

"Please, we won't hurt you. We just want some food," he said.

The farmer held out the bucket of milk, and Peter gulped it down as Emmanuel kept watch.

Then the woman said, *"Boche! Boche!"*

Peter dropped the bucket immediately upon hearing the slang term for Germans, and he and Emmanuel ran out of the stable. But they ran right into two German soldiers with their guns cocked. Peter and Emmanuel raised their hands and then saw more soldiers approaching with the rest of their captured comrades.

The Germans marched them a few miles away to a fenced-in area where prisoners were being kept.

"What are they going to do with us?" Emmanuel asked. He was only seventeen years old. "We aren't French."

"I guess they'll lock us up and send us back to Spain in a few months," Gutiérrez said.

Hearing them speak in Spanish, one of the guards came up and asked in stuttering Spanish, "You Spaniards? I fight Condor Legion. Hitler and Franco good friends."

Peter went up to the soldier and asked, "May I speak with an officer? I'm a citizen of the United States, and my country remains neutral."

The soldier laughed and spoke in broken English. "Cowboy! You, good friend!"

An SS officer barked at the soldier for speaking with the prisoners.

"But this man is American," the soldier explained.

"It doesn't matter. They're all Communists, you idiot."

Just then a soldier in a Polish uniform tore off running, and several Germans went after him. He had been part of a small contingent that had escaped Poland and joined the Allies. The SS officer took aim and shot. The Pole fell down, writhing in his own blood. The officer went up to him and observed his slow death without putting him out of his misery. Then he walked away from the fenced area.

Peter turned back to the soldier who had fought in the Condor Legion. "What are you going to do with us?" he asked.

"All prisoners go to Lyon," he answered in Spanish.

That response made Peter feel slightly better. The farther south they went, the closer he would be to Isabel. At least he had survived thus far in a second war. Surely the British would surrender soon, the war would be over, and he could return to the United States and get on with life. He threw himself on the ground and closed his eyes. He tried to call up Lisa's face, but the precise details had faded from his memory. He did not even have a picture of her. To his horror, he found that Isabel's face had also started to slip away from his memory. He forced himself to go inch by inch down her body the way he had last seen her at the maternity hospital. He swore that as soon as they were back together, they would never be separated again.

Elisabeth

ELNE MATERNITY HOSPITAL

July 23, 1940

The avalanche of humanity had already arrived some months before, but life in the maternity hospital was unaffected by it until well into the summer. Friedel Bohny-Reiter, one of the Swiss volunteers, started bringing pregnant Jewish mothers and their sick children from the Rivesaltes internment camp to Elne. That completely changed the dynamic in the hospital. The new mothers and children took up a lot of space, and everyone else had to make room. Many of the women arrived sick and at high risk of miscarrying due to the terrible conditions at the camp.

One morning a Polish couple showed up at the door. They had managed to travel a long journey without being picked up by the authorities. Elisabeth ushered them into her office. The woman was almost full term.

"Thank you for receiving us," the man said. "My name is Mikołaj Spiel, and this is my wife, Ruth. She'll go into labor any day now."

"How did you make it this far?" Elisabeth asked, incredulous.

"It hasn't been easy. We escaped from Poland after the invasion. From there we went to Hungary and then to Slovakia. The plan all along was to get to France. We thought we'd be safe here—ha." The man gave a dry laugh and shook his head. "We made it to Italy and from there to Lyon. When the Germans invaded France, we kept moving south. Now we've been hoping to get to Spain, but my wife can't keep traveling."

"Of course, of course. Tell me, why did you leave Poland?" Elisabeth asked.

Mikołaj and Ruth looked at each other for a long moment, as if it were too painful to recount aloud.

"Can it be that you don't know what's happening in Poland? Poland has been torn apart since the Nazi occupation started last September. Hitler started by getting rid of the political and economic elite. Then he came after us. They put race laws into effect, and now they're shutting up the entire Jewish population in ghettos. Things aren't as bad in the Soviet-occupied zone, but thousands or hundreds of thousands of our brothers and sisters are dying because of overcrowding and food shortages," Mikołaj said. Ruth gripped his hand and started to cry.

Elisabeth was speechless. She feared something similar would happen in France. The Jewish community was not as large as in Poland, but the Nazis and their collaborators might lock them all up in camps or send them to Germany as cheap labor.

Elisabeth swallowed to steady her voice and looked at Ruth. "You'll be safe here. We don't have men in the house, except for a few of our workers, but you and your husband can stay in a little hut that was once used by guards. It's not fancy, but you'll have privacy, and then you can continue your journey to Spain."

"Thank you. Thank you so much," Ruth said, getting to her feet and kissing Elisabeth's hand.

"This is what we're here for. The world is sinking into perhaps the darkest hour of history, and it makes the light we shine seem so small."

Elisabeth left the couple in the hut out back after some of the volunteers got it ready for them. Back in the main house, she ran into Isabel.

"Who are they?" Isabel asked.

"They're Polish Jews. They need a place to stay until the woman gives birth."

"Are the Nazis looking for them?" Isabel's voice trembled.

"I'm afraid so. Who knows what those beasts are capable of, but even thinking about it chills my blood." Elisabeth clasped her hands together to steady herself and then returned to her office. Work helped take her mind off the fact that France was no longer a sovereign nation and that they were at the mercy of the evilest man to rise to power in perhaps all of human history.

THIRTY-THREE

Isabel

ELNE MATERNITY HOSPITAL
September 1, 1940

The war had been going on for a year. Daily life proceeded as usual despite the horrors occurring elsewhere. British cities were being bombed constantly, and everyone was holding their breath waiting for Prime Minister Churchill to surrender.

The delight of watching Lisa grow was tempered by my ceaseless anxiety about Peter being buried in some far-off ditch, never to be seen again.

María came to the hospital with her husband one day and searched the house until she found me in the kitchen.

"Dear Isabel, I came to . . ." She trailed off. We had grown apart since she had moved out of the maternity hospital. Her life had gone on: she was with her husband and daughter in their own home. Meanwhile, my life was still in suspense, ever at the mercy of a letter that may or may not arrive or, worse, an anonymous message with bad tidings.

"What is it?" I asked, seeing her tear up. I took her baby girl in my arms, and the cook pulled out a chair for her before leaving us to talk.

"We're leaving."

I had not expected to hear those words. The last time we had spoken, she had talked about not wanting to go back to Spain after all.

"To Mexico. We've booked passage, and my mother is going to join us later this year in Veracruz with my son."

I was stunned. Of course, I was happy for her, but in comparison, fate had dealt with me unfairly, and I was bitter.

"Oh. Oh! I . . . I'm so happy for you. You'll get to start from scratch without the shadow of the war constantly hanging over you. Your daughter is just adorable, and when you're with your son again, it'll be just like before the war, when we all used to be happy."

María hugged me, and we wept together. Her daughter stared at us in confusion.

"Listen, Carlos can get two more tickets, one for you and one for Lisa. You'd do well in Mexico. Elisabeth would have our address, and she could give it to Peter when he gets back. Come with us."

My tears came harder, and a knot in my throat threatened to choke me. I was touched that she had thought of me. "Oh, María, thank you; that means so much to me. But I can't. I just can't leave France until I know what's happened to Peter. I know—I think—I hope he'll be back soon. The war will be over, and we'll be back together. It'll be easier to travel, and we'll go to live with his family. Mexico and the United States are right next to each other, so we'll see each other."

She understood. We hugged again, and I handed her daughter

back. The child was as healthy and beautiful as Lisa. We both owed so much to the maternity hospital. It had saved us from the horrors of the camp and had given us back the dignity we lost on the journey over the Pyrenees. Every time I went to the camps and saw the refugees, I was acutely aware of how privileged I was.

María started up the stairs but then turned and looked back at me. "I'll never forget you, Isabel. I won't forget América or any of the others we lost along the way. I pray every day for Peter to return and for you to get out of this country and this continent. There's no future for Europe. I love you, my friend."

María's final words broke my heart. I ached with longing for Spain, for the early days of our marriage before Peter went off to fight, for that dawn we shared on the beach before they took him away again, and for the last time we saw each other, when his eyes lit up beholding Lisa.

I collapsed into a chair and did not hold back my tears. I needed all the suffering to get outside of me and stop hurting.

Peter

The Montluc prison was in downtown Lyon. All the prisoners captured on the front were taken there. Peter and his comrades were crammed together in a small cell. After some time, the Nazis had handed them over to French authorities, who wanted to be rid of the Spaniards. As the months dragged on, one after another was set free. Most returned to Spain or went back to southern France to find their family members. But Peter and Lieutenant Gutiérrez were still being held.

Inspector Moreau called for Peter to come to his office. He was a heavyset Frenchman with bug eyes, curly hair, and a cold look. Politely, he asked Peter to sit down and then read his file.

"Citizen of the United States, married to a Spaniard, soldier with the International Brigades in the Spanish Civil War. I can't blame you. In my youth I was as impetuous and revolutionary as you. Every generation wants the same thing—to change the world and build a new one in its own image, but most of them fail. I hope you soon see the error of your ways. Fascism offers the only chance this world has for survival. This doesn't mean I necessarily agree with everything Hitler and Mussolini are doing—their anti-Semitism is absurd, and I despise their theatrics when it comes to ideology—but at the core, the new Vichy France represents the essence of French society: work, family, and fatherland. And you, what will you do if I set you free? Will you go join the Red army, become a terrorist?"

"As soon as I get to Perpignan, I'll get my wife and daughter and take the first boat we can find to the United States," Peter assured him.

Moreau dabbed at his brow. The room was very hot despite the crisp autumnal air.

"I've looked into things with your embassy. It seems your exit visa is in order, they have authorized your marriage, and they have recognized your daughter. The consulate should be working on your papers, so you will be able to leave the country."

Peter smiled, incredulous. He could not believe he might actually, finally be free.

"I'll give you a letter of safe passage for your journey south. You'll have thirty days. If you haven't left the country by then, you'll be considered illegal immigrants once again and liable for detention. Do you understand?"

"Yes, sir. Thank you so much."

The inspector handed over a signed, sealed document and then put a few francs on the desk. "Call me sentimental, but I'd rather people like you get out of my country. The last thing we need is a civil war like Spain. The Nazis will clear out after the war—there's no reason for them to occupy half the country—and things will get back to normal, but we'll have rid ourselves of the Popular Front and all of the Soviet Union's minions for good. Safe travels to you."

Peter stood, and they shook hands.

"Go back to the United States," Moreau said, "the land of liberty and opportunity. Over here the world is too old to be happy. Yet a new France will rise from these ashes."

Peter walked out of the office as light as air, gathered his few belongings from his cell, and half an hour later was walking the streets of Lyon a free man. It felt so strange not to be running and hiding. Now the only thing that mattered was getting to Isabel and Lisa and going home at last.

THIRTY-FOUR

Isabel

ELNE MATERNITY HOSPITAL
February 2, 1941

Most of the internment camps for Spanish refugees had closed, so it seemed that the mission Elisabeth had started over two years ago would be coming to an end. I had been receiving letters from Peter again for a few months. His first came at the end of the previous October, and my whole disposition changed after that. He was alive. He was in a jail in France, but he was alive. And that was much better than if he had been in one of the terrible Gestapo prisons everyone was talking about.

Lisa was a darling. For Christmas Elisabeth had given her a beautiful white dress that made her curly red hair stand out. Everyone adored her, and she was the favorite pet of the nurses and volunteers.

"Isabel, can I speak with you?" Elisabeth's voice called me out of my reverie. I had been staring at the snow-covered yard and waiting to go help in the kitchen for snack time.

"Yes, of course. I was, well, just thinking about Peter."

"Do you have more news of him?"

"Yes. He was released a few days ago and should be here soon, though the roads are difficult with the ice and snow. And the buses aren't running like they used to. But he might try to get all the paperwork taken care of in Lyon first."

"Oh, wonderful. After such a long wait, you'll hardly notice a few more days." She smiled at me, and I smiled in return. Lisa waddled up to her and gave her a big hug.

Elisabeth scooped her up and spun her around. "Lisa, you're getting to be so big and so pretty!" She placed her back down and then joined me at the window.

"Winter makes me think about crossing the Pyrenees. It seems like eons ago, but it was just two years," I mused.

Elisabeth shuddered. "I remember it all too well. I've been away from home for too long. My father is ill, but I can't get back to see him."

"Why don't you take a few days off? There are fewer women in the hospital now that most of the camps have closed. And the rest of the refugees are getting folded into French society."

"That's the problem. The Vichy government is holding a lot of the new refugees at Rivesaltes, near the old military quarters. You'll see it soon. We've already got one Jewish mother from there as well as several of your fellow Spaniards."

I nodded.

Elisabeth went on. "I'd like you to go there with Elsbeth Kasser and Elsa Lüthi-Ruth. Now that we're officially part of the Swiss Red Cross, we have more resources than before, and they won't turn us away from that camp."

"But how can I help? I can't leave Lisa here alone."

"You'll just be there for a few days, taking stock of the situation and negotiating permissions with the camp authorities for pregnant women and young children to get transferred here. After that, I'd like you to go once a week with the team to identify high-risk pregnancies."

"What will happen if Peter comes while I'm gone?"

"Don't worry," Elisabeth said. "I'll send for you immediately."

I did not love the idea, but I could not say no to Elisabeth. She and the other volunteers had done so much for me and Lisa that it would have been terrible of me to deny the same help to other women.

The next day we headed for Rivesaltes. I left Lisa under the care of my colleague Amalia, though I knew that the entire household would watch out for her.

The camp was about an hour north of Elne, built on a deserted flatland where the wind blew fiercely all year long. It was roasting hot in the summer and freezing cold in the winter. At the main gate, two soldiers stopped us. Elsa showed them our authorizations, and they let us through. A large avenue ran down the middle of the camp. Here the barracks were built of brick instead of wood. They were tall and had staircases leading up to them. The bathrooms were in a separate building.

We parked the van and went to the Red Cross building. As we walked, people in the camp noticed our uniforms and started begging us for supplies. They were surprised when I answered them in Spanish.

"You're a Spaniard?" a woman named Tomasa said. She lived in the family area with her daughter and two granddaughters.

"Yes, ma'am. I work with the Elne maternity hospital." Elsbeth and Elsa waited for me as I spoke with the woman.

"Can you help us? We don't have much food or any soap. When we got to France we were in Argelès, and now . . ."

"I was locked up in that horrible place too," I said.

She nodded. "Things are a bit better here, but it's so cold, and the heaters are never on. They say there's not enough money for firewood."

I took her cold hand in my own. "I'll do what I can. We need to meet with our Red Cross colleagues now, but then I'll come see you in your barrack. Why have you decided not to return to Spain?"

Tomasa's face clouded over.

"My son-in-law is working outside the camp and has promised to get us out soon. I write letters with my sister Juanita in Castellón. Her letters get censured, but I understand well enough. They're starving over there, and the dictator makes life unbearable. My granddaughters will have a better future here."

I cocked my head in skepticism. "But the Nazis are the masters of France now."

"They'll move on, my daughter; they'll eventually let us be."

I squeezed her hand and continued on with my group from the hospital. We met with Dr. Harold, a Canadian who had been working for two years in the refugee camps. After introductions, he gave us an overview of life at Rivesaltes.

"The camp has 150 barracks. There is no access to potable water, and the wind blows all day and night. The buildings have no insulation or heat. There are currently 6,475 refugees, half of whom are Spaniards, but the authorities are bringing more and more refugees who've come from Germany, Poland, and other countries. At this rate, we'll reach max capacity by the summer. We don't have enough of anything we need: food, medicine, blankets, warm clothing, books for the children, shoes, and, most of all, hope. Some of the people have been shuttled around from one camp to another, and many no longer know any other way of life."

"Are there many pregnant women?" Elsa asked.

"Yes, as well as infants and sick children. We don't have the means to treat them all. Several organizations, like the Quakers, the Mennonites, and other groups, are taking some of the children to shelters and other camps where they get better care, but it isn't enough."

"We can take ten pregnant women and another ten children and mothers," Elsa said. The doctor's face fell to hear how little we could host.

"Well, something is better than nothing."

"We've also brought some clothing, food, blankets, and other essentials," I said in French. I was getting the hang of the new language.

"Thank you. I'll help you unload the things now."

After that, I filled two small bags with supplies and took them to Tomasa's barrack.

"Thank you, my daughter. Come meet my granddaughters. This is Rosa and this is Gemma. This is my daughter, Soledad, and these are all our friends." Tomasa pulled out a chocolate bar from the bags I had given her and shared it among the children.

"There are people here from all over," she said, "and a lot of Gypsies. At first it was just us Spaniards, but now it's a veritable Tower of Babel. We have to wait in long lines for everything, and it's so cold."

One of the girls came up to me. Looking at her face, I realized she was sick.

"What's going on with your granddaughter?" I asked.

Tomasa shrugged. "She's run down."

MARIO ESCOBAR

"Well, she's not likely to get better here. Do you want me to take her with me to Elne? We'll bring her back when she's gotten better and has put on some weight."

Tomasa looked at Rosa and then at her daughter, Soledad. She sighed, torn. "I . . . we . . . we don't want to be separated. We're a family, and we'd rather be together."

I understood completely. I knew what it was like to have loved ones far away. I nodded, hugged her goodbye, and went back to Elsa and Elsbeth.

THIRTY-FIVE

Elisabeth

ELNE MATERNITY HOSPITAL
February 10, 1941

The prefect had sent several inspectors to the maternity hospital. Several neighbors had reported seeing immigrants near the building, and he had not authorized a change in the organization's status to being a refuge. Elisabeth called Karl. They had been out of touch for some time, as Karl was working full-time in the camps where orphaned children were being held and was as overwhelmed as Elisabeth with the arrival of new immigrants.

"Karl, it's Elisabeth. The prefect wants to close the hospital, and I don't know what to do."

Her tone surprised him. He had always known her to be determined and sure.

"Are you all right?" he asked.

"Yes, just overwhelmed. I haven't slept in a few days. The Germans are trying to requisition our supplies at the border, and donations are few and far between. The reality that this war is going to drag on has dissuaded many people from donating what they've got saved up. And . . . I think the authorities have figured out that we're giving Jewish children Spanish names so they don't get sent to the concentration camps."

"I'll come see you," Karl said. Within an hour, he was parked in front of the hospital, surprised to find a police car there as well.

He strode across the garden with growing concern, went up the stairs, and heard two gendarmes arguing with Elisabeth at the front door.

"We've got to come in and take a look around. There's a report that you're sheltering certain individuals illegally," the corporal said. He was holding out a document signed by the prefect.

"You can't search this building. There are pregnant women and babies here."

The gendarme pushed her, and Elisabeth almost fell. That was when Karl made his presence known.

"Excuse me! What is going on?" he said loudly, putting himself between Elisabeth and the officers.

"I've got orders to search this building for undocumented refugees," the gendarme said.

Karl blocked the man with his arms. "This building belongs to the Swiss Red Cross, and you cannot enter without permission from the Swiss government. What you're doing is equivalent to raiding the embassy."

The gendarmes looked at each other. The corporal tsked and shook his head. When they had gone, Karl and Elisabeth went inside. Several nurses and mothers were just inside the door.

"Those Jewish women are going to ruin everything," Ester

snapped. She was a very young Spanish mother who had just given birth. She had been transferred from Rivesaltes and had not had positive experiences with the foreigners there.

"In this house, there are no Jews nor Spaniards nor Gypsies. We are all one family," Elisabeth clarified.

Ester left with her baby for the living room, muttering under her breath. The rest of the group also dispersed. Elisabeth nodded toward her office.

After closing the door, she let down her guard. "I don't know how much longer we can hold out. The Vichy authorities are as racist as the Nazis."

"They keep saying the United States will enter the war. If they do, the Nazis are bound to lose."

"Ugh, I'm so tired of rumors. Supplies are running out. There are so many Jewish mothers coming to us from Rivesaltes. We're sending help to the camp there, but now this happens." She waved vaguely toward where the police car had been.

Karl hugged his friend, and she calmed down.

He stepped back and asked, "Any word from Lucy?"

At the mention of her dear friend, Elisabeth's face fell again. Lucy had gone on a mission to serve in a camp in the occupied zone, and it had been weeks since they had heard from her. Elisabeth missed her terribly. She shook her head.

Karl took a seat and quietly suggested, "I think you might need some time off."

"What? No—how? I can't leave now with everything that's going on."

Karl switched tactics. "Why don't I go see the prefect? I might be able to persuade him."

"How could you possibly convince that petulant racist to

change his mind? I thought he hated the Spanish, but Jews—you have no idea!"

"Sometimes things can be easier than they seem. I can get him to turn a blind eye. Rodolfo can send me some money."

Elisabeth's eyes bulged. "You mean bribe him?"

"Call it what you want, but it's worked for my orphanage. Sometimes we have to do things we wish we didn't in order to keep the children safe."

Karl stood back up and studied his friend. He could not put into words what exactly he felt for her, but it included admiration, affection, and perhaps love. They had both chosen a difficult path in life. Their priority was renouncing their own happiness in order to give themselves for the sake of others. Yet as he drove away, Karl could not keep himself from imagining the what-if: life with Elisabeth, two or three children, a home with a garden in a small city in Switzerland, helping serve the needy from their Calvinist parish, watching the years go by slowly and their love deepen with age.

===

Peter

Peter was exhausted as he got off the bus. He had spent several trying days in Lyon getting all the visa paperwork together, and then it had been challenging to find transportation to Perpignan. But now he had arrived, and everything was in order. He just needed to get Isabel and Lisa and get out of there.

There was a police checkpoint at the station exit. Peter approached with no concern. He had nothing to hide and had all his papers. Two country policemen asked to see his documents.

"You're from the United States?" the one in a green trench coat asked.

"Yes. Everything is in order."

The agent whispered something to his colleague and then put Peter's documents away.

"What's going on? I need to go meet my wife. She's waiting right outside." Peter pointed to the door where Isabel was holding Lisa. He could see her face tighten with worry. "Look," Peter insisted. "That's my wife!"

Instead of turning to look, the officer pulled out his pistol and aimed at Peter. "You're under arrest," he said while the other officer pulled out handcuffs.

"Arrest? Why? What have I done? I'm just a citizen who wants to return to his own country."

The agent did not answer but grabbed Peter and put him in handcuffs.

Isabel burst through the door and through the checkpoint to reach Peter. Her beloved husband was greatly changed. His beard was bushy, and gray hairs had appeared at his temples.

"Peter! What's going on?" she called.

Peter started struggling, trying to get to his wife, but the policemen held him firmly.

"I don't know! But I'll figure it out, and we'll get out of here soon, Isabel!"

Isabel screamed the entire time the agents were stuffing

Peter into a black car. Lisa, too, screamed and cried in terror. Isabel was running alongside the car. She watched Peter through the small window. He was completely crestfallen. She reached out to touch the glass, and he bowed his head toward her hand as they drove off.

THIRTY-SIX

Isabel

ELNE MATERNITY HOSPITAL

February 13, 1941

I was beside myself. I had been so close to Peter, almost close enough to touch him, and those horrible policemen took him away. They had not even allowed him to kiss his daughter.

When I got back to the hospital, Ruth saw my face and immediately took Lisa and handed her to one of the volunteers. I broke down crying and ran to my room.

"Isabel, what's going on?" she asked gently, following me inside.

My face was buried in my pillow, but the whole first floor could hear my sobs. It took me a long time to calm down and catch my breath to be able to tell her what had happened.

"But surely there's been some mistake. The Vichy police are hunting down all the foreigners in the country. They'll probably just question him then let him go free."

Ruth's words did not cheer me up. "Free France" was a euphemism for the Fascist regime that aligned itself with Hitler and Mussolini.

"Why? Why does this keep happening to us? Elisabeth talks about love and justice, but while things somehow work out for other people, we keep suffering."

Ruth sat down on the edge of my bed. "The sun shines on the just and the unjust, honey."

"So what good does it do to follow a belief that ignores people?"

"Human beings are the ones doing all these terrible things. We are free to do good or evil, and many times we choose evil."

I sat up, and Ruth hugged me tight.

"We'll understand more in a few days," she said, stroking my hair.

I tried to believe her, but my endurance had run out. Lisa was the only reason I got out of bed every morning. Without her, I did not know what I would do.

THIRTY-SEVEN

Peter

PERPIGNAN
December 3, 1941

Peter was accused of being a spy. He was held in preventative detention until his trial in December. The police interrogated him for weeks trying to force a confession, but they could not break him. Isabel was not allowed to see him, though she sometimes walked by the prison with Lisa in hopes that Peter might look out and see them.

Isabel had gotten in touch with Peter's family so that they could pressure the government to intercede on their son's behalf. Fortunately, there had been a change at the consulate the previous year, and the new consul took an interest in Peter's case. He had requested Peter's release several times.

Elisabeth, Ruth, Karl, and Isabel were present the day of the trial. Friends of their organization had paid for the lawyer, and they hoped to get Peter off, despite the unjust legal system of Vichy France.

Everyone stood when the judge entered the courtroom. He had a stern face with imposing cheekbones and sunken cheeks.

At a sign from him, they all took their seats again. The district attorney stood to read the charges and briefly present the facts of the case.

"Peter Davis is an American agent who has infiltrated our country for the purpose of acquiring important information for our enemies. These are the so-called 'Allies': the English pirates that destroyed our fleet and massacred over a thousand of our countrymen, together with the Yankees who claim neutrality yet who have armed the Bolsheviks and the British pirates. As an undercover agent, Peter Davis also infiltrated Spain, and that woman there is his cover. But I will soon demonstrate to the court that he is guilty of espionage and merits the death sentence."

The room was silent. Then the defense attorney stood. He was a pudgy, friendly-looking man.

"Your Honor, the defendant, Peter Davis, is a citizen of a country with whom we hold friendly diplomatic relations and with whom we are not at war. He has served in our army as a volunteer offering support to our troops, and he is the father of a child born in our country, Lisa Davis, who is also the daughter of his wife, Isabel. The only thing Mr. Davis is guilty of is being in the wrong place at the wrong time. The police had received information from the Gestapo about a suspected foreign spy. The agents who detained Mr. Davis confused him for this spy. He has been held prisoner for eleven months without trial due to this error. I will now present proof of the reports sent to the embassy in Paris and to the most excellent United States ambassador, the consul's report, and a request from the president of the United States Senate requesting the immediate release of the accused. Mr. Davis is the son of a Christian minister and comes from a faithful, highly respected Christian family. His father has served as a chaplain in the White House."

The trial followed the typical procedures. The two police officers who had arrested Peter were questioned, as was the consul, and finally Isabel was called to testify.

"Isabel Dueñas, Mrs. Davis, you have sworn before this court that everything you say is the absolute truth."

"Yes, sir." Her voice trembled before the defense attorney.

"Did you meet your husband in Spain?"

Isabel told about the first time she and Peter met, their wedding, and their eventual escape from Spain.

"Have you ever witnessed violent or strange behavior from your husband?"

"Even though my husband has fought in a war, Peter is a good, gentle man. He longs for peace. Ever since we got to France, we have been trying to get a visa to travel to the United States, but up to now bureaucratic red tape has prevented us."

The defense lawyer approached the judge and held out the proof of each attempt to secure their visas over the years.

"So your intention is to leave this country as soon as your husband is released?"

"Yes, sir," Isabel answered. The lawyer rapped his fingers on the banister and sat down.

The district attorney stood and approached Isabel.

"Is it true that your husband, the accused, went to Spain to compete in the People's Olympiad in 1936 in Barcelona?"

"Yes, sir."

"Those games were organized by the Communist Party and other extreme left parties," he declared.

"I couldn't say, sir," Isabel answered.

"Is it not true that your husband is a member of the Communist Party?"

"No, sir, he is not."

"Isn't it true that he fought for the Communist government of the Spanish Republic?"

Isabel held Peter's gaze for a moment before answering. "I am a Spaniard, and I can assure you that the day the Republic was declared, everyone poured out into the streets to celebrate. Extremists from many different groups stirred things up and opened the way for the coup d'état. Then foreign powers took advantage of the situation to drag the war out. My husband fought only for a just cause. It was the cause of freedom. Since I've been in this country, I've been taught that equality, fraternity, and liberty are the foundations that France is built on."

"For your information, madame, our foundations are work, family, and fatherland," the attorney spat out.

The judge massaged his cheek and leaned back impatiently.

"My husband and I both believe in the equality of all people. We have all been created equal. Our free will is based on the freedom we all share and on our brotherhood, which tells us that we all belong to one human race."

Voices of protest rose in the courtroom, and the judge hammered his gavel. "Silence, or I'll clear you all out." He turned to Isabel. "Go on, madame."

"I only want to add, Your Honor, that my husband is a good man who cares about his family. All he wants to do is hug his daughter and go home."

The judge left for a few minutes to consider the case. Isabel was allowed to speak with Peter while he was gone.

"I love you, and I will always love you," she said, tears spilling down her cheeks.

"I love you too," Peter answered as the judge returned. Everyone rose.

The judge took his seat and looked at Peter, then at the full courtroom.

"Peter Davis, citizen of the United States of America, I find you innocent of all charges. This case is closed."

The judge smacked the gavel and stood. The district attorney started to protest, but the judge had already left the room.

Isabel ran to Peter and threw herself into him. They kissed and hugged a long time while their friends clapped and cheered. Finally, they were free to go home.

THIRTY-EIGHT

Isabel

ELNE MATERNITY HOSPITAL
December 12, 1941

None of us could have foreseen that Japan would attack the United States a few days after the trial and bomb Pearl Harbor. We had planned to leave for Bordeaux the very day that the United States declared war on Japan and its allies.

The consul called to urge us to leave immediately, but our exit visas were no longer valid: Peter's country was now at war with Germany, the de facto rulers of France.

Elisabeth and Karl examined every option for getting us out through Spain, but we were at risk there too. For fighting against Franco, Peter would be arrested the moment he stepped foot on Spanish soil.

After we had been shut up indoors for two days, Elisabeth knocked at our door and told us her plan.

"The only thing we can do is transport you in a Red Cross vehicle to Bordeaux. From there, with false passports, you can get on a ship going to Cuba. We just need a few days to get the paperwork ready."

Elisabeth was not worried for my safety, but she knew the police could arrest Peter any minute.

We tried to carry on with regular life. Peter spent every moment closed up in the little hut at the back of the garden, and Lisa and I spent the night out there with him.

The next day, a German Jew came to the hospital to give birth. She was in a terrible state when she arrived. The police had found her in a train station and taken her to Rivesaltes.

"Isabel, can you help me with Ilse? Can you get her ready for delivery?" Elisabeth asked.

Since our trip to Bordeaux had been canceled, my mind had not been able to concentrate on anything but our situation. But I shook my head to clear my thoughts and started helping the woman before me. Her skin was dark, as was her hair, and she could barely walk. She was so thin that her belly hardly protruded. She was a pitiful sight, so weak and exhausted, I helped her get to the delivery room and undress. I cleaned her off and put a new gown on her.

As she endured the racking pains of labor, I noticed a young child outside the door.

"What's your name?" I asked in French. He told me his name was Alois. I offered him a piece of candy, and he smiled at me.

Ilse gave birth to a waif of a baby girl who looked like she had little chance of survival. For her part, the mother looked half dead after the delivery. Yet within a week, the baby was opening her eyes, gaining weight, and grabbing onto the finger of who- ever stroked her little face. One of the Spaniard mothers offered to nurse her, as Ilse's poor body was too weak and malnourished to produce milk.

Close to Christmas Eve, two men in trench coats knocked at

the door of the hospital. Ruth answered the door, but when they insisted on coming in, Elisabeth went to see what was going on.

"Ma'am, we are Gestapo agents, and we've been told you have a female Jew in this house."

We had many more than one, though Elisabeth falsified our records to give them and their children Spanish names.

"Yes, she's recovering from giving birth. Why do you ask?"

"We need to take her with us."

"Oh, she's far too weak for that," Elisabeth answered.

"That's of no matter. We must take her and her children to a detention center."

I started trembling as I listened. If the Gestapo entered the hospital, they would find Peter as well.

"I'm sorry, but I can't let you in."

"It seems you don't understand the gravity of the situation, ma'am," the one who seemed to be the boss said. He looked like a stereotypical government employee: bald with round glasses.

"You can come back in a few days for her, but if she tries to leave now, she won't even make it to your car." Elisabeth made to close the door, but the agent stuck out his foot and pushed it back open.

"We'll be back, and we'll close this haven for Jews down. Mark my words!" he yelled, turning on his heels and storming back to their car.

The Swiss flag was waving right out in front of the hospital. Perhaps that was why they hesitated. From then on, there were two Gestapo agents posted at the front door. We were truly trapped. We could not leave the building without risking arrest. The Nazis did not have jurisdiction over Vichy France, but the authorities did not lift a finger to protect us.

THIRTY-NINE

Isabel

ELNE MATERNITY HOSPITAL

December 24, 1941

The inhabitants of the maternity hospital felt like prisoners again for the first time in a long time. The house in Elne, which had been a paradise for us over the past couple of years, became our jail and perhaps our tomb. Elisabeth and her team of volunteers were exhausted. They hardly left the grounds and made sure that the women who came to us had all their papers in order. The Gestapo continued watching the entrance day and night. Furthermore, a letter had arrived from the prefecture requesting that my husband present himself at the commissary. They were detaining all US citizens. Most were being deported, but with the accusations against Peter for espionage, it was a risk we could not take.

In those days Peter also received a moving letter from his father. That Christmas Eve we stretched out on the bed in the little hut. As he read it aloud to me, I tried to imagine what life in the United States would be like.

Dear Peter,

After being separated for years by distance and time, I cannot deny my heart's desire to see you again. I don't know if I've been a good father. I can at least assure you that I have tried to be. And I can assure you that I love you more than my own life.

When you were a boy, you would flop down next to me on the couch on Sunday afternoons. We would listen to the radio or read a book out loud. I didn't understand then that those little moments were some of the happiest times in my life. To have you and your siblings together at home, to see you grow up, to see your personalities start to come out—those were the greatest gifts given to me.

Your mother and I have prayed a lot for you, especially that no bullet would pierce your loving, generous heart. When you wrote to us about Isabel, at first I was angry. I didn't want you to be with a woman who doesn't share your beliefs and values. But now I know she is part of your soul. Together you are forming a beautiful family. All of us here are eager to meet her. We're sure that, if you've picked her, she must have a soul as tender as yours.

Thank you for the picture of Lisa, our granddaughter! Even at a distance, being grandparents has given us something we'd lost: the excitement of seeing your eyes in hers, of feeling a parent's deep love again, and of watching the next generation grow up.

We are praying that soon we'll be reunited and that, together again around the table, we can give thanks for our blessings and gifts in this life.

It will be hard to go through this Christmas knowing you

three are not yet safe, but we trust that very soon you'll be by our side, and all our sadness will turn to joy.

We love you,

Dad and Mom

Peter and I were both crying by the end of the letter. Lisa stared at us and then joined in with her own tears, clinging to us.

"I miss them so much, and every day I'm afraid I'll never see them again. My dad and I didn't part on good terms. He didn't want me to come to Spain, and he certainly didn't want me to fight in the war. I didn't understand him at the time. He had fought in the Great War, but now I know that he was trying to spare me a lot of suffering. We all want to keep our children from going through pain, but I guess we have to accept the fact that they, too, have to suffer like the rest of us."

His words made me think about my mother. Her life had been hard and lonely, and she had no one to lean on. I regretted all the times I had been rude to her and made her cry.

"We'll be with them soon. For me, they're already family. They're the family I never had."

In a few hours, we would celebrate our Christmas Eve feast and try to hold on to peace and calm in the midst of the fear and anguish the past several months had brought.

Elisabeth

ELNE MATERNITY HOSPITAL

December 24, 1941

Everything looked lovely: the table, the flickering candles, the bright ornaments, and the huge Christmas tree. The mothers and the workers sat around the table, though some who were too weak stayed on the couch. Most of the babies were already asleep. Elisabeth stood and began to speak.

"Once again we're blessed to celebrate Christmas, while Europe bleeds out in a terrible war that, with the entry of the United States, has turned into a worldwide conflict. Yet here we are, thankful for this house and the peace we share. We have over twenty nationalities among us. We're a veritable League of Nations! We have different faiths, or none at all, but what brings us together is our love for one another and our longing for peace. I want to thank every one of my coworkers for the love and passion with which they care for the children and their mothers. I want to thank all of our volunteers and all the mothers who help us out in every way. Together, we truly are a family."

She raised her glass, and everyone stood.

"Today we celebrate the birth of a baby who was born in a humble manger. There was no place like this hospital for Mary, a first-time mother, to go. May humankind come back to our senses and put a stop to the war this very night!"

Those gathered all raised their glasses, but the noise of loud beating at the door interrupted the toast. Ruth and Elisabeth went to the door. The Gestapo was about to beat it down.

"Peter, get to the coal cellar," Elsa whispered. Isabel went with him and held open the trapdoor so he could slip through.

"Ilse, take your baby and Alois and go hide," Elisabeth said.

Ilse grabbed Alois's hand and ran outside, her eyes crazed with fear.

Elisabeth steeled herself, then opened the door. Her eyes met those of the same Gestapo agent from a few days before.

"You're going to beat the door down. It's Christmas Eve. What do you want?"

"We've got orders, and we're going to search the building." He pushed the door open, and a dozen agents spread throughout the house. "Where are the dirty Jew and the Yankee?"

"They're not here," Elisabeth said, following the agent through the foyer. Everyone at the table was stock-still when they entered the dining room.

"Everyone, papers, now!" he barked.

The women pulled out the passports and visas they kept with them at all times.

The agents scrutinized every detail until they heard a noise from the backyard and ran toward it. Ilse and Alois were trying to get through a broken part of the fence. The barking of the Gestapo's dogs released clouds of vapor into the air. The dogs were let loose.

"No!" Elisabeth called, running after the dogs. If they reached the boy or the baby, the dogs would tear them to pieces.

The agents were also running, and everyone else stood

paralyzed with fear. The dogs reached Ilse when Alois and the baby were already balanced on top of the fence. They tore at her dress, and she could not shake them off.

"Get down from there!" the Gestapo officer commanded.

Ilse did not obey, but an agent grabbed at her, and she fell to the ground. Two others grabbed Alois and the baby.

"Please, at least leave the children here!" Elisabeth begged. The chief turned and slapped her so hard she fell to the ground, her lip dripping blood.

"You damned meddling fool! I'll be back in a few days to shut this place down and take you all away!" he roared.

The men regrouped and resumed searching the house with the dogs. They went down to the basement. Ruth and Isabel went with them to open the doors they pointed to. Isabel's heart was beating out of her chest as they approached the boiler room.

"Open that door!" the Gestapo agent yelled.

Ruth tried to, but her hands were trembling. The officer pushed her aside and shot the lock off the handle. It burst into pieces, and he pushed the creaking metal door open slowly, never lowering his gun.

FORTY

Isabel

ELNE MATERNITY HOSPITAL
December 31, 1941

We decided that New Year's Eve would be the best time to escape. The Gestapo agents had been drinking for hours. We watched them carefully from the hospital windows for a good time to sneak out.

Peter had been in hiding at the abandoned house next door to the hospital for a week. Before the Gestapo agent had entered the coal cellar, my husband had felt his way up the ramp, pushed open the trapdoor, and escaped through the garden. While the Nazis were chasing Ilse and her family, he had jumped the side fence into the yard next door and hidden in the building.

We did not know where he was until the next day, but then we starting leaving food and supplies on the other side of the fence, and he would sneak out at night to get them.

We prepared to celebrate New Year's Eve at the hospital as if it were a typical holiday. The threat of Max Diem, the name of the Gestapo chief who wanted to arrest all the volunteers and close the building, hung over us all. Yet I tried to enjoy those last moments with Elisabeth and our friends.

Peter had returned to our building for the dinner, and we planned to sneak out from under the Nazis' noses at four o'clock in the morning.

The table was not as elegant as it had been on Christmas Eve, and we did not celebrate it all together this time. The mothers had eaten first and were already in bed with their children. Then the volunteers and workers gathered to eat.

"This is our last night with Isabel and her family," Elisabeth announced to the group. The women looked at me with sadness. We had lived through so much together, and it was hard to think of parting. "Isabel and Peter, would you like to say anything?"

Elisabeth's invitation caught me completely by surprise. Peter looked around and stood up.

"I just want to thank you all from the bottom of my heart for how well you've taken care of my wife and my daughter. I don't know what would've become of us without this maternity hospital. Thank you to Elisabeth and to the rest of the team for much more than a wonderful place to sleep. Thank you most of all for the love and tenderness you show to mothers and their babies."

Everyone applauded, and I thought I was off the hook. But Ruth prodded me to get to my feet and say something.

"I, uh, well . . . becoming a mother is the most beautiful thing that has ever happened to me. I never thought I would feel this way. Now nothing makes sense without Lisa. She's my first thought in the morning and my last thought at night. I know that one day she'll have to fly away from our nest and start her own life, but she will never stop being my little girl. When Elisabeth found me, I was a lost woman. I was so desperate that I have no idea what would've become of me. This dear friend has taught me so much over the past couple of years. I have learned that faith is not just a set of beliefs. Above all, it is trusting. I've also learned that the best advice we can give others is our example and that love is able to open doors, even when it looks like fate has sealed them shut. From all of you I've learned that it's so much better to give than to receive, and . . ."

I was crying too hard to keep speaking. Everyone stood to hug me. One by one they kissed me and said how much they would miss me and that they would never forget me.

"I'll never, ever forget you all," I said, bidding farewell to the rest of the volunteers.

Then Peter, Lisa, and I went down to the bottom floor and out the back door. A Red Cross ambulance was waiting for us two blocks away. It would take us to Carcassonne, and from there we would board the train to Bordeaux at eight o'clock in the morning. We would be in the city by the afternoon, in time to take the first boat to Cuba.

Peter helped us get over the fence. We crept through the overgrown yard next door and went out to the street through a hole in the fence. We carefully made our way to the ambulance. We could hear the Gestapo agents laughing and drinking in the distance.

The ambulance crept along the street and did not pick up speed until we were several miles from the maternity hospital. Lisa fell asleep immediately. I leaned back against Peter and thought about all that we were leaving behind: the months of separation and worry, the interminable flight from France, the months on the sand at Argelès, and the time in Elne. So many experiences and emotions were flashing through my brain I could hardly breathe.

We got out at the beautiful Carcassonne train station. We walked to the platform with our tickets ready and waited for the first train to arrive. When the whistle blew and the column of smoke approached, the rest of the passengers stepped toward the railway. We got on quickly, as the train did not stay long at that stop. We located our compartment and saw that inside there were empty seats next to a priest. We smiled and sat down beside him. A minute later, two German soldiers opened the door noisily and plopped down in front of us. One of them, a young man with hair so blond he looked to be albino, stared at us for a moment but then turned and kept chatting with his comrade.

The train clattered its way through cities, mountains, fallow fields, and bare vineyards, and Lisa constantly begged for food. Finally I took out some bread and butter and gave her some.

"She's a lovely child," the blond German said in perfect French.

"Thank you," I said, steeling my voice.

"Where are you traveling to?"

I hesitated but finally answered Bordeaux. I did not want Peter to speak and give them the opportunity to hear his accent.

Almost five hours later, the train finally reached the outskirts of the city. As the two soldiers stood up, one of them dropped his hat. Peter automatically reached for it and handed it to him.

"Thank you," the soldier said, eyeing Peter closely. "Where are you two from?" he asked.

Peter and I exchanged looks. "My husband is from Beijing. He's the son of missionaries."

The soldier saluted us and left the compartment. We let out a sigh of relief, and the priest, who had not spoken up until then, handed Lisa a piece of candy.

"Beware of those Boche. They may act like fools, but they

aren't. I'd advise you to get out now by the back door, run down the platform, and leave on the other side."

"Thank you," I said to him. We grabbed our few belongings and did just as he had said. When we were at the front of the station, I looked back and saw the Germans from our compartment talking to the passport-control agent. We had barely slipped through.

A taxi dropped us at the Garonne port. From there we traveled by a small passenger boat to Royan, where the transatlantic boats docked.

It was late by the time we got to Royan, and the boat we had hoped to take had left some hours before. Our only option was to wait two more weeks for the next one or try to find passage on another ship.

We went up and down the port to learn which boats were headed for the Americas. Most were taking cargo to Amsterdam or North Africa, but we found one small cargo ship named *La Habana* that was taking French wine to Cuba. We went on deck and asked to speak with the captain.

The sailors took us to the control room where a dark-skinned man with shiny gelled hair and a gray goatee smiled and asked us to take a seat.

"My name is Ismael Cala Pérez. I'm sorry to tell you that we don't take passengers on board. We aren't equipped for that."

I addressed him in Spanish, and he seemed to take a liking to me. He nodded all the while as I explained our situation.

"Before we leave tomorrow morning, our cargo will be inspected. Cuba is a neutral country in this war, but we're not allowed to transport passengers."

"I understand, Captain. But if the Nazis catch us, we'll end up in one of their camps," Peter said in Spanish. "I've been in too many camps already, and I'm begging you to get us out of here."

"My grandfather was a Spaniard, from the Canary Islands. I've always wanted to visit his mother country." He sighed heavily. "Very well, we'll hide you in the cellar until the boat sets sail."

We jumped for joy. In a few hours we would be far from France, going to the other side of the ocean, where the world was still a free place and human life still mattered for something.

Captain Pérez offered us coffee and Danish pastries. I let out a long sigh as we enjoyed those delicacies. I wished with all my heart for Elisabeth and the maternity hospital to be okay. As the war continued and the monster of violence spread across the world, that little haven of peace and love had snatched a number of lives back from the jaws of death.

FORTY-ONE

Elisabeth

Karl knew that the inevitable could not be delayed much longer. Since Germany had invaded the previously unoccupied zone the previous November, the Nazi authorities were constantly harassing the orphanages. They wanted to take all the children and adolescents to Germany and Poland, supposedly to put them in work camps; yet rumors were already circulating about mass killings, especially in Poland.

Karl called Elisabeth to see if she could hide some of the orphans at the maternity hospital. The Swiss flag still flapped proudly at the facade of the hospital, which had been officially part of the Swiss Red Cross since January of 1942 and was no longer under the umbrella of Swiss Aid to Spanish Children.

Elisabeth took the faithful Rocinante and, together with Ruth and another volunteer, drove out to the château where Karl was caring for the children. A few hours later, they were in front of the huge house on the outskirts of town. They parked at the entrance and looked inside for Karl, but there was no sign of him.

Finally they found one of the groundskeepers and asked about their friend.

"He's taken the children up to a cabin in the woods. The Gestapo has come by several times, and they've got nowhere else to go."

"But it's the middle of winter," Ruth said. Snow already covered the mountains.

"Can you tell us how to get there?" Elisabeth asked.

The man pointed out the road that left from the back of the grounds and curved steeply up the mountain.

"Let's go," Elisabeth called, and the women returned to the van.

"Rocinante can't make it up that road in this weather," Ruth said.

"Well, we can try. It can't be that far. Karl called me just this morning."

"But he knows the way better than we do."

Elisabeth shrugged and pulled out. There was no snow for the first mile, but as they began to climb, the way became more difficult.

For the next half hour they steadily climbed, and Rocinante threatened to stall several times. At the top, they could see a large wood cabin. It took them twenty more minutes to get there and park behind another van. There was just enough room for both on the stretch of flat ground.

Karl came out to meet them. He was sweating and wearing short sleeves despite the cold on the mountain. "We've been playing inside with the children. Thanks for coming," he said, leading them into an open room. The women looked at the faces of some fifty children between the ages of eight and fourteen. They waved to them all. While the volunteers stayed with the children, Elisabeth followed Karl into the kitchen.

"It's the same guy who was after you a few months ago, that accursed Max Diem. He's after us now. He wants to send all the children to Germany. I've gotten the Vichy authorities to forbid it until recently, but now the government belongs to the Nazis. We have to hide them."

Elisabeth understood Karl's predicament, but she could not do much to help.

"Karl, I can take ten or fifteen with me, twenty at the most. It will be hard to feed them, but if we can feed ten, we can feed twenty. But my hands are tied when it comes to changing their names in the records. Max Diem is watching me like a hawk for any irregularities in our records, just looking for an excuse to close the hospital and lock us all up."

"I know, I know. All we're doing is dragging out the inevitable."

Elisabeth tried to cheer Karl up. "The Allies are already in North Africa, and there's talk of a landing soon in Europe. There's a chance the war could wrap up within months."

"No, the Nazis are still strong on all the fronts. They've started losing to the Russians, but this thing could go on for years. Having the children at your hospital for a few weeks isn't enough. You'd just be fattening them up for the Nazis to kill them regardless."

Elisabeth shrugged and shook her head sadly. "It's all I can do."

"I know. It's all right. Okay, take twenty of them with you, and try not to do anything on the records until you absolutely have to."

"Done," Elisabeth said as Karl fixed some tea. "So how are you holding up?"

"All right, though I'm not sleeping much these days. You know what's going on in the east. The damned Nazis are killing off all the Jews in the countries they've invaded."

"We can't change the course of this war, my dear Karl. All we can do is lessen a few of the blows."

"It's not enough."

"Yes, it is. Each life is irreplaceable," Elisabeth said, starting to lose patience. She felt like the roles had been reversed in their relationship.

"I know. You're right. I'm sorry."

They carried the trays of tea into the cold room. Karl looked out the window at the sunset. "You three should be moving along before it gets dark."

Elisabeth nodded while taking a sip of steaming tea. "Yes, but I've got good news for you."

"I don't get enough of that these days. What is it?"

"Isabel and Peter made it to Bordeaux safe and sound. They sent me a letter saying they had found room on a ship going to Cuba. They should have arrived weeks ago."

Karl teared up, not just for Isabel and her family but for all the people he and Elisabeth had given hope to and helped to escape from hell.

"That brings me such joy, Elisabeth—thank you."

"Our work is not in vain, Karl."

Karl dried his tears and looked out the window at the pine trees that rose majestically all around the cabin. The beauty on that mountain always helped him forget the terrible things humanity was capable of. He sometimes felt he could stay on that peak forever. He started reciting Psalm 121 from memory:

"'I will lift up mine eyes unto the hills, from
whence cometh my help.
My help cometh from the LORD, which made
heaven and earth.
He will not suffer thy foot to be moved: he that
keepeth thee will not slumber.
Behold, he that keepeth Israel shall neither slumber
nor sleep.
The LORD is thy keeper: the LORD is thy shade upon
thy right hand.
The sun shall not smite thee by day, nor the moon
by night.
The LORD shall preserve thee from all evil: he shall
preserve thy soul.
The LORD shall preserve thy going out and thy
coming in from this time forth, and even for
evermore.'

FORTY-TWO

Isabel

It took my spirit a long time to settle down. That cold January morning we sailed away from France, and I thought that tragedy was behind me. The ship did not move very fast, and to avoid any conflict we stayed away from the coasts of Ireland and England. Eight days in, Lisa started having a fever. Several of the crew became ill over the next couple of days. It became apparent that scarlet fever had started with her and spread to some of the adults. I spent every day and night by her side. Peter brought me food, but I could not eat. I tried everything I knew to bring her fever down, but she was burning. After three days she seemed to improve and we all rejoiced, but twenty-four hours later, it came back with a vengeance. She was so weak. My poor child had not eaten for days and could not keep any liquids down. She grew delirious by day five. The only intelligible word her dry, white lips murmured was to call me *"Mamaíta."* On the morning of the sixth day, she died. I clung to her and felt the fever lowering. Eventually Peter tried to pull her away from me, but I refused.

He told me our daughter was no longer in that lifeless body and that one day we would be with her in heaven, but I refused to let her go until that night.

The captain presided over the brief funeral, and we surrendered her precious little body to the waves, two days out from Cuba. I did not even have a grave to visit later.

We arrived in the United States a week later. We went ashore in Miami and then took another boat to New York. I barely ate anything and spent all my time lying down in our cabin. When we reached the city of skyscrapers, we took a train to Cleveland. It was still bitterly cold, as cold as my heart deadened by pain.

I vividly recall the first time I set eyes on the white house where Peter grew up. It was in the middle of a snow-covered yard surrounded by a short wooden fence. Peter's parents came out to meet us. His father was a heavyset man, shorter than Peter with a reddened nose and eyes as gray as the ocean in the winter. His mother had her hair pulled back in a bun. When she turned her kind eyes to me, I saw Lisa's eyes and started sobbing.

They looked after me for weeks like I was their own sick daughter. They babied me and did not stop to judge or reprimand me. A few months after our arrival, when the flowers started to spring up in the fields around the church and their house, my mother-in-law invited me to go for a walk. By that time I understood English quite well, though I still struggled to speak it.

"Death is the most painful reality we have to face, Isabel," she said as we meandered down a nearby path. "I lost a baby, just before Peter. They put him cold and dead on my lap after the delivery. People tried to comfort me with promises about eternity and heaven, but right then that was not what I needed. Nothing goes against nature as much as a mother having to give up her child.

Months went by, and Peter's dad didn't know what to do to help me. Frankly, I had abandoned our other children and didn't want to keep living. Then, on a day like this one, he took me out to the country, and we sat down on a blanket. *'I love you,'* he said. *'Life has stolen our son, but it can never steal our hope.'* I started crying, of course, but that was the beginning of the wound starting to heal. It won't be easy. You'll never be the same. But you will get better."

She hugged me tight. Back at the house, I came down that night and sat at the dinner table with everyone else for the first time. Peter had found a job working construction, and he was remodeling a house. He showed up with paint all over his blue-jean overalls. He saw me and just grinned. We spent three months fixing up a little house for ourselves. I was finally ready then to write Elisabeth. I told her what had happened and also how often I remembered her and all her advice.

I followed the events of the war with a great concern. I was terrified that Peter would get drafted and fearful for my friends in France. But little by little the Germans began losing. We started to have a ray of hope.

Elisabeth

ELNE MATERNITY HOSPITAL
May 23, 1943

Threatening letters from the prefecture kept arriving. The Red Cross office in Bern also wrote to pressure Elisabeth to follow all regulations to the utmost. But they were not there seeing what Elisabeth saw every day.

A few months after offering to house some of Karl's orphans, Elisabeth had been forced to hand the children over. The Gestapo had also raided the house and dragged out a young Jewish mother name Lucie right after she lost her baby. Things were worse by the day, and the increasing strain on the Nazis' nerves translated into harsher demands.

Elisabeth understood full well that sometimes it was necessary to disobey orders for the purpose of saving lives. She had hidden a Belgian baby whose mother had died after the birth. She had also passed Guy Eckstein off as the son of one of her Spanish volunteers since October of 1941, though he was actually Jewish. His only crime was being born into a certain ethnicity. Every time she saw him, she felt she had at least managed to snatch one beautiful, helpless creature from the fire that was devouring Europe.

That day Max Dließm returned to the maternity hospital and beat on the door with his characteristic rage. Ruth went to answer that time. He burst past her and demanded to see Pedro Alcalde, the gardener.

"And what business do you have with Mr. Alcalde?" Elisabeth asked, emerging from her office to relieve the terrified Ruth.

"I need to take him from the premises immediately."

Elisabeth stood in the middle of the hallway and stared at the German. He gave her a cruel smile and waved to his men to start the search. They went out of their way to leave things in disarray.

A few minutes later Pedro appeared from the back door. He was a gray-haired man with slouching shoulders. He carried his hat in his hand.

"This Communist, this Red Republican, is coming with us. But we'll be back soon for the rest of you. You hear me?" he shouted at the volunteers. They dared not look up at him.

As soon as the Germans had gone, several of the mothers broke down crying.

"It's all right. That brute can't do anything to you as long as that Swiss flag is flying out front," Elisabeth comforted them. Back in her office with the door closed, she, too, broke down in tears.

Her new boss, Maurice Dubois, stood up for her and her work, but the Red Cross in Bern wanted to close the maternity hospital immediately. She did not know how much more time they had. The members of her team were exhausted and wanted to go home, but no one would leave until Elisabeth herself did.

FORTY-THREE

Isabel

CLEVELAND, OHIO, UNITED STATES
March 12, 1944

The gift of life is the most beautiful thing heaven has given us. Men are only capable of snuffing it out, but women produce it. Peter was drafted at the beginning of 1911, but they gave him a short leave in March after basic training so that he could meet our son, John. He arrived at the hospital just moments after the birth. That modern hospital, so bright and clean with nurses wearing spotless uniforms, made me think of the maternity hospital in Elne. I had not heard from Elisabeth in several months. Her letters had to go through Switzerland first, and they took a very long time to reach me.

Peter came into the room and stared at us, momentarily speechless. He looked so handsome in his uniform, though he had sworn not to fire a single shot. He was the chaplain of his squadron. He bent over us and kissed my forehead, then picked up our baby. Watching him cuddle and kiss little John brought back so many memories of Lisa. I tried to hold back my tears but could not.

My mother-in-law took my hand, and her smile told me everything.

"He's as handsome as his father," I babbled, trying to bring my mind back to the present.

"No, he takes after his grandfather!" Peter's father said, and we all laughed.

"When are you shipping out to Europe?" his father asked. Peter beat around the bush but finally admitted that he would be leaving the next day. Some important operations were being planned for the next several months. He would be joining the parachuters, and they had to take strategic positions before the troops were deployed.

We hugged. Even though he would not be armed, he would still be facing enemy fire.

"Please take care of yourself, and come back safe and sound."

"I will, Isabel. I promise." He flashed me his smile that could light up a whole room.

The next day he left for Europe. I followed the news assiduously. Every advance and retreat unnerved me, though little John kept me happily busy. I could not bear to face another loss. My heart, so full of scars, may have seemed strong, but I had learned long ago just how weak it really was. I could only bear the weight of it all if I trusted and rested.

FORTY-FOUR

Elisabeth

ELNE MATERNITY HOSPITAL

April 13, 1944

Elisabeth looked around at the maternity hospital. It was as empty as the day she found it a few years before. Her heart sank. She touched the chimney in the living room and remembered the Christmases and birthday parties. For several years, that place had been full of laughter and happiness. Now it was a cold, dead shell. Trucks had taken all the equipment and supplies to the train station, where they were carted off to Montagnac. There they would be used to help starving French people who had learned the hard way what the Spaniards learned in 1939: sooner or later in life, everyone needs a helping hand.

Elisabeth closed the gate. The German army had requisitioned the building for military use since they feared an imminent invasion of France. Nearly four years after the German invasion, it looked like the country would again become a battle zone, and the hunger and desperation of the population would send them to the brink of death.

She went down the stairs and saw Karl, who had stayed back to give her time to say goodbye to the hospital.

"You all right?" he asked.

She shook her head and let the tears fall. She was no longer the bright, young, carefree girl who had left her country full of hopes and dreams. Two wars were enough to change anybody. Yet she still held on to her deep faith in humanity.

They got into the car and drove north. As long as the winding highway allowed them to see the Mediterranean, she thought about the hundreds of thousands of refugees trapped on the beaches. Their distracted looks had captured their accumulated fear and desperation. Sometimes silence had reigned in those camps. Deep sadness is generally quiet, not demanding loud expression. Now the wind was blowing, and the waves were pounding into the cliffs. Elisabeth understood then that, while sadness silenced the people, the majestic creation all around kept roaring. It roared out the promise that calm comes after the storm, that things can begin again, that the mystery of life is always miraculous.

FORTY-FIVE

Elisabeth

Everything was exactly as she had left it in the winter of 1939. Switzerland seemed immune to the changing times. Elisabeth had left the maternity hospital in Montagnac in the capable hands of a colleague and had finally returned home. She did not know what she was looking for yet. Perhaps her own self.

Johann and Marie were eating at the kitchen table when they heard the door open. Their daughter paused on the threshold a moment as she took in the sight of the house. Then she wiped off her feet, left her shoes by the door, and entered.

Marie reached her first, then Johann came up to complete the embrace. They got her seated in the living room and began asking questions.

"We weren't expecting you. Are you hungry? Shall I fix you something?" Marie began.

"No, I'm just fine with what you've served me."

"How are things in France?" her father asked.

Elisabeth thought about how to answer and summed it up

with, "The country has been liberated, but so many people—too many—have died."

"And you—how are you, Elisabeth?" Her daughter's sunken eyes, jaundiced skin, and feverish look worried Marie.

Elisabeth sighed. "I've seen so many things. I don't know that I'll ever get them out of my mind."

"Many things heal with time and distance," Marie said, going to the kitchen to make some tea.

"Oh, Father, I never dreamed the world could be such a cruel place."

The aged pastor scooted his chair closer and stroked his daughter's face. "As long as children keep being born, there's still hope for the world, my dear."

She had helped bring hundreds of them into the world. Now they were all hers, in a way. Though they came from vastly different lands, they were all brothers and sisters.

Her father stood and put a record on the old player. The tune that Beethoven had given to Schiller's poem "Ode to Joy" began softly. They listened to the beautiful melody together and closed their eyes as before an angel chorus when the words began:

Oh friends, no more of these sounds!
Let us sing more cheerful songs,
More full of joy!

EPILOGUE

Mrs. Jackson's voice halted in the waning afternoon light. The tears in her eyes shone in the growing darkness. The beautiful story of my grandmother's life had moved us both. After a month of visits to my new older friend, I now understood what had happened to my grandmother during the wars and why she had never spoken about the past.

"Thank you. Thank you so much for telling me her story."

"I owed it to your grandmother."

"I still wish she had talked to me about it."

"It was just too painful for her," Mrs. Jackson said, getting to her feet with some effort. She opened a box on top of her dresser and handed me a tattered notebook. "This is where she wrote all her memories. I've read it a hundred times. She gave it to me long before she died, as if she didn't want to keep those things with her anymore."

I sucked in my breath and held out my hands for the diary. The paper was cold and damp. The ancient diary looked like it had survived a shipwreck.

I thanked Mrs. Jackson again and left the nursing home. It was very cold, and my car was covered with a crust of snow. I drove carefully back to my house and swore to get that diary to an editor in New York. The world needed to know about Elisabeth Eidenbenz. Now more than ever, the world needed the story of my grandmother, of my grandfather, of Karl and Ruth and Lucy, of América's tragic end. I did not want them to disappear with the death of the last person who knew and loved them. Their memories needed to fill the lives of other people and show us all that in the midst of the horror of war, there was a maternity hospital in southern France where life found a way to flourish.

REFERENCES

"¡Ay Carmela!" Original translation of a popular folk song. Public domain.

Donne, John. "Meditation." Devotion XVII in *Devotions upon Emergent Occasions*. Ann Arbor: University of Michigan, 1959. https://www.gutenberg.org/files/23772/23772-h/23772-h.htm.

Fernández de San Miguel, Evaristo. "Himno de Riego." 1820. National battle hymn of the First Spanish Republic. Public domain. Original translation.

Machado, Antonio. "Espanolito." Poem 53 in *Proverbios y Cantares: Campos de Castilla*. 1912. Original translation.

Mohr, Joseph. "Silent Night." 1818. Translated into Spanish by Federico Fliedner (d. 1901). Public domain.

Montella, Assumpta. *La Maternidad de Elna*. Barcelona: Now Books, 2007. Page 9. Original translation.

Schiller, Friedrich. "Ode to Joy." 1785. Public domain.

Tremlett, Giles. *The International Brigades: Fascism, Freedom and the Spanish Civil War*. London: Bloomsbury, 2021. Page 512.

CLARIFICATIONS
FROM HISTORY

This novel about the Elne maternity hospital is based on real events. Elisabeth Eidenbenz was a Swiss teacher who helped orphans during the Spanish Civil War and, after the defeat of the Republic, crossed the Pyrenees Mountains. In 1939 she opened a maternity hospital to care for Spanish Republican women who were pregnant and forced to give birth in terrible conditions at the refugee camps. Toward the end of her life, she received several honors and recognitions for her labors during the Spanish Civil War and World War II. She was declared Righteous Among the Nations by Yad Vashem and the Cruz de Oro de la Orden Civil de la Solidaridad Social by the government of Spain, awarded the Creu de Sant Jordi by the government of Catalonia, and inducted into the Legion d'Honneur by the government of France.

The assistance of Quakers and Mennonites in humanitarian aid work during the Spanish Civil War and in the various internment camps set up for Spanish refugees was vital.

The camps at Argelès-sur-Mer and Saint-Cyprien, to mention just two, were terrible places where hundreds of people died due to poor sanitary conditions and insufficient food.

Rodolfo Olgiati, general secretary of Service Civil International (SCI), founded the Swiss Aid to Spanish Children organization in

1937. Both he and his wife helped during the war and later concentrated their efforts on administration and fundraising.

This novel mentions only a few of the many workers from Switzerland and other countries who helped throughout the maternity hospital's duration.

Karl Ketterer and Ruth von Wild were real people. Isabel's friend María is based on the life of a Spanish immigrant and her doctor husband, who worked in the maternity hospital after she gave birth there.

The description of the final military actions in Catalonia is based on history, as is the story of the International Brigades and the famous Abraham Lincoln Brigade comprised mainly of citizens of the United States.

An estimated 475,000 Spaniards fled the country in early 1939 and crossed the Pyrenees Mountains in the dead of winter. Some 100,000 were forcibly detained at the Argelès-sur-Mer camp.

Many of the stories of Spanish immigrants narrated herein are based on real testimonies of survivors.

The Elne maternity hospital assisted in the live birth of some 597 children, 200 of whom were Jewish.

Elisabeth Eidenbenz eventually retired to Austria before returning to Zurich, where she lived until her death in 2011 at age ninety-seven.

TIMELINE

1939

January 26: Barcelona falls to Franco. Thousands of
Spaniards, both soldiers and civilians, flee to France in
what was called the *Retirada*.

January 30: France opens the Argelès-sur-Mer camp on the
beach. Other similar camps follow.

February 13: France closes the border with Spain and does
not allow any more refugees to cross. The *Retirada* is
over.

April: The maternity hospital in Brouilla opens, before being
moved to Elne.

September 1: Germany invades Poland and World War II
begins.

September 3: Great Britain, France, Australia, and New
Zealand declare war on Germany.

December: The first births take place at the Elne maternity
hospital.

1940

June 14: The Wehrmacht enters Paris. Germany occupies
France and controls it through the Vichy government.

June 22: France signs an armistice with Germany.

1941

November 25: Germany attempts to attack Moscow.

December 5: The Germans halt their offensive against Moscow.

December 7: Japan attacks the United States military base at Pearl Harbor.

December 8: The United States declares war on Japan.

December 11: Germany declares war on the United States.

1943

May 12: Axis forces surrender in North Africa.

July 25: The Fascist government of the Italian Benito Mussolini falls.

September 3: Italy signs the armistice with the Allies.

September 11: Germany occupies Rome.

October 13: The official Italian government declares war on Germany.

1944

April: The Elne maternity hospital is closed.

June 6: The Normandy landings begin.

August 15: The Allies land in southern France.

August 25: The Allies free Paris.

1945

April 30: Faced with the impending arrival of Soviet troops to his bunker in Berlin, Adolf Hitler dies by suicide.

May 7: Nazi Germany surrenders unconditionally to the Allies. World War II ends in Europe.

DISCUSSION QUESTIONS

1. Would you consider Elisabeth Eidenbenz a hero, or would you consider her a regular member of society? How might her actions and her demeanor defy the typical definitions of what it means to be heroic?

2. What is the purpose of hope in this story? How does someone like Elizabeth or Isabel or Peter maintain hope when all seems lost, when no day seems better than the one before?

3. When asked about having children of her own, Elisabeth is purported to have said, "I already have them." How does this change or enhance your view of motherhood?

4. Consider how Elisabeth and Isabel see the world—both in their differences and in their similarities. Do you relate to one more than the other? If so, how and why?

5. What does this story tell you about the power of love? About the power of mercy and sacrifice?

6. Of the many losses portrayed, what do you consider the greatest loss in this story?

7. Which character did you connect with the most? And who do you admire the most?

8. How much did you know about the Spanish Civil War before you read this novel? What did you learn, and what

did the story teach you about the nature of civil wars in particular?

9. The novel ends with Isabel's grandchild vowing to make sure the story was told. Do you think there are instances of everyday heroism that have been lost to time and circumstances? How does that affect how you view history and your own story?

10. The author based this novel on the real Mothers of Elne—the maternity home that saved an estimated 600 children. How does the truth of this story change the way you read and experience it?

International bestselling author Mario Escobar captures
the strength of the human spirit and the enduring
power of kindness in this moving novel based on
the true story of a brave Polish teacher who cared
for hundreds of orphans in the Warsaw Ghetto.

Available in print, e-book, and audio

HARPER MUSE

Through letters with a famous author, one French librarian tells her love story and describes the brutal Nazi occupation of her small coastal village.

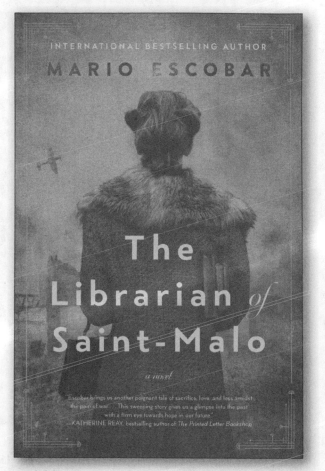

Available in print, e-book, and downloadable audio

From international bestselling author Mario Escobar comes a story of escape, sacrifice, and hope amid the perils of the Second World War.

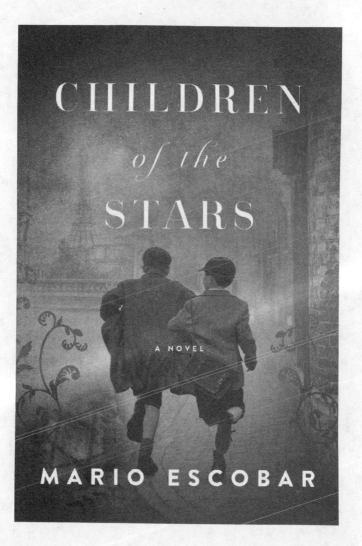

CHILDREN *of the* STARS

A NOVEL

MARIO ESCOBAR

THOMAS NELSON
Since 1798

Available in print, e-book, and audio

Based on the true story of a brave German nurse tasked with caring for Auschwitz's youngest prisoners, *Auschwitz Lullaby* brings to life the story of Helene Hannemann—a woman who sacrificed everything for family and fought furiously for the children she hoped to save.

ABOUT THE AUTHOR

Photo by Elisabeth Monje

Mario Escobar, a *USA TODAY* and international bestselling author, has a master's degree in modern history and has written numerous books and articles that delve into the depths of church history, the struggle of sectarian groups, and the discovery and colonization of the Americas. Escobar, who makes his home in Madrid, Spain, is passionate about history and its mysteries.

Visit him online at marioescobar.es
Twitter: @EscobarGolderos
Instagram: @marioescobar.oficial
Facebook: @MarioEscobar

ABOUT THE TRANSLATOR

Photo by Sally Chambers

Gretchen Abernathy worked full-time in the Spanish Christian publishing world for several years until her oldest son was born. Since then, she has worked as a freelance editor and translator. Her main focus includes translating/editing for the *Journal of Latin American Theology* and supporting the production of Bible products with the Nueva Versión Internacional. Chilean ecological poetry, the occasional thriller novel, and audio proofs spice up her work routines. She and her husband make their home in Nashville, Tennessee, with their two sons.